Praise for
MONEY, MURDER, MAYHEM

Money Murder Mayhem book is a great read!

"Suspenseful, funny and lots of twists. Couldn't put it down until I finished it. Never knew what was going to happen next. Can't wait for the next book."

Carol Abby, Amazon

Medium rare!

"Medium rare, as in perfectly prepared. A wonderful combination of compelling characters, witty banter, and intrigue that keeps the pages turning and leaves the reader anxiously anticipating the next installment. The perfect read for a dreary winter afternoon or a day at the beach!"

Gabe Holmes, Amazon

Loved it!

"Fabulous characters and an intriguing plot with suspenseful twists and turns. I can't wait to see what happens next for Lord and Lady Crosswick in *Art, Wine, and Crime!*"

Sue Hodges, Amazon

A Great read!

"Fun mystery, a charming family you wish you could join! Likable characters in a wonderful setting. Can't wait to see what the future holds for Lord and Lady Crosswick!"

MAC, Amazon

What a delightful book!

"From the very beginning, I was so caught up in the story that I could not stop reading! *Money, Murder, Mayhem* checks all the boxes for a great movie, as well! I am anxiously awaiting *Art, Wine, and Crime* in France."

G. Bowers, Amazon

Many Twists and Unique Characters

"Super loving couple Philip and Genevieve provide insight into becoming extremely wealthy suddenly in England. Owning an estate with a ghost and then having their closest friend nearly murdered changes their lives even more. Trying to be accepted into the life of being royalty while there is a murder investigation adds humor and excitement to the story…. Many twists and unique characters keep the mystery exciting."

KSHYDOG, Goodreads

Cannot put it down!

"To me, the sign of a great book is when you come to the end of it and you want to know what happens next to the characters! That is how I felt after reading this book! I have to say that I am not a reader of mysteries, but *Money, Murder, Mayhem* held my attention all the way through…. The characters were so well developed that by the end of the book you felt like you knew them…. But best of all, Ms. Boerger is writing a sequel to this book and I can assure you that I will be among the first to buy it! Enjoy!"

Steven L. Amazon

Agatha Christie couldn't have done it better!

"A delightful read with just the right mixture of humor and mystery. Can't wait for the Warwick's next adventure!"

Janice Daniel, Amazon

Finished the book

"WOW! Wish I could give this book ten stars. Author keeps the reader not only engaged but makes them feel like they are a part of the story line. Fantastic read!"

Debbie L. Campbell, Amazon

"I love mysteries, and this one did not disappoint!

"Greatly enjoyed this debut novel, and true to genre I was kept guessing as to whodunit until the secrets were revealed! Great and accurate descriptions of the English countryside and the trials, tribulations, and delights of inherited treasures! I liked getting to know these characters, they were quite obviously written and created with love and care, and I look forward to the next install-ment of the Crosswicks!"

Mark Haggerty, Amazon

Riveting Read

"This book grabs you right from the first page. Love how the characters interact and are developing. Look forward to book 3."

Booklover, Amazon

C'est magnifique!

"Thoroughly enjoyed Tana's 2nd book. Never knew about giclee, counterfeit wine and la chanteuse, Zaz. Quelle merveilleuse lecture but it's over so quickly. I hope the 3rd edition is coming soon!"

CLG, Amazon

Fun Characters

"Book 2 is a delight. Great characters follow the new Lord and Lady on their next journey to their wine estate. Mystery follows.

Tazmania, Amazon

A Lord and Lady Crosswick Mystery

VENGEANCE
at the
VINEYARD

Tana L.H. Boerger

Altta Publishing
2 The Pointe
Sanford, NC, 27332

Printed in the United States of America

Paperback ISBN: 979-8-9919220-2-9
Hardcover ISBN: 979-8-9919220-1-2
Ebook ISBN: 979-8-9919220-0-5

First Edition

To my family: you have never tried to rein me in. Perhaps occasionally you should have, but I'm grateful you didn't.

VENGEANCE
at the
VINEYARD

PROLOGUE

T INY NEEDLES OF ice pricked the back of his neck. He flipped up his collar and pulled it tight. Not even the wool scarf could keep the wind from cutting through his fine, black-worsted overcoat. His rasping breath was loud in his ears and he was grateful there were only a few steps from where he'd parked the black Mercedes to the entrance of Blain Lodge.

Head down, he pushed on through the intensifying sleet and stepped over a patch of ice, hugging the package tighter inside his coat. Grunting as he heaved open the glass door, he was careful not to let the wind catch it. Even the warm air that kissed his cheeks as he stepped into the vestibule couldn't thaw his icy anger. He unclutched his collar, pulled the gift box from his coat, then brushed frozen beads from each shoulder with a gloved hand.

Eager to see the woman and take her to task, nerves churned his stomach. He wanted her to regret everything she had done to his family: the terror and chaos she had caused them to live under for weeks.

He nodded to the prim woman behind a mahogany reception desk. She bobbed her head in response, spoke into the phone, and motioned to the lounge just off the foyer. He pushed through the heavy paneled doors into an elegant waiting room and walked to the wall of paned windows that overlooked a perfect lawn sloping down to the stone riding center. Sleet tapped against the windows, sending a shiver down his spine. He leaned forward, squinted, and watched a lithe figure stride up the path from the stables to the main building, head down against the freezing rain. Her snug breeches accentuated her long, elegant legs and she held the neck of her Barbour quilted riding jacket closed with a gloved hand. There was no question; it was she. Watching her enter the main building, his palms dampened and he took a deep breath as he waited for her to join him.

He had told no one of the tongue-lashing he intended to give her. When he was finished with her, she would regret the anguish she had caused all of them. Of that, he was certain.

ONE

From the stone walls lining the allée to the front door decked with evergreen swags and a holly wreath, Château Beaulieu was dazzling and dressed for a holiday wedding.

Duncan glanced at his wrist where his Rolex usually told him the time, but it was bare. "Damn!" he cursed under his breath. "I must have left my watch on the dresser."

Checking the time on his phone, he saw he was running late and turned his long stride into a lope. He rapped three loud knocks on the door to his father's study before opening it. His smile broadened at the bride's entourage bustling, primping, smoothing, adjusting, and organizing themselves to walk down the aisle.

"Ten minutes to show time, ladies," he said. "Is everyone ready?"

"I'm as ready as I'll ever be." Fighting back a happy tear, the bride grabbed her daughter's hand, lacing her fingers through Olivia's, and squeezed.

"Ouch!" Feeling a pinch, Olivia lifted Becca's hand and saw the offending ring, a square-cut ruby Becca had been given years ago. "Don't you think you should take this off? You don't want it to compete with your wedding ring" Olivia smiled at her mother, arching a teasing brow.

Becca glanced at the jewel that held generational history. "I suppose that's a good idea. This represents my past and I'm heading into my future." As she tugged, the ring resisted, so she slid her finger into her mouth. When she tried again, it slipped over her knuckle with ease.

"Give it to me," Olivia said. "I'll take care of it." She took the precious heirloom from her mother and smiled to herself.

"I'll be back in ten, ladies." Duncan left the salon of chattering beauties and made his way to the orangerie where guests from England, France, and the US gathered to witness the marriage of Sir David Spencer Frederick Weatherington of the United Kingdom and Rebecca Harris Conway of the United States, a union of two people with a long, rocky history, but a promising future.

As the wedding guests anticipated the start of the ceremony, their excitement began to build. The orangerie was decked to perfection—fanciful but sophisticated and filled with the fragrance from Douglas fir boughs swagged around the room. A string quartet played Vivaldi's popular "The Four Seasons", setting the mood for a high-energy, elegant event. Every guest held a flute sparkling with Champagne, and spirited voices full of laughter swirled around the salon.

Mrs. MacIntosh, the house manager from Wilmingrove Hall, the Warwick's family seat in Yorkshire, drained her glass. As she licked a drop of Champagne from her lips, Wallace, the Hall's butler and her long-time friend, put his flute on the sideboard and plucked the crystal from her hand. He strode toward the bar at the far end of the orangerie where several people waited for drinks. Seeing the crowd, he walked out into the hallway and into the kitchen where he exchanged the empty glass for a filled flute sitting on a silver tray, waiting to be delivered to thirsty guests. He nodded to the chef, who returned the courtesy.

Barely breaking his stride, he swept through the kitchen door and back into the hall, where, in the middle of the corridor, Olivia squatted next to Cooper, the Warwick family dog, fluffing and fiddling with the blue bow around the pup's neck. Her violet eyes rounded at the sight of Wallace before they narrowed to slits. She stood, blocking Wallace's way, and he stopped abruptly. Champagne sloshed over the sides of the crystal and streamed onto his fingers.

"Wallace," she said, more like a challenge than a greeting.

"Miss Conway," he returned, his voice cool. "Shouldn't you be with the bridesmaids?" He glanced at his watch. "The ceremony is about to begin."

Images of Olivia out of control and murderous at Wilmingrove Hall just a year ago flashed through his mind. From the moment he saw her yesterday when he and Mrs. MacIntosh arrived at Château Beaulieu, he'd been unable to tamp the gnawing fear that Olivia was here to agitate, at the very least. And if, as Shakespeare said, the past was prologue, it would not surprise him if her intention was to torment someone—or, perhaps, everyone.

She leaned over and adjusted Cooper's bow one last time before fixing the elegant butler with a sweet smile. "Of course,

Wallace. I should go. But," she tilted her head to the side, "they won't start without me, will they?" Though her lips tilted upward, the corners of her mouth were pulled tight. With her chin high, she turned and sauntered back toward Philip's study, Cooper trotting at her side.

He shook his head at the beautiful young woman's retreating back. She was up to no good, he feared. But maybe he was wrong. He strode back through the door into the orangerie, buzzing with anticipation of the wedding about to begin. He swept up his glass from the sideboard just where he had left it, and searched the crowd for Mrs. MacIntosh. When he saw her across the room, his heart gave a little flutter and he began to weave his way through the crowd.

"Aha, here he is," Mrs. MacIntosh said, accepting the glass he held out to her. "You were gone a while. What took you so long?" Her eyebrow arched into the salt-and-pepper wave of hair that dipped onto her forehead.

Wallace leaned close to her ear. "I ran into that horrible Conway girl. I know she's up to absolutely no good."

A quiet chuckle gurgled in her throat and she shook her head at Wallace. "Will you never forgive Olivia? She seems to me to be trying very hard to overcome her demons." She slipped her hand through the crook of his arm. "I see Alex with his gong." She smiled across the room at the handsome young man. "Let's go find our seats," she said, and tugged on his arm. They strolled over to where they had been told to sit, in seats reserved for the family, and nestled in.

As if he had been waiting for the pair to settle, Cooper trotted to where Wallace sat and stretched out by his chair. Wallace reached down to scratch the well-brushed pup behind the ear and was surprised to feel metal and heavy paper against his wrist. He looked down at Cooper's neck and rooted between the loops of his blue bow. When he parted the ribbon, a watch face caught the candlelight flickering on the candelabras lining the aisle. A red smear slashed across the crystal of the Rolex, which was tied to a heavy linen notecard. He turned the card so he could see the words and drew a sharp breath as he read the bloody scrawl.

"Vengeance is justice and it's time for mine!"

Surprised to hear Wallace's gasp, Mrs. MacIntosh leaned into him. "What's the matter?"

"Nothing, Bertie. Nothing that won't wait until later," he said under his breath, just as nine-year-old Alex began to move through the orangerie, striking his small brass gong.

"Everyone! Everyone!" he called out with confidence, commanding the attention of the group. "The wedding is about to begin," he said, urging people to be seated. With that job completed, he ran back to the vestibule where the bride's party was ready and stepped into the line just behind his sister, seven-year-old Ella, and in front of three attendants: his mother, Julia; his beautiful grandmother, Genevieve; and Becca's daughter, Olivia. Though she was a troubled young woman working through her issues at a psychiatric clinic in York, England, Becca was elated Olivia could be with her on this significant day.

Keeping his fingers entwined in Cooper's silky blond fur, Wallace felt the card again and glanced down to confirm what he had seen. The message was clear to him and he was almost certain he knew who had written it. He gave Cooper a pat and tried to drag himself back to the beautiful ceremony about to take place, but his head throbbed with the knowledge that someone might be planning to harm the Warwick family. That, he simply couldn't allow.

The pendulum on the brass Morbier clock swung to the left, pushing the long hand to the top of the hour, and four chimes rang out. David stepped into his place on the right side of an arch draped in holly berries, evergreens, and tiny sparkling lights, next to his best man, Philip Warwick, the 13th Earl of Crosswick. David's eyes were glued to the paneled doors through which his future was about to walk.

Watching the ceremony unfold, beads of perspiration slicked Wallace's forehead. His tuxedo shirt suddenly felt too tight, and he stuck his finger in the neck and pulled it away from his throat. As he downed the last of his Champagne, he felt Mrs. MacIntosh's eyes on him and did his best to smile.

The string quartet slid from Vivaldi into Delibes' stunning chorus from "Duo des Fleurs". As two sopranos hit the first soaring notes, the double doors to the vestibule opened.

Ella paused, as she had been schooled. Twisting in their seats, every guest watched as the little beauty in an indigo velvet gown counted under her breath. Her curly hair was bunched atop her head, with jasmine blossoms intertwined and a few wispy ringlets tickling her neck. She clutched a sterling silver basket filled with coral rose petals and, on the count of five, she took her first step into the room as the music swelled. She walked slowly up the aisle formed by one hundred guests seated in petit point-covered chairs, smiled at her audience, and dropped rose petals one at a time. Five steps behind her, Alex held the ring pillow high and steady, looking older than his nine years in a small version of his father's black tuxedo. He was followed by the three beautiful attendants, beaming as they made their way down the aisle.

And then came the bride. When Becca stepped into the doorway, David heard a low "aaaah" murmur through the room, and his eyes misted as every guest stood. Heads swiveled between David and Becca, his eyes blinking back tears, her smile radiant.

For several seconds she paused, standing between her two brothers: Conner classically handsome and James boyishly charming. But she was the star, dressed to shine in deep periwinkle that matched her eyes. A bateau neckline sat high on her collarbone then dipped midway down her back. A close-fitting bodice with long, tight sleeves gave way to a billowing skirt filled with every color of a winter sunset: pinks, oranges, and icy blues. Then she began her walk down the aisle, her blonde blunt-cut hair swinging with each step. When she arrived at the arch, she kissed each of her brothers on the cheek before they left her side to sit with their spouses. Becca stepped forward, handed Ella her bouquet made of a single blue hydrangea and a short trail of ivy and ribbons, then turned to face David. The music hushed to its glorious last notes and there was silence.

Duncan stood tall and imposing in front of the bride and groom, a dazzling blend of his parents, Philip and Genevieve Warwick. "As everyone knows," he began in a clear voice, "it's taken David and Becca over twenty years to get to where they're standing today." A low rumble of agreement rippled through the audience. "This gathering of people who have traveled from near and far to be with them is a celebration of that journey, right?"

Several people offered a quiet "right".

"You can do better than that," Duncan's voice demanded. "I said, this ceremony is a joyous celebration, right?"

This time, the crowd exploded, yelling "right," clapping and whooping. Alex and Ella jumped up and down, David threw his fist in the air, and Becca laughed as she turned to look out at the guests.

"Good job." Duncan took Becca's hand and placed it in David's. "I believe you two have things you want to say to each other." He stepped back.

David looked out at the glowing faces of the people he considered family. A lump rose in his throat and tears stung his eyes. When he turned back to Becca she was beaming at him and he was ready.

"My darling girl, we have known each other for many years. We have traveled roads together and separately that have led us to this very moment, this moment when I choose you. I choose you to be by my side until we are very old, but never decrepit." He smiled at the crowd and was rewarded with laughs. When the noise died down, he continued. "I will love you, support you, and cherish you for the rest of my life. You are my everything." He raised her hand to his lips and kissed it. "Your turn," he said with relief.

Becca's strong voice rang out. "David, my love, I am the luckiest woman on the planet. Against all logic I'm standing here with my hand in yours, ready to spend the rest of my life with you." Her eyes grew cloudy as she looked deeper into David's. "I promise a life filled with laughing and crying, building and growing, arguing and making up. I promise to fill your life with romance, and I promise to love you forever. To quote a wise woman," she smiled at Genevieve, "ours is a romance that was forged in fire and will smolder forever." Tears trickled down her blushing cheeks.

In the audience, Mrs. MacIntosh dabbed her eyes. Sitting next to her, Wallace reached for her hand, squeezed it, swiped a tear from his cheek, and patted Cooper. There were few dry eyes in the orangerie.

Duncan said the magic words, "With that, I now pronounce you husband and wife," and David took Becca's face in his hands, gazed at her for a moment, then leaned down and pressed his lips to hers.

The crowd stood and applauded, and the quartet struck up a string version of the Beatles' "All You Need is Love" as the couple moved into the crowd to hugs, kisses, slaps on the back, and well-wishes.

"Bertie, sit back down will you, please?" Wallace heard his voice quiver as he spoke.

"Something's wrong, isn't it? I knew it." She sat on the edge of her chair and rested her folded hands in her lap. Her knee bumped up and down under the long navy-blue skirt of her gown. "Well?" she said, looking up at Wallace, waiting for him to reveal his news.

Still holding Cooper by his bow, Wallace sat again and guided the dog from his side around to Mrs. MacIntosh. The pup put his head on Bertie's lap and looked up at her with happy brown eyes. "Cooper, you sweet thing," Mrs. MacIntosh cooed, leaning over to ruffle the fur on his neck.

"Go a little deeper," Wallace said.

"What?" Bertie swiveled her head to look at Wallace.

He gave his chin an upward jerk. "Go on. Dig into the bow."

Two deep lines wedged between her brows and she stared at Wallace for several seconds before looking back at Cooper, his long tail wafting back and forth. Unsure what to expect, she danced her fingertips along the top of the ribbon loops.

"Bertie," Wallace hissed. "Feel down in the bow." Exasperated, he covered Mrs. MacIntosh's hand and pushed it into the center of the ribbon. "There. What do you feel?"

As Cooper watched on, his tongue hanging to the side of his mouth, looking as if he were grinning, she felt the cold metal of the Rolex and the rigid thickness of the notecard. "What in the world?" She parted the loops to reveal the watch and paper.

Expecting a message of good wedding wishes, when Bertie saw the bloody scrawl, she jerked her hand back.

"Oh my word," was all she could say. "Oh my word," she repeated.

But when she looked up at Wallace, her eyes were filled with all the emotions she couldn't speak: confusion, fear, anger. "What is this all about? What are you going to do?" she hissed, then shook her head, continuing: "What are *we* going to do?"

"I've had the entire wedding to think about the correct course of action and I believe I should wait until the festivities are over to share this with Lord and Lady Crosswick."

Expecting an argument from Mrs. MacIntosh, Wallace was surprised when she said, "I think that is absolutely the right thing to do. We don't want to spoil Sir David and Ms. Conway's lovely day." She untied the watch and card. She tucked the watch into her evening bag, stood, and smoothed the wrinkles from her skirt. She handed the card to Wallace. "Put that in your inside pocket and we'll deal with this unpleasant situation this evening when everyone has left. I just hope I can contain myself until then."

"I know what you mean. It's unnerving to have this secret." Pleased to have an ally, he did as he was told then patted his right lapel, feeling the card in his tuxedo pocket. "You know, Bertie, I don't know what I would do without you."

"I know," she said, with a little wink that brought heat to his cheeks. She slipped her hand through the crook of his arm and gave him a shove with her hip. "We'd better get in there. We don't want to miss anything," she said, and they followed Cooper, who trotted ahead of them.

The wedding party and guests had made their way to the Château dining room. All the colors in Becca's dress were reflected around the room. On the sideboard, the head table, and in the center of the ten circular guest tables, ivy, jasmine, peonies and hydrangeas entwined soaring candelabras. Only candlelight lit the room, splashing off every surface.

Wallace and Mrs. MacIntosh found their place cards at a table where eight other guests were already seated and engaged in lively conversation. The newcomers walked around the table greeting those they knew and introducing themselves to guests they had not yet met, when they arrived at a sixty-something woman who, it appeared, had never met an injectable she didn't love. Her brows arched in permanent surprise, her skin stretched taut over ping-pong ball cheeks, and her lips were like tiny pillows beneath her blood-red lipstick.

With his hand on the small of Bertie's back, Wallace made an elegant introduction. "Good evening. I don't believe we have met. I am Reginald Wallace and this is my dear friend Alberta MacIntosh." He inclined his head and was about to extend his hand when the woman screeched and threw her arms around his neck.

"Wallace! Mrs. MacIntosh!" She gave him la bise, kissing first one cheek then the other, then did the same to Bertie. "I am Elise Beaufoy, an intimate of Lord and Lady Crosswick. We have never met, mais je sens que nous sommes de vieux amis! I am so sorry! En anglais! I feel we are old friends. I know all about the two of you. Oohlala. I have wanted to meet you for such a long time. You must sit here." She patted the chair next to her, which was occupied by her husband.

Much to Wallace and Mrs. MacIntosh's embarrassment, Michel Beaufoy stood, looked at the person next to him and shrugged as if to say, "what can we do?" And so it went, with everyone shifting to the right until they got to Bertie and Wallace's empty seats. For the entire dinner, they were captives.

When it appeared everyone was seated, Philip Warwick, the 13th Earl of Crosswick and patriarch of the House of Crosswick, stood at one end of the head table, raised his Champagne glass, and tapped it with his fork. It took several tries for the din to quiet, but finally each face turned toward the master of Château Beaulieu. He looked to the opposite end of the table and held out his hand. Genevieve, his wife of forty years, stood and walked behind the seated wedding party, stopping to kiss a cheek, squeeze a shoulder, or whisper a private word in an ear. When she arrived at Philip's end of the table, she leaned into him and kissed his lips. The crowd applauded and she offered them a sly smile and a coy nod, then began.

"You two," she said and shook a finger at David and Becca. "You two have defied the odds. What Philip and I wish for you on this journey is that you wake every day exhilarated to be with each other, thrilled to see what the day holds and how you can support each other through it. When the days are exciting and glorious, celebrate them. When the days are dark and difficult, hold each other tightly. But whatever you encounter along the way, cherish each other, always."

Not missing a beat, Philip carried on. "It seems impossible, but a year ago," he swept his gaze around the room, "few of us knew each other. In those twelve months, not only did everyone in this room become friends, but we became family, as well.

"Château Beaulieu is a world Genevieve and I never imagined we'd be a part of, but here we are. Like Wilmingrove Hall, our family seat, Château Beaulieu is part of the great history of our family. And, like the soil here at the Château, this family," he gestured to everyone at the table, "is full of grit and will continue to hold fast the roots of the Laney clan. Duncan, Julia, Alex, and Ella are the future and the next heartbeat of Château Beaulieu. How fitting that tonight, we celebrate two new beginnings: the start of David and Becca's new life together and Duncan and Julia taking the helm at Château Beaulieu. We wish you all a glorious odyssey." Philip raised his glass toward the bride and groom. "To David and Becca: may you always be awed by each other.

If you are, every day will be an adventure. And to Duncan and Julia: embrace the challenge, love the journey, and always trust in the process. If you do those three things, Château Beaulieu will flourish for many generations to come and David and Becca will always have a place to celebrate their anniversaries."

Everyone stood and "Santé" rang out from all the family and the friends who had become part of that family.

As he sat down, Wallace pressed his hand to feel the notecard in his pocket and the words flashed through his mind. He leaned into Bertie and whispered in her ear, "No one had better try to undermine this family or they'll have me to answer to."

He glanced from table to table, studying each elegant man and woman in the room. He was quite sure he knew who was responsible for the disturbing message and, as his gaze settled on the head table, his eyes lingered on one person. He would be watching carefully until he could confirm his suspicion.

"A penny for your thoughts." He felt Mrs. MacIntosh's warm breath on his cheek as she leaned over and whispered in his ear.

A chuckle bubbled from his throat. "I was just speculating about who did the unpleasant deed." He patted his pocket again. "You know," he said, raising his brows.

"Of course I know," she shot back. "I may be getting older by the minute, but I haven't lost my memory completely. Try to put it out of your mind until we talk to Lord and Lady Crosswick."

"That's a tall order, Bertie, but I'll do my best."

"I know," she said. "But we decided there was nothing to be done until later. If you're not careful, you're going to spend all evening lost in your thoughts and miss this lovely event."

"You're right, of course," he said, offering the best smile he could muster. He patted her hand then turned to Elise Beaufoy, who was chattering on about something of little interest to him.

With the last course of the sumptuous wedding feast served and eaten, guests began to drift back into the orangerie, which had been transformed from the site of David and Becca's ceremony into a magical world of holly trees, fairy lights, and music.

For their first dance, Becca had changed into a figure-hugging black dress with a thigh-high slit. For weeks, she and David had been taking dance lessons and were about to show off their newly honed skill as the trio played "Mi Confesion," a sultry accompaniment to the sensual steps of the Argentine tango. The crowd cleared the dance floor as the couple held each other in a close embrace, leaning into one another so their legs could move freely. As the music began, David and Becca locked eyes. David took a step forward and Becca ran her foot up the inside of his leg.

"Oohlala," rippled through the onlookers.

Lost in the sensuous music and moves of the tango, it was a long moment before Wallace felt the discomfort of being watched. When at last he turned to see whose eye might be on him, he looked directly into Olivia's frosty stare. And, though he pulled his attention back to David and Becca immediately, he could feel Olivia's eyes boring into him.

The crowd gasped and cheered as the beat drove the dancers around the circle in a smooth glide, with Becca's legs whipping in and out of David's. Olivia stared at Wallace and he stared at the couple. The pulse in his temple matched the beat of the music and the tension built, throbbing in his head until David and Becca twirled three times, froze in place and Wallace thought his head would explode.

Becca slid her foot seductively down the outside of David's thigh. She held his gaze, heat searing the space between them, then, as the musicians played their final notes, she took his face in her hands and slowly, slowly drew his lips to hers.

The crowd erupted. Stomps and whistles of appreciation rewarded David and Becca's seductive performance and Wallace nearly collapsed from the release of the pent-up tension.

Wallace looked back to where Olivia had been but she was nowhere to be seen.

Exhilarated, bride and groom twirled, swept into a dramatic bow, then bowed again as the applause surged and finally waned. With the wedding couple's dance complete, guests poured onto the dance floor, refilled their drinks, and clustered into chattering, laughing groups. The elegant atmosphere during the ceremony and dinner had morphed into a joyous party and guests moved in and out of noisy groups, picking up threads of conversation, tossing in a jovial word then moving on to the next laughing clutch of friends.

In the midst of all the music and the din of merrymakers, Cooper wandered from group to group getting a pat here, a scratch behind the ear there, until he spied two faces he knew. Trotting toward David and Becca, his long blond coat swayed and his tail wagged until he arrived and sat at their feet, the jaunty blue bow making him look like a gift.

From nearby, Wallace saw the newlyweds smile at Cooper's surprise visit. He held his breath as Becca squatted to give him a cuddle and ruffle the fur on his neck. When he heard her say, "Cooper, you darling boy," Wallace exhaled, confident there had been no more surprises buried in the dog's ribbon. With that assurance, he decided to take Bertie's advice. He'd do his best to enjoy the rest of the evening before sharing the nasty business of the note.

He glanced around the room and felt a happy glow when he saw Mrs. MacIntosh standing with a group near the dance floor. He crossed the room and stood just behind her until she felt his presence.

"Reg," she said, surprised. "How long have you been standing there?"

"Just a moment," he said. "Is there any chance you would like to take a turn on the dance floor?"

The wording was old-fashioned, but the invitation was welcome. "Absolutely," she said, taking his arm before he could have second thoughts.

They sidled between twirling, wiggling, jiggling dancers until they found a space to stand. With enough distance between them for Wallace to feel proper, he put his right hand on the small of Mrs. MacIntosh's back and held up his left for her to slip her palm into his.

"Wallace," she said laughing and scooting back another few inches. "This is not a waltz and this is not a tea dance." She bounced her shoulders to the band's rendition of ABBA's "Money, Money, Money".

How appropriate, Wallace thought, moving his hips slightly, and trying to appear as if he knew what he was doing.

TWO

WITH THE MUSIC loud and the mood boisterous, Genevieve pulled Becca into a bear hug. "I'm so glad you wanted to have your wedding here at Château Beaulieu. What a wonderful day this has been, don't you think?" She looked around the circle where three of the four Warwick family members and their two closest friends had gathered amidst music, dancing, laughter, and people they loved. "Didn't Ella and Alex do a spectacular job?" she said with grandmotherly pride.

One of her great joys this year had been to have their son, Duncan, his wife, Julia, and their children decide to live at Château Beaulieu. After the vineyard's general manager died, Philip and Genevieve were thrilled when Duncan suggested he and his family take over the running of the Château and its revered vineyard.

Two years ago, David Weatherington, chief executor of the estate of Jonathon William Wallace Laney, the 12th Earl of Crosswick, had located and secured Philip as the heir to the House of Crosswick with its vast holdings and title. David, Philip, and Genevieve instantly became fast friends. And with Becca's reintroduction into David's life, they had all grown to be as close as family. Last year, they had weathered Becca's daughter Olivia's murderous intentions and, now that she seemed to be coming out the other side, they were thrilled for Becca that she might be getting her daughter back.

David planted a loud kiss on Genevieve's cheek, flushed from the warmth of the room and several glasses of Champagne. "Everything has been absolutely brilliant, Genevieve. We can never thank you and Philip enough for this extraordinary beginning to our married life." He interlaced his fingers with Becca's and kissed her forehead.

"Look at Olivia." Duncan pointed into the throng of bobbing, dipping dancers. "She looks like she's having a great time."

Becca and Duncan scanned the dance floor until they lasered in on Olivia. They watched her head bounce up and down as her high, blonde ponytail whipped back and forth. Becca felt a surge of optimism as she watched her daughter move her hips and pump her arms in rhythm with the drums of the dance band that had taken over from the tango trio. Olivia's partner, a lanky, stylish Parisian boy, had moves that could only have been cultivated by hours on the dance floors of Paris's best clubs. They danced together. They danced apart. They teased and laughed, wiggled and twirled, until, at last, the music stopped. They were two young people enjoying good music and a good time.

"We're very proud of Olivia," David said, hoping he sounded convincing. "She's really doing well in her recovery."

"God, I hope you're right," her mother said, with less conviction.

David put his arm around Becca's shoulders and pulled her to him. "Darling, the fact that she's been moved from a secure floor to the open residential floor at Blain Lodge tells us she's made enormous progress."

Becca tilted her pretty face with its delicate features so she looked into her husband's eyes. "And it's a very good sign that Dr. Morgan's allowing her to spend time here at Château Beaulieu over the holidays," she said, with all the certainty she could muster. But she kept her eyes on her daughter, who was flushed from dancing and fanning herself with her hand while she and Émile waited for the next song. "They seem to be having fun." She allowed herself to smile.

"Ah, to be twenty-one again!" Genevieve laughed, knowing she wouldn't turn back the clock for anything. She loved her life just as it was.

"What about Émile? How is he doing?"

"Are you asking because of his high jinks with our Jackson Pollock when the little prankster tried to extort five million euros from us?" Genevieve's eyes were wide with mock surprise.

Becca barked a laugh. "Since he's getting cozy with my daughter, who is trying to work her way out of a criminal conviction, I guess I am."

Less than a year ago, Philip and Genevieve had taken Émile under their wing after he had committed what he considered a prank and Lord and Lady Crosswick had considered an attempt at grand larceny. After Émile's father begged the Warwicks to allow his son to work at their vineyard rather than go to prison, Philip and Genevieve agreed if he promised to work hard and do everything asked of him, they would give him a chance. If he did not, it was back to Paris and straight to prison. And they had been rewarded. Émile was not only growing into a valuable member of the vineyard staff, but he was becoming a part of the Warwick family as well.

Duncan searched the crowd and when he finally saw his father, he caught his eye and waved him over.

As the band bounced its way into Wilson Pickett's "Land of 1000 Dances", Philip snaked his way through the throng of guests swarming on the dance floor. He paused to twirl Madame Morier, the commanding head of their Avenue Foch Château in Paris, then passed her into the arms of Becca's brother, James. He stopped and gave Mrs. MacIntosh a hip bump and a smile before emerging from the crowd.

With his hands in his pockets, he sauntered toward the little group filled with people he loved.

"Where have you been, Philip?" Julia sparkled, keeping beat to the music by bouncing in place.

"I was just in the kitchen thanking Lizette and her staff for doing such a wonderful job today."

Duncan grinned at his wife. "Julia, my darling, it looks to me as if you're ready to get out on the dance floor."

"What was your first clue?" She batted her lashes at him and pumped her shoulders in time to the music. Then, realizing she hadn't seen their children since dinner, she scanned the crowd for Alex and Ella, spying them wiggling around the dance floor with Wallace and Mrs. MacIntosh. "I'd better go rescue those two wonderful people. Dancing with two wild kiddos is definitely not in their job description."

As he watched Julia join their children on the dance floor—slender hips swaying to the music and arms overhead punching toward the ceiling, head thrown back, laughing with abandon—he marveled at what a lucky man he was. Fifteen years of marriage and Julia could still knock his socks off. The band whipped into a frenzy of the last notes of "Land of 1000 Dances" and everyone chanted, "Na-na-na-na-na-na-na-na-na-na-na-na-na-na-na!" at the top of their lungs until the end. The musicians paused long enough to gulp their drinks and mop perspiration from their brows and the dancers swilled whatever filled their glasses, trying to recover before the music began again.

Duncan squeezed himself between the dancers crammed on the floor, making his way to Julia and the kids. He hefted Ella into his arms and bounced in place waiting for the next song.

The band hit the first iconic notes of "Proud Mary" and the vocalist brought Tina Turner to life. With her three backup beauties pumping and grinding behind her, she started slowly, building tension as she lured her audience with sensuous promises. With full lips snarling and a deep sultry laugh, the seductress growled, "I never, ever seem to do anything nice and easy. That is to say, I like to do it nice and rough!"

The crowd erupted, then quieted, softly clapping to the steady riff of the guitar until, at last, she began to sing. "Left a good job in the city." The dancers could hardly contain themselves, their muscles taut with anticipation. Their shoulders dipped and rolled, hips following as their bodies kept rhythm to the irresistible buildup of what was to come.

With the last, slow, "Rollin' on the river, river, river," the horn blared, the drummer doubled the tempo and the room exploded with frenzied dancing.

Next to the writhing Warwicks, Mrs. MacIntosh and Wallace swayed sedately. She smiled at her partner and his eyes crinkled back in a grin. Giving over to "Proud Mary's" driving beat, Wallace gently pumped his shoulders and lifted his feet, taking small steps to turn in place. As he rotated away from Mrs. MacIntosh, he found himself face to face with Olivia.

Her brows drawn together, she looked up into his face. "Are you all right, Wallace? You don't look at all well," she said. She frowned at him for several seconds, then, turning her attention back to Émile, flashed a dazzling smile at her dance partner, and fell into the music.

Wallace completed his slow spin so he was again facing Mrs. MacIntosh. He pulled a linen handkerchief from his pocket and mopped his sweating brow. As a wave of nausea swept over him, he panicked at the idea of vomiting right here on the dance floor and clapped his hand over his mouth. As he swayed, feeling unsteady, Ella grabbed his other hand, raised his arm over her head and twirled like a ballerina on top of a music box. She twirled until she was so dizzy she began to stagger, then collapsed into a mass of giggles.

Wallace bent to pull her up, but instead of reaching out to the little girl, he clutched his chest, his eyes startled wide and his face scarlet. He gasped, trying to draw a breath, fear flooding through him as he clawed at his collar, struggling to loosen the button and locking on Bertie's terror-filled eyes just before he crumpled to the floor.

Julia was the first to see his distress and knew instantly what was happening.

"Duncan, call an ambulance!" she snapped at her husband. Two steps and she was at Wallace's side, squatting beside him, grabbing his wrist, searching for his pulse. She looked at the sweep hand on her watch and counted the weak beats.

He looked up at Julia, his half-lidded, glazed eyes relieved to see her. "It's lucky you're a doctor, my lady."

"Lucky indeed, Wallace." She smiled at the aging man she had adored from the moment they met at Wilmingrove Hall. She lay a comforting hand on the side of his face. "An ambulance is on its way. We'll get you to the hospital and into expert hands." She leaned forward and whispered conspiratorially, "You know, Wallace, I'm not licensed in France yet, so don't tell anyone I took your pulse." She winked into his wan smile, wary of the pallor that had replaced his flushed complexion.

Sensing a presence standing over them, Julia looked up at sturdy Mrs. MacIntosh, whose eyes brimmed with tears, her lower lip gripped between her teeth. The other half of the duo that had kept Wilmingrove Hall running like a machine for decades, Mrs. MacIntosh stood motionless except for fingers that twisted and untwisted her linen handkerchief.

Julia reached up and intertwined her fingers with Mrs. MacIntosh's to still her nerves. A siren's cry could be heard in the distance, growing louder with each passing moment until an EMS team bolted through the door. In an instant they assessed Wallace's condition and expertly eased him onto a gurney. Before they whisked him out of the Château, Wallace grabbed Julia's hand, clearly wanting to tell her something. She brought her ear to his lips and he mumbled in a feeble voice, "I know who did this to me."

Unsure what she had just heard, Julia watched as the emergency workers wheeled Wallace out of the room and were gone, leaving a hundred devastated guests in their wake.

THREE

AS THE AMBULANCE screamed down the driveway away from the house, Genevieve issued orders to Julia. "Keep the party going if you can. Keep the Champagne flowing and the music playing. We'll call you as soon as we have any news." She wrapped Julia in a ferocious hug. "Thank you, darling Julia." As she looked at her daughter-in-law, her eyes swam with tears. She mustered a small smile. "I'm sure you saved Wallace's life."

Julia returned the squeeze. "I wish I could say he'll be fine, but I have no idea," she said.

Genevieve's stomach clutched with fear. "At least he's in good hands now," she said, and kissed Julia on the cheek before rushing Mrs. MacIntosh to the foyer where Delphine, Château Beaulieu's house manager, stood at the ready with their coats. They flew out the front door and down the wide steps to the Purosangue, where Philip waited with the engine running. He stood by the open passenger door and held Mrs. MacIntosh's hand as he guided her into the front seat of the Ferrari. Before he could turn to open Genevieve's door, she was seated, belted, and ready to go.

At eight o'clock on a Saturday night, Hôpital Public in

Libourne was a quick eleven-minute drive from Château Beaulieu. It was not known for outstanding care, but it was close. At each of the four roundabouts, Philip accelerated into the circle then shot out onto his exit road, happy to have the speed of the powerful SUV at his command. From the back seat, Genevieve kept a comforting hand on Mrs. MacIntosh's shoulder until they arrived at the hospital emergency entrance.

When the three rushed through the ER door, the smell of disinfectant was like a slap in the face. The waiting room overflowed and the noise from patients waiting to be seen and their caretakers rivaled the din of an airport during a busy holiday.

Philip advanced through the chaos to the high counter announcing RÉCEPTION. He leaned on the desk and loomed over the nurse on the other side. Furiously scribbling on charts, she didn't acknowledge his presence. He cleared his throat. Nothing. He cleared it again, louder this time.

The woman held up a finger, signaling for Philip to wait.

Not in a waiting mood, he said, "Excusez-moi," louder than he meant to.

Still holding her finger in the air, the nurse raised her head, brows arched. "Oui?" she said, annoyance dripping from the word.

Undaunted, Philip forged on politely. "Je suis Lord Crosswick de Château Beaulieu. Je veux des informations sur Reginald Wallace. Il est arrivé en ambulance il y a quelques minutes." He wanted information about Wallace and he wanted it now. He stared into her unblinking eyes, narrowed his, and hardened his jaw.

Just as Genevieve stepped forward to intervene in the power struggle, double doors with a sign reading "Personnel Seulment"—"Staff Only"—parted and a chic, white-coated woman strode through. She wore her hair in a tight chignon, and an escaped salt-and-pepper strand fluttered as she barreled toward Philip, Genevieve, and Mrs. MacIntosh. Her expression gave nothing away.

Genevieve blinked, trying to control the tears stinging her eyes. Mrs. MacIntosh sniffled, and Philip held his breath for the few seconds it took for the docteur to walk down the hall and stop in front of them.

"Lord and Lady Crosswick?" she said. Philip and Genevieve nodded. "Et vous?" She turned to Mrs. MacIntosh.

"This is Mr. Wallace's dearest friend, Bertie MacIntosh," Philip answered for the housekeeper.

She nodded. "Je suis Dr. Aubert." She offered her hand to each of them, then turned and said over her shoulder, "Allez avec mois."

The three followed her down the hall to a small windowless room. Rather than antiseptic, the smell of lilies hung in the air. The docteur motioned for them to be seated and they obeyed like school children. Genevieve leaned forward, her hands on the arms of her chair. Mrs. MacIntosh was as stiff and erect as a flagpole, her fingers laced together in her lap. Philip sat back against the cushion of his chair, ankles crossed, right foot bouncing, his jaw clenched with tension.

Dr. Aubert remained standing. "Français ou anglais?" she said, arching her brows in question.

"Anglais, s'il vous plaît." Though Philip and Genevieve were fluent in French, Mrs. MacIntosh was not.

The docteur began, her voice rushed and detached, as if she were lecturing a class. "When Monsieur Wallace arrived at the Emergency Room, he had suffered a massive heart attack. Though our medical personnel did everything they could, he was pronounced dead shortly after he arrived at the hospital. Je suis désolé. I am sorry for your loss." She extended her hand to Philip. "Someone from administration will call you tomorrow with next steps."

She turned and was gone, leaving Philip, Genevieve, and Mrs. MacIntosh alone, stunned, and speechless. The three looked at each other, not understanding what had just happened.

"Did she say Wallace is dead?" Mrs. MacIntosh almost whispered.

Genevieve hesitated. "I think that's what she said. But how is that possible?"

Through a curtain of tears, she watched Philip slide across the faux-leather sofa to Mrs. MacIntosh. He put his arm around her slumped shoulders and pulled her into his side. The stoic Scot collapsed into Philip's chest and Genevieve watched her shake in silence, releasing her grief. Philip's face clouded with the same sorrow that shrouded Mrs. MacIntosh's, her own emotion compounded by decades of working side by side with this lovely man, this unexpectedly dead man.

When their gaze met, Genevieve's cheeks were streaked with tears and Philip's eyes glistened. He shrugged his shoulders in response to Genevieve's unspoken question, "What do we do now?"

FOUR

The mournful creaking of Château Beaulieu's massive front door reflected the sorrow of the three people who trudged into the foyer. The clock began to chime. Philip held Mrs. MacIntosh's coat as she struggled to pull her arms from the sleeves. He doffed his topcoat, took Genevieve's heavy cape from her hand, and tossed them all on a bench by the front door.

When the last of the ten bongs quieted, silence filled the grand hall, except for the ticking of the clock. Taking Mrs. MacIntosh by the elbow, Philip steered her into the grand salon, made cozy by comfortable overstuffed furniture and warm colors. He led the housekeeper to a chair next to the fireplace where coals still glowed on the hearth.

"Mrs. MacIntosh, please sit," he said. Taking a poker from the tools standing at the ready, he poked and pushed unburned bits of wood around until small flames flickered to life, then chose two logs from the copper woodbin. As he laid them across the embers, they crackled and shot sparks at the old brick at the back of the firebox.

While Philip tended to the fire, Genevieve brought a tray with a decanter of whisky and three cut-glass tumblers from the sideboard. She set it on the coffee table in front of the down-filled sofa, which faced the fireplace where the flames were beginning to dance. Before sitting, she pulled a camel, cream, and white Afghan from the back of the sofa, walked to Mrs. MacIntosh, and draped it over her knees. She squeezed the housekeeper on the shoulder and when Mrs. MacIntosh looked up, Genevieve saw her eyes were full of gratitude and sorrow.

"You know how much we all loved Wallace," Genevieve said.

"And he adored you, my lady. You know he thought you were the perfect lady of the manor, don't you?"

Genevieve handed Mrs. MacIntosh a glass and she took it with a nod of thanks.

Genevieve sat next to Philip on the sofa. She chuckled before she took a sip of scotch. Staring into the fire, she was far away for a moment. "When Philip and I first arrived at Wilmingrove Hall, we were so worried we would make a misstep. You frightened us when you met us at the helicopter that first day."

"No! That's not possible, my lady." Mrs. MacIntosh smirked, her Scottish brogue thick.

Philip raised his glass to her. "It's more than possible. That was your intention," he laughed. "And you were determined to dislike us. Two obnoxious Americans coming to sully generations of Crosswicks with our coarse behavior. That's what you thought, wasn't it? Admit it, Mrs. MacIntosh."

"My lord, I shall never admit such a thing." She paused to empty her glass and a tiny sparkle returned to her eye. "I will say, however, Wallace did Google the two of you as soon as we learned of your inheritance. He was very good at Googling." She smiled.

Genevieve's cheeks pinked. "What did he find?" she asked, not sure if she wanted to hear the answer.

"I have to say, he was quite disappointed. There was nothing untoward about you two. In fact, quite the contrary. Everything he found was about business successes and charitable donations. There was even an article about how years ago you started an art school for underprivileged children in Washington, D.C. similar to what you've done at your museum in Paris." Her smile crinkled the corners of her eyes. "In fact, Wallace was so disappointed he was quite difficult to live with until you arrived."

Genevieve whooshed out the breath she'd been holding. "Whew," she said, then turned to Philip. "Looks like we were able to cover up all the terrible things we've done recently."

"I'd say those were dollars well-spent." Philip kissed Genevieve on her nose and patted her thigh, leaving his hand to linger a moment before rising to refill all three glasses and toss another log on the fire.

It may have been the scotch or perhaps it was reminiscing about Wallace, but Genevieve wanted to prolong the warm mood that had settled over the room, replacing the bleakness of just a short while ago. "Mrs. MacIntosh, do you remember the day we arrived and you and Wallace gave me a tour of the house?"

"Of course I do. We were so impressed with your knowledge of many of the great artists and artisans whose works fill the Hall. It didn't take long for you and Lord Crosswick," she smiled at Philip, "to win the two of us over."

"Well, I'm grateful for that. I'll never forget when we arrived at the music room and the Hall's historian, Fenton Morrisey joined us to share some of the wonderful stories about the artists who had performed there. Remember, he brought a stack of volumes in his skinny arms. I loved his curly ginger hair and how it bounced when he walked. I remember he didn't watch where he was going, tripped over a small footstool, and dropped some of the books. When I stooped to pick up the volumes, another book fell and smacked me on the head. I fell to the floor and thunked my nose on the hardwood." By now Mrs. MacIntosh and Genevieve were wheezing with laughter.

"And Wallace came back into the room," Mrs. MacIntosh gasped.

Genevieve lowered her voice an octave and mimicked Wallace's posh accent. "What's going on here?" she bellowed, imitating the butler. "Remember, he was carrying a bottle of Château Margaux in each hand. When he saw me lying face down on the floor, he almost had a heart attack." When she heard the words come out, she clamped her hand over her mouth. She and Mrs. MacIntosh stared at each other, eyes round with horror until several seconds later they fell back into laughter at the irony. They snorted with giggles that exploded into belly laughs. They gasped for air but couldn't stop howling.

Cozy and relaxed on the sofa, Philip watched with amusement from his corner of the couch. He marveled at the resilience of human beings and their ability to withstand tragedy. Just an hour ago, they had received terrible news about a man they loved, and now their spirits were buoyed by sharing Wallace stories, laughing at memories of him, and weeping as they talked about how they would miss him. Without looking, Philip felt a presence enter at the far end of the room.

"What's going on?" Duncan asked as he, Julia, David, Becca, and Olivia walked the length of the room, surprised Genevieve and Mrs. MacIntosh were in the throes of hilarity.

"Your mother and Mrs. MacIntosh were telling some wonderful Wallace tales. We're all still in a state of shock." He motioned to the bottle sitting on the coffee table. "Grab a glass, sit down, and tell us what went on here after the ambulance left."

The kids, as Philip and Genevieve called them, each hugged Philip and Genevieve, then squeezed Mrs. MacIntosh's hand, kissed her on the cheek, and leaned over to hug her before flopping into the remaining empty chairs, all except Duncan. As they passed the whisky bottle around, he stood in front of the fireplace and described the scene at Château Beaulieu.

"After the EMTs whisked Wallace away, everyone was on tenterhooks, hoping for the best."

David splashed scotch into a crystal tumbler, handed it to Duncan and he continued. "After you called with the devasting news, people held each other, sobbed together, grappled with their disbelief, but they didn't linger long. No one could grasp what had happened."

"I still can't believe he's gone." Olivia's eyes were red-rimmed. "I know he didn't approve of me but I loved his very English elegance."

Mrs. MacIntosh searched Olivia's eyes for several seconds trying to confirm whether or not the girl was genuinely sorry for Wallace's death. When Olivia realized Bertie was staring at her, she returned the favor, setting her jaw and narrowing her eyes to menacing slits. Bertie glanced away then looked back, saw a sad, angelic face, and wondered if she had imagined Olivia's malevolent glare.

Duncan raised his tumbler and surveyed each person in the tight circle. "Though none of us knew Wallace as long or as well as you, Mrs. MacIntosh," he smiled at the housekeeper, "each of us loved him. There will never be another Reginald Wallace and I pity the poor bastard who tries to fill his shoes at Wilmingrove Hall. To Wallace."

A boisterous "To Wallace" echoed through the vast salon.

FIVE

THE COLD DRIZZLE that had moved in the night before was a perfect metaphor for the pall that had descended on Château Beaulieu. With guests arriving for Christmas in three days, Genevieve couldn't imagine how they were going to provide a happy holiday for Alex and Ella. Mrs. MacIntosh was still at the Château along with Olivia who was staying with them while David and Becca took a few days' honeymoon in Tenerife before coming back on Christmas Eve. Lillie Langdon would arrive from Paris, and Finnegan Mountbatten, an old Warwick family friend, would be joining them. With Duncan, Julia, Alex, and Ella, they'd be a group of twelve, with the adults putting on a brave face for the sake of two children who deserved a happy Christmas.

Genevieve tapped her Mont Blanc pen on the edge of her computer and stared out the windows of Philip's study. Beyond the terrace the naked vines shivered in the frosty haze. She pulled her pashmina tighter around her shoulders, closed her eyes, and listened to the fire crackle on the grate.

The devastating sorrow she felt when they were told Wallace was dead kept flooding back. The sting of tears made her blink and a fat drop oozed from the corner of her eye. It trailed down her cheek and slid to her jaw, where it sat for a moment before plopping onto the sheet of paper, spreading a freshly penned word into an inky puddle.

Buried in thought, her phone startled her as it vibrated toward the edge of the desk. A picture filled the screen: Becca and her taken at Château Beaulieu last fall. In the photo they sat on the terrace just outside these very windows, but the day was sunny and warm and the two friends smiled into the camera, looking glamorous in dark glasses.

"Becca, I'm so glad you called." She rubbed the damp from her cheek with her knuckle. "You're just what I need."

"I can hear in your voice you've been crying." Becca flooded the distance between them with love. "I'm so sorry I'm not there to give you a hug."

"Do I sound that bad?"

"You sound pretty bad," Becca said.

"I assume Mrs. MacIntosh is staying for Christmas."

"If you can imagine, she was making noises about going back to Wilmingrove Hall on Friday, but Philip and I insisted she stay. But that's not why you called. What's up?" Genevieve could tell Becca had something on her mind.

"You are so perceptive, darling friend. I do have a favor to ask of you." Becca's voice tensed. "The other day just before the wedding procession began, Olivia suggested I take off my ruby ring."

The stunning square-cut blood-red stone, surrounded by diamonds, flashed into Genevieve's mind. The former Laney family heirloom had a storied past and she chuckled under her breath to think of its journey over the last twenty-five years.

"That was a wise decision," Genevieve said. "Your wedding ring is a stunner, but that ruby, whoa!"

"The problem is, I hadn't thought about it until I was unpacking my bag last night." She paused. "And I can't find it. I gave it to Olivia and assumed she took it upstairs and put it in my jewelry organizer. You know, that beautiful tapestry roll you gave me last year for Christmas?"

"I remember it well. I loved it so much I almost kept it." Genevieve smiled into the phone. "You have the organizer, right?"

"I do. But the ring isn't in there."

"You're sure?"

"Genevieve." Becca's voice had an edge to it. "You don't think I'm capable of looking through a jewelry holder and finding a ring if it's there?"

"And you've checked with Olivia?"

"Of course I have. I called and woke her this morning. She said she put it in the jewelry roll, just as I thought," Becca snapped.

"Sorry, sorry." Genevieve put a defensive hand up at her end of the phone.

"No, *I'm* sorry." Becca's voice sounded on the edge of tears.

"Becca," she soothed. "We'll find the ring."

Sniffles crept through the line, then a shaky breath. "Of course you're right. I'm just so sorry to cause you all this trouble, particularly now."

Genevieve snorted a laugh. "Becca Conway Weatherington. You have caused me nothing but trouble since we met!"

There was silence at the other end of the line for several beats before both women laughed.

"Could you please ask Delphine to check our room? I'm sure I left it somewhere there. Maybe it's in the corner of a dresser drawer, or maybe it slipped down the side of the cushion of that wonderful, overstuffed chair. I'm not panicking yet." But as she spoke, Genevieve could tell she was anxious.

"Don't worry about a thing." Genevieve's voice caressed her friend with calm assurance. "We'll find it. We can't let that heritage piece disappear." Genevieve chuckled to lighten Becca's mood. "That ring has more stories to tell than Dr. Seuss."

Genevieve heard her friend's feeble laugh and knew until the ring was found, Becca wouldn't sleep.

"I'm going to hang up right now and go look myself." She was already out of the study and on her way to the staircase. "I'll call you the moment I find it. Fear not, mon petit chou. Super sleuth is on the case."

"Thank you, thank you. You're my heroine, Genevieve. You always have been."

Genevieve skipped up the stairs, taking two at a time until she got halfway to the top. Gasping, she grabbed the banister and slowed her pace to one step at a time. When she reached the top she bent over, standing with her hands on her knees. "Jeeze, girl. You need to work out more," she said, panting. She closed her eyes and calmed her breath.

Feeling a presence hovering above her, she opened her eyes and saw two black Chucks peeking out from under a pair of well-faded jeans.

"That was quite a sprint—until you petered out," Philip said, humor edging his voice. He reached down and eased Genevieve to stand. Unable to resist her flushed cheeks and pink mouth, he pulled her into a warm kiss that promised more. "What's the rush, G?" His voice was husky.

Not wanting to break the seductive spell, she tipped back in his arms and hoped he thought her heavy breathing was excitement for him and not the aftermath of her dash up the stairs. She reached up and brushed a strand of hair from his forehead. "How are you still so handsome?"

Philip had changed little since he and Genevieve met over four decades ago, she a second-year law student and he a graduate student in art history. They had fallen in love quickly and deeply and were among the lucky ones who had survived the long haul. Through difficult times as entrepreneurs there had been robust disagreements, but they had always encouraged each other's dreams and buoyed each other, and to this day they shared a life filled with adventure and laughter; always laughter.

When Philip received the call telling him he had inherited a billion pounds and an earldom, their lives had changed but Philip and Genevieve had not. True, at one point Philip had been ready to give the inheritance back and return to their previous, less complicated lives. But after surviving several frightening and disruptive challenges, they were committed to assuring the House of Crosswick would flourish for their son, their grandchildren, and well beyond.

With their newfound wealth they were accomplishing things on a grander scale than before their windfall, changing lives and contributing to their shared passion, the arts. And they were having a spectacular time. At this point, they were prepared to fend off any dangers that might come their way but hoped that was all behind them.

Philip wiggled his brows. "Do you have a few minutes? I have something I want to show you in our room."

Tiny lines crinkled at the corner of Genevieve's eyes as her smile appled her cheeks. She kissed Philip on the mouth, then pressed out of his arms. "I'll have to take a raincheck," she said, and giggled at the disappointment on his face. "Becca called and can't find her ruby ring. She asked me to look in their room."

"You must be kidding," he said. "She's misplaced the Laney ruby ring?"

"Philip, it hasn't been the Laney ring for a long time. Anyway, I need to go scour the room. Do you want to come?"

"Tempting as that sounds, if I can't lure you to our room, I'm going to meet Duncan in the wine office. He's teasing me with an idea he says I may or may not like."

"That sounds mysterious, but I have my own mystery to solve."

"While you're looking for Becca's ruby ring, keep your eyes open for Duncan's Rolex. Did he tell you it's been missing since the day of the wedding?"

"He did not but I bet it's in his room somewhere. I have bigger fish to fry." Genevieve stretched up on her tiptoes and gave Philip a loud kiss on his lips, then turned to head to the room where David and Becca had stayed.

Before she was out of reach, Philip gave her a smack on her bottom. "I'll see you later," he promised.

"You most certainly will," she assured him.

SIX

G ENEVIEVE SAT ON the guest room floor. Duvet, sheets, and pillows were strewn across the bed and every drawer was pulled out. The light from the dressing room poured through the open door and painted a yellow rectangle on the floor. Genevieve's hair stood out with static electricity where her head had rubbed the carpet as she searched under the bed. She had combed every inch of the room, turning everything she could upside down.

All the while, though there were no flowers in the room, the fragrance of roses hung in the air. Sensing Charlotte Chaubert's presence, she called out twice to the family ghost, hoping the spirit would use her supernatural power to find the ring.

She puffed at a strand of hair tickling her nose. It fluttered up then wafted back to where it started. She ran her fingers through her locks, tugging her hair to the top of her head and slipping a scrunchy around it, tying it into a messy bun.

Not willing to admit defeat, she hoisted herself to her feet and returned to the bathroom. She turned in a slow circle, taking in every inch of porcelain, tile, and chrome. She even looked at the ceiling, wondering if the ring could have somehow made its way from the jewelry roll and into the bowl-shaped fixture above her. Not likely, she decided.

Unable to conjure any reason to postpone her call to Becca, she pulled her phone from her jeans pocket and punched in the number. After two rings, Becca answered. "Genevieve?" Her voice was bright, hoping for good news.

"It is," Genevieve said.

"Did you find it?"

"Not yet. But it has to be here, doesn't it?" Genevieve tried to keep her tone upbeat. "Is there somewhere else in the Château Olivia could have put it?"

Silence filled the other end of the line for several seconds. Genevieve could almost hear Becca thinking.

"Let me talk to Delphine and ask her to keep her eyes open. And I'll check with Olivia again. It was just before the wedding started. Maybe she was going to run it upstairs but got sidetracked. It won't hurt to check with her again," Genevieve said. "There's no reason to give up hope. It's got to be here somewhere. On the bright side, I doubt if David would be sad if the ring never turned up, would he? After all, it was a gift from Philip's cousin, your lover." She snickered.

"Genevieve Warwick, you're absolutely wicked." Though her tone was harsh, Genevieve knew she was smiling at the joke. "I'll be there in a couple of days to continue the search if you don't find it before we come for Christmas."

"I'd better get your room put back together before Delphine sees it. I'll be in real trouble if she walks into this mess."

"Je t'aime, mon amie." Genevieve still heard worry in Becca's voice.

"I love you too. A bientôt." Genevieve ended the call.

With her mind racing, she began putting the room back together. Since 1850, the square-cut ruby ring had decked the finger of one Crosswick countess after another until more than twenty years ago Philip's cousin Jonathon, the 12th Earl and the man from whom Philip inherited his fortune and title, gave the ring to Becca.

She smoothed the duvet and was surveying the room with a critical eye when the fragrance of Rose Otto hit her like a gust of wind.

"Charlotte," she whispered.

Today was the first time Genevieve had felt her presence since encountering the magnificent ghost at Wilmingrove Hall. It made sense that Charlotte would take an interest in the missing ring. The magnificent French wife of the 9th Earl of Crosswick had stood out among the exceptional lineage of Crosswick countesses. She had often worn the ring while she charmed London society for decades as a magnificent hostess, a patron of the arts, and a well-known animal lover.

She picked up a small petit point embroidered pillow from the chair next to the dresser. "Charlotte," she said again, hugging the pillow to her chest. "Do you know where the ring is?"

She stood looking out the window. Feeling Charlotte in the doorway, the skin on her neck prickled and she inhaled a deep, rose-fragrant breath. Not wanting to frighten the spirit away, she turned slowly until she faced the door. There, his hands in his pockets, a broad smile on his face, Philip stood leaning casually against the jamb.

"Did Charlotte find the ring?" he said.

Genevieve hurled the pillow at Philip and he snatched it out of the air with one hand. "You and Charlotte have quite a close relationship, don't you?"

"How long have you been standing there?" she said, her cheeks hot with embarrassment.

"Long enough to catch most of your conversation and I have to say, I found it pretty entertaining." His grin was irresistible.

She turned away from him, wiggled her hips, and, looking over her shoulder with a bat of her lashes, threw him a coquettish pout. "I am nothing if not entertaining."

Philip shot across the room toward his vamping wife. Genevieve shrieked with laughter as she ran to the bathroom to escape her advancing husband.

"You can run, my pretty, but you cannot hide." Philip wrung his hands villainously, threw back his head laughing a Snidely Whiplash laugh, strode through the bathroom door, and closed it behind him.

SEVEN

LYING ON HIS side on the huge, plush bathmat, Philip propped himself on his elbow and tickled Genevieve's nose with a strand of her hair. Her eyes were closed and she was almost dozing. She brushed the hair away and he did it again.

She could feel a sneeze building. "Will you please stop that?" The sneeze rose then evaporated. Her eyelids fluttered open and she grinned into Philip's elegant face. "That was fun," she said, referring to their playful lovemaking. She stretched like a cat then curled into him. He nuzzled her neck.

"I'm sad to say we need to get dressed and go downstairs." He looked at his watch. "We're having lunch with Mrs. MacIntosh and Olivia at one, then Duncan and I are spending the rest of the day working on vineyard business."

"What time is it?"

"Quarter 'til. You have fifteen minutes."

"Yikes! It's going to take longer than that to pull myself back together." She jumped to her feet, leaving Philip lying naked on the floor. She turned the shower faucet on full and squealed as she stepped into the cold blast of water.

When Genevieve arrived in the petit salon just off the kitchen, Mrs. MacIntosh, Olivia, and Philip had already started the party. In an effort to cheer everyone up, Delphine had decked the small round table with blue and yellow linens and plates decorated with hand-painted Breton figures, each one unique. In a cutglass bowl in the center of the table, pretty yellow faces of daffodils peeked out from behind stalks of delicate lavender foxglove. Light from the fire flashed in the facets of the crystal wine goblets, but barely shone through the rich ruby red of Château Beaulieu's best cabernet sauvignon.

"I see you three didn't wait." Genevieve's throaty chuckle matched her dazzling smile. Her fresh-from-the-shower glow was enhanced by her creamy cashmere sweater topping graceful wide-legged trousers that fluttered as she walked to her chair. She adored that, after forty years of marriage, she still saw a healthy lust in Philip's eyes whenever he saw her.

She eased herself into the empty seat next to him. "Now tell me, what have I missed?"

Before Philip could rise to get the bottle of wine from the sideboard, Delphine was pouring a glass for Genevieve.

"Thank you, Delphine. Everything is so beautiful. The flowers are stunning."

"Don't you just love the foxglove?" Olivia said, her eyes shining. She touched the trumpet of one of the daffodils and smiled. "How cheerful. And the foxglove is perfect with it."

"It's lovely, isn't it?" Genevieve smiled thinking how much Olivia had changed since filling their lives with threats and chaos just over a year ago. She was lovely to have around and Genevieve was thrilled she seemed well on the path to recovery. "Are the flowers from our greenhouse, Delphine?" Genevieve asked.

"They are, my lady." Delphine flushed with pride. For years, she had been responsible for assuring every inch of Château Beaulieu was maintained to the highest standard, and it was gratifying when the owners noticed her efforts.

She replaced the wine bottle on the sideboard. "Sophie will bring your déjeuner tout suite. Let me know if there is anything else you need, Lord Crosswick, Lady Crosswick," she said, and nodded at them both.

"We're very lucky," Genevieve said to Mrs. MacIntosh. "Without all of you we couldn't manage all of this." Tears pricked her eyes and her throat tightened. "I'm so sorry," she said, offering an embarrassed apology. "I don't know what we're going to do without Wallace. I can't imagine our lives without him."

"He really was the epitome of a gentleman, wasn't he?" Olivia dabbed at her eyes with her linen napkin. "Shortly after I went to Blain Lodge, he came to visit me and brought a package from my mother. He was so kind to do that after the havoc I caused at Wilmingrove Hall." Olivia sniffed and bit her lower lip.

"That's all in the past," Genevieve said to Olivia, and hoped it was true. "I do have a question for you, though. As you know, your mother can't find her ruby ring. I tore her room apart this morning looking for it and came up with nothing. Is there any chance you might have put it somewhere other than her jewelry roll?"

Genevieve saw Olivia's jaw clench just before she forced her mouth into a smile that didn't reach her eyes. "As I told my mother, Genevieve, I took the ring to her room and put it in the pouch with her other jewelry. I can't help it if she lost it between here and London."

"All right, then." Genevieve's eyes widened and she raised her brows. "I guess we'll just have to keep looking."

Mrs. MacIntosh caught Genevieve's eye and she pursed her lips.

Genevieve took a drink of her wine, put her glass down with a loud thump, and sat back in her chair just as the newest addition to the kitchen staff came through the door carrying a small platter of lamb lollipops and well-toasted Brussels sprouts. A local, pretty young woman named Sophie had replaced Chloe, the previous kitchen maid. The smell of succulent meat and nutty vegetables filled the small room and Sophie moved from person to person, holding the dish just right so diners could serve themselves with ease.

As she moved around the table, Philip told a joke: "Why do the French only have one egg for breakfast?"

Olivia was game. "I don't know, Philip. Do tell. Why *do* the French only have one egg for breakfast?"

"Because one egg is an oeuf," Philip deadpanned.

Genevieve groaned, Mrs. MacIntosh looked confused, and Sophie giggled under her breath.

"You see, Sophie is a woman with a well-honed sense of humor." Philip took a bite of his lamb then hummed with pleasure as he chewed.

"Actually, that was quite funny," Genevieve said as she cut into a Brussels sprout. "But I'd venture to say Sophie was just being diplomatic. Right, Sophie?"

The slim girl widened her gamine eyes in mock innocence. "Ç'est possible, Lady Crosswick. Çest possible." She finished pouring water, gave Philip, Olivia, and Mrs. MacIntosh a splash of wine, and returned to the kitchen.

"Isn't she a breath of fresh air after Chloe?" Genevieve said.

"Who was Chloe?" Olivia said.

Before Genevieve could explain, Mrs. MacIntosh leaned toward Olivia, her elbows on the table, and said, "I never met her, but as I understand it, she was quite the treacherous coquette. As I recall," she looked at Philip, "she spied on the family and shared household information with those dreadful people who were trying to steal your wine."

"Well, something like that," Philip said, choosing not to correct the story.

"I can tell you, Wallace was furious when he heard someone on the household staff would do such a thing." Mrs. MacIntosh nodded for emphasis.

"That would be so like Wallace. His standards were impeccable." Genevieve smiled as she remembered how he had little tolerance for anything but perfection and loyalty.

"How awful she must have been," Olivia said, more with admiration than disgust. "Why did she do it?"

"She was well paid, of course," Philip said with a sneer. "People do a lot of unsavory things for money."

"You fired her, didn't you?" Mrs. MacIntosh said.

"We did. We couldn't prosecute her. The police said her crime was basically gossiping for money."

"She must have been quite a cheeky besom."

"Besom? I don't know what that is." Genevieve scrunched her forehead.

"A besom is a thoroughly awful woman who does unpleasant things." She wrinkled her nose and shook her head as if she had smelled something malodorous.

"That about sums it up," Philip said.

The unpleasant events of last year weren't Philip's favorite topic of conversation and he was ready to move on. "Changing the subject, Duncan has an interesting proposal we're going to talk about after lunch."

The three women brightened.

"Oh, tell us about it, Philip." Olivia leaned forward, eager to hear.

"I don't know the full scope of it yet, but it has to do with the wonderful dessert wine our neighbor Hank Shou created before he had the trouble that landed him in prison."

Olivia sat up straight and her eyes widened with interest. "How exciting. Wine and crime, what a great combination." She laughed and her blonde ponytail bounced. "You have a neighbor who's a criminal?"

"We do," Genevieve said. "Quite a claim to fame, isn't it?"

"I'd love to meet him. Is there any chance I could?"

Philip narrowed his eyes and said, "Of course not, Olivia. As I said, he's in prison. I'm sure neither Dr. Morgan nor your mother would be enthusiastic about you fraternizing with a criminal."

"I just thought—"

"Well, you thought wrong," Philip snapped back.

Genevieve raised her eyebrow and she and Mrs. MacIntosh exchanged a surprised look.

"Philip, perhaps Olivia could go with you and Duncan if you meet with Lian," Genevieve said, hoping to smooth over Philip's obvious annoyance with Olivia.

"Who is Lian?" Olivia was anxious to hear more.

"Lian Shou, Hank's wife. I have no idea what Duncan has in mind, but we'll see," Philip said reluctantly. "Maybe we'll have her over for dinner. We could introduce the two of you."

"That's a great idea. We'll invite Kim and Jing Wang too. We haven't seen them in ages." Genevieve was already planning the party in her mind.

Olivia pushed out of her chair and wrapped her arms around Philip from behind. "Oh, thank you, Philip. I'd love to meet the wife of a criminal. And I'm sure your other neighbors are interesting too." She kissed him on the cheek. "Thank you for a lovely lunch. I'm going to take my Ducati and go for a ride. I'll be back later," she said, and dashed out of the petit salon.

"I can't imagine why she had her motorcycle shipped here to France. It seems too cold to ride a motorcycle," Genevieve said. "And that whole thing about wanting to meet the wife of a criminal was strange."

"It certainly was," Philip agreed.

"I think she's a very scary young lady," was Mrs. MacIntosh's opinion.

EIGHT

A FTER WHAT SEEMED to be an endless day, Genevieve washed the last of the exfoliant from her face. She heard the Morbier clock downstairs in the foyer chime eleven. She patted away the last droplets with a fluffy white towel, then opened a jar of cream that smelled like a spring bouquet. She dabbed a line of dots over her cheekbones and along her jawline, then massaged the moisturizer into her skin with gentle, upward circles, all the while humming "I Feel Pretty". Cozy in jersey-knit pajamas, a fleece bathrobe and wool socks, she was exhausted from the day's drama and ready to collapse into bed.

Philip and Duncan had been buried in Philip's study all afternoon and evening, discussing future plans for Château Beaulieu, plans which would take the vineyard into the next decade. *They could be there all night,* Genevieve thought to herself.

Still humming, Genevieve pulled a tube of Penhaligon's Blenheim hand cream from the drawer of her bedside chest and squirted a dab into her palm. As she massaged the rich balm into the backs of her hands she breathed in the elegant scent. She plucked her wedding rings from the top of the chest and walked to her jewelry box where it sat on a carved chest of drawers at the far side of the room. Just as she touched the lid of the box, the smell of Rose Otto swirled around her.

"Charlotte," she whispered. "Charlotte, are you here?"

As quickly as the aroma had wafted into her bedroom, it was gone. She closed her eyes and breathed deeply. The only fragrance was the smell of her hand lotion.

"Honestly, Genevieve, you need to get a grip," she said out loud. She raised the lid of her jewelry box, ready to put her rings away, and dropped it as if it were as hot as smoldering coals. She squeezed her eyes shut and willed her head to stop swimming. Maybe she had imagined it. She opened her eyes and watched her shaking hand reach toward the leather tooled box she bought years ago in Florence. She felt the rich smoothness of the aging leather, then slowly, slowly she raised the lid again. There, nestled deep in the green velvet, was Becca's huge, square-cut ruby ring.

With her gaze riveted on the red stone sparkling in the lamp light, and her heart pounding in her ears, Genevieve backed toward the door until the doorknob pressed into her back. Still keeping her eyes glued to the leather case atop the dresser, she reached behind her, pressed the lever down, inched forward, and opened the door just enough to squeeze around it. As soon as she was on the other side, she tugged the door closed and bolted down the hall. She raced past the rooms where Alex and Ella were nestled, cozy in their beds. Her robe peeled open and flapped at her sides as she tore past Duncan and Julia's room, down the stairs, and across the foyer. When she reached the closed door to Philip's study, she pressed the wrought iron lever and threw the door open without breaking stride.

At the sound of the door smacking against the wooden chest behind it, two heads flew up.

"I found it! I found it!" Genevieve croaked between gasps.

"My watch?" Duncan said. "You found my watch?"

"No, Duncan. I found Becca's ruby ring." Her breath was beginning to calm.

"I didn't know it was missing."

"Of course you didn't," Philip said. "While your mother was tearing the guest room apart, you, Julia, and the kids were at Marché de Noel in Bordeaux."

Genevieve plopped into an overstuffed chair by the waning fire. Her hair was wild from running and the color in her cheeks raged from the shock of finding the ruby.

"Well, where did you find the ring?" Philip had returned to the report he'd been reading before Genevieve made her grand entrance and he was barely paying attention.

Genevieve looked like a child about to reveal an enormous secret. She blinked at Philip, then Duncan. She leaned forward and whispered. "I found it in my jewelry box."

"You what?" Philip lifted his head from his papers.

"I found it in the leather case where I keep my jewelry. Remember the one I bought in Florence at the leather school?"

Once again, she had Philip's attention. "I don't understand." He cocked his head to one side and his brows drew together. "How did it get there?"

Overwhelmed with emotion, Genevieve pushed out of her chair and walked to the fireplace. She snugged her bathrobe around her and cinched the belt, then grabbed the poker and stirred the smoldering embers into small flames. When she turned around, tears streamed down her cheeks.

"Mom, why are you crying?" Duncan said. "Shouldn't you be happy you found Becca's ring?"

Genevieve smiled at him through her tears. "I'm just so relieved. But I don't understand how the ring got in my jewelry box."

Philip rose, walked around his desk, and pulled Genevieve into a hug. She melted into him; he tightened his embrace and stood quietly. At last, he tilted her away from him and studied her face: her cheeks were wet, her nose running and her eyes sparkling.

"So you have no idea how the ring got into your case?"

"Absolutely none. When I saw it, I was stunned. And I swear, Charlotte was in the room just before I found it."

"Charlotte Chaubert, the Crosswick ghost?" Duncan laughed as he said the words, but sobered when his mother shot him a scathing glance. "I, um, just, um…" His words dissolved into mumbling.

Genevieve sniffed away the last of her tears and poked her finger at Duncan. "Go ahead and laugh," she said. "You may not believe in ghosts…" She stopped for a second. "Actually I don't either, but I believe in Charlotte. I don't know why she has chosen to be my spirit, but she has. I know when I smell her Rose Otto perfume, and when I feel icy fingers on the back of my neck, I know it's Charlotte. I smelled her perfume twice today. Both times it was connected to the ruby ring. Don't forget, it was once hers, so I'm not surprised she's lurking around Château Beaulieu looking after her interests."

Philip and Duncan glanced at each other. Though their faces were sober, their eyes twinkled.

"Stop it, you two!" Genevieve pushed out of Philip's arms, huffed back to her seat and plopped down, pulling a cashmere lap robe from the back of the chair and over her knees. "Is that scotch?" She pointed to the glass on Philip's desk.

He plucked it up. "It is. Would you like it?" he asked and handed it to her.

She drained the glass in two gulps and set it down on the round, burled table beside her.

"There just isn't any other explanation besides Charlotte, is there?" She looked from Philip to Duncan and waited for a response. When none came, she went on. "Becca left early yesterday and discovered her ruby was missing this morning when she was unpacking. The ruby wasn't there when I put my rings away last night. The ruby wasn't there when I took my rings out of the box this morning, but it was there when I put them away tonight." She scrubbed her face with her hands.

"Maybe Olivia didn't have a chance to put it in Becca's room and by the time she remembered, she put it into your jewelry box?" Duncan said.

"Nope." Genevieve shook her head and tugged the lap robe up to her shoulders. "When I asked her about it at lunch, she was emphatic that she had put it in Becca's jewelry roll." Genevieve stared into the dwindling fire. "She could be lying, I guess," she said, almost as an afterthought.

Philip tossed a dried oak log onto the embers and they flashed to life, snapping and spraying sparks around the firebox.

Genevieve felt warmer just watching the flames lap higher and higher until the blaze was robust again.

"Do you think she would just lie to me?" She looked at Philip, a deep furrow between her brows.

"Of course she would," Philip said, as a matter of fact. He stood in front of the sideboard and poured another glass of whisky, then turned to Genevieve. "I'm sure if we think about this in the light of day, we'll be able to come up with a logical explanation that doesn't involve Rose Otto, Olivia, or Charlotte Chaubert." She held up her glass and he splashed two fingers of scotch into her tumbler. "G, as alluring as the idea is of a beautiful spirit inhabiting our homes, I can't quite bring myself to believe the spirit of the 9th Countess of Crosswick is concerning herself with Becca's ruby ring."

"Mom, isn't it possible one of the housekeepers found the ring and put it in your jewelry box?" Duncan said.

Before she answered, Genevieve scowled into her glass. "I suppose it's possible. But I can't imagine they wouldn't have mentioned it to Delphine."

"But Delphine's been at her sister's since early yesterday. She only came back late this afternoon." Duncan's logic couldn't be denied.

"True." Genevieve sighed and swirled the caramel-colored Macallan 18 in her glass before drinking the last of it. "I suppose you're both right. Maybe my imagination has gotten a bit out of hand."

Philip held out his hand. "Let's go to bed, G."

She slipped hers into his, palm to palm, and gave him an exhausted smile. "Yes, let's."

He pulled her to her feet, took the lap robe, tossed it on the chair, and put his arm around her slumped shoulders.

"Duncan." She kissed the top of her son's head. "Don't you need to get to bed?"

"Thanks, Mom." He indulged her maternal fussing. "I'll head up shortly, but I want to finish looking at this report from Edouard. He has some interesting ideas for increasing yield over the next five years. For such a young vigneron, his knowledge is unbelievable. We need to get him involved with our plan for the dessert wine. We're very lucky to have him. Don't you think, Dad?"

"No question. Daniel LaGrande did us a huge favor bringing him to Château Beaulieu."

Genevieve sighed. "I miss Daniel. He was a wonderful friend and he managed our vineyard to perfection."

"Yes, he did. And now it's up to Duncan to do the same." He squeezed

Duncan's shoulder. "Come on. Let's go, darling girl."

As they started up the stairs, Genevieve stopped abruptly. "Philip, do you smell it?"

"Smell what?" Philip drew in a deep breath.

"Rose Otto." She looked at him, searching for any sign he smelled it too, but there was none.

Rain pelted against the windows and thunder growled in the distance. Cozy in a duvet cocoon, Genevieve's breath was slow

and rhythmic. When she felt a cool hand caress her forehead, she burrowed deeper into her warm covers, pulling the comforter over her head. Wafting almost to consciousness, she saw Charlotte's elegant face wavering in front of her, as if she were looking through water.

The grande dame of Château Beaulieu held up a glass of wine as if toasting Genevieve, but instead of drinking, she threw the Bordeaux into the air. In her dream, Genevieve put her arms over her head to avoid getting wet, but the wine evaporated.

When Genevieve looked up, Delphine had appeared and was holding Charlotte's hand, looking smug, as if she had stolen Genevieve's friend. Genevieve opened her mouth to speak, but no words came. She tried again, but Charlotte put her finger on Genevieve's lips to still her.

Charlotte blew her a kiss, then dissolved into a million tiny stars and Delphine sneered at Genevieve as she faded into darkness.

Genevieve nearly woke. She heard herself whimper and shivered, then fell back into a dreamless sleep.

NINE

WITH HER HANDS cradling a mug of steaming coffee, Mrs. MacIntosh sat by the window in the kitchen remembering how every morning for nearly forty years, she and Wallace would enjoy their first cup of coffee together before starting their day running the great household of Wilmingrove Hall together. She watched the terrace's yellow-potted lemon trees bob and bow to the wind as it gusted from the north. How strange it was that in the midst of her grief, the kitchen staff bustled around her, preparing breakfast and baking ahead for Christmas, just two days away. Cinnamon, nutmeg, chocolate… all the aromas that announced Joyeux Noël filled the Château kitchen.

"Madame MacIntosh." Lizette, the head cook, refilled the sturdy Scot's cup.

"Bertie," she said. "Please call me Bertie."

Lizette smiled, pleased at the friendly gesture.

Feeling the warmth from both the kitchen's energy and the heat of the ovens, Mrs. MacIntosh shrugged out of her beige Shetland cardigan and draped it over the back of her chair.

In black pants and tweedy sweater, sleeves pushed up to her elbows, Delphine charged through the kitchen door. "J'en ai marre! I've had enough!" she snarled, sweeping her right hand over her head. When she saw Mrs. MacIntosh, she stopped abruptly. "Madame MacIntosh," she said, and nodded her respect.

Throughout the House of Crosswick estates, the Crosswick staff of more than a hundred knew Reginald Wallace and Bertie MacIntosh were the longest serving and most influential of Lord and Lady Crosswick's staff. They were legends. And now it was just Mrs. MacIntosh.

Delphine pulled out the ladderback chair across from the Wilmingrove Hall housekeeper and sat down. "Pardon, Madame. Please forgive my outburst. I am dealing with les imbéciles d'Orange, our internet provider. Our Wi-Fi keeps going out. J'en ai ras le bol!" She held her hand up over her head, indicating she had had it "up to here" with the faltering internet.

The words were foreign, but the gesture was clear. Mrs. MacIntosh nodded. "I understand completely. I'm sure you can imagine what a time we have at the Hall. We're constantly calling BT and, though it's better than it used to be, our Wi-Fi is still far from perfect."

Delphine squinted at Bertie. "Have you had breakfast?"

"I have not, but I'm fine." Bertie brought her mug to her lips and wrinkled her nose as she drained the tepid coffee.

"Lizette." A ferocious frown burrowed into Delphine's forehead and she narrowed her eyes at the head cook. "I can't believe Mrs. MacIntosh has had no petit-déjeuner. Tu dois t'en occupier immédiatement."

Though Mrs. MacIntosh had no idea what Delphine said, the harsh tone was unmistakable. But when she saw Lizette shrug and raise one eyebrow, she was quite sure the staff was used to this behavior.

Delphine pushed her chair back and stood. "Madame MacIntosh, if there is anything I can do for you at this difficult time, you must let me know. Anything." She turned and was out the door before Bertie could say a word.

"Omelette avec fromage et jambon?" Lizette offered the French staple as if nothing had happened.

"I certainly don't want to inconvenience anyone. Everyone has so much to do before Father Christmas arrives."

"You mean Père Noël?" As Lizette grinned, her cheeks rounded into rosy apples.

"Oui. Père Noël."

"Omelette?" Lizette asked again. "Fromage et jambon?"

"Ah, s'il vous plaît," Bertie said, her Scottish accent murdering the elegant French. Feeling a gnawing in her stomach, she realized she hadn't eaten since lunch yesterday. "I must say, ham and cheese is my favorite omelette." She ran her finger around the rim of her mug several times before she asked, "Lizette, is Delphine always that crabbit?"

"Crabbit?" Lizette plopped into the chair Delphine had just vacated.

"Bad tempered. Out of sorts," Bertie said, to explain the Scottish word.

Lizette poured coffee into Bertie's mug, set down the pot, and crossed her hands on the table. She shrugged and her lips pouted as she said, "Baahh, oui. I would say most of the time."

"I'm surprised," Bertie said. "I got the impression from Lady Crosswick that she was genial and quite lovely."

"Mai, oui." Lizette nodded. "She is always charmant when she is with Lord and Lady Crosswick or their famille."

"Has she always been so unpleasant to the staff?"

She shook her head. "Non, absolument pas." She leaned forward and lowered her voice. "Before the new heirs came to Château Beaulieu, she was never like that. She has always run the Château well and has always been friendly with everyone who worked here. But when Lord and Lady Crosswick arrived last winter, she became a different person to all of us." She hushed and leaned back in her chair as Sophie approached the table, a plate and napkin in her hand.

"Voilà." She set a perfect, fluffy, pale-yellow omelette in front of Mrs. MacIntosh. As the fragrance of the steaming eggs oozing with Gruyère wafted to her nose, saliva flooded her mouth. "Thank you, Sophie. I didn't realize I was so hungry."

"Mon plaisir." She strode back to the huge kitchen island and returned carrying a tray with two mimosas, a basket of baguettes, a crock of creamy butter, and a bowl of diced fresh fruit. She put everything on the table, then placed the mimosas in flutes in front of Bertie and Lizette. "Bon appétit," she said, and returned to her other duties.

Lizette held up her glass. "Let's drink a toast to Reginald Wallace, shall we?" They clinked, drank, and exchanged smiles.

"Lizette, thank you for this. You're a kind soul."

"I'm glad Lord and Lady Crosswick insisted you stay at Château Beaulieu until après Noël." She patted Mrs. MacIntosh's hand. "Don't worry, Bertie. We shall all take good care of you while you are here." She started to leave the table, then turned back. "Bertie," she said, studying the icon for a moment. "Was Wallace votre amant, your lover?"

Mrs. MacIntosh had just taken a gulp of mimosa and it sprayed out of her nose, soaking the table linens in front of her. She began to cough. She coughed into her shoulder, gasping for air, then wheezed again, this time into her elbow.

Lizette grabbed Bertie's hands and held them over her head. "Lève les yeux! Lève les yeux. Look up, Bertie, look up!"

Finally, the hacking subsided and her raspy breathing calmed. She drank several gulps of water from the cup Lizette handed her, wiped her face with the yellow and blue linen napkin in her lap, sniffed several times, then plucked a tissue from the sleeve of her white Oxford blouse and blew her nose.

"Lizette," she croaked, her voice failing her. She cleared her throat and tried again. "Lizette, why did you ask me that?" This time she was able to get the words out.

"Ah, ma cher, you and Monsieur Wallace seemed to be so close. It was obvious you cared for each other. You lived in the same house for decades." She shrugged her shoulders. "It is only logique, non?"

Still trying to regain her composure, Bertie stared at her hands resting in her lap for several seconds, her eyes catching on her ringless finger.

"Je suis désolé," Lizette said, regretting the distress she had caused Mrs. MacIntosh. "I am so sorry, Bertie. This is not of my business."

Mrs. MacIntosh looked up. "*None* of my business."

"Eh?"

"You said 'This is *not* of my business.' You actually meant, *none* of my business."

"Aha. I see. So it is none of my business. I should not have asked."

The stoic housekeeper smiled a wan smile. "You are most perceptive, Lizette. Wallace and I were dear friends for many years. There was a time when I thought we would be more than friends, but apparently I was the only one. Wallace has… well, had a strong sense of loyalty and duty, and he believed he could not fulfill his obligations to the House of Crosswick and have a family of his own as well."

Sympathy flooded Lizette. She leaned forward with her elbows on the table and reached out, taking Bertie's hands in hers. "Ma pauvre, chère amie."

"Poor me, indeed." Bertie waved her hand in the air. "It is all, as they say, water under the bridge, and it was decades ago. Wallace and I never had a passionate relationship, but we had a long and caring one. Rather like brother and sister." She chuckled. "To a French woman, that must sound very sad indeed!"

"Ah, oui." Lizette sighed dramatically and brought the back of her hand to her forehead. "Ç'est tragique!"

She was holding her pose as Philip walked through the kitchen door. "There you are, Mrs. MacIntosh. I hope I haven't interrupted anything," he said, smiling at Lizette's dramatics.

"No, Lord Crosswick. We were just talking about Wallace."

"Perfect timing, then. I just got a call from our friend, Frederic Picard, the Chef de Police in Saint-Émilion. He's on his way here with some urgent news, something to do with Wallace, and he's bringing Dr. Aubert and the chief hospital administrator. Would you please join us in the grand salon when they get here?"

"Of course, my lord. Do you have any idea what this is about?" Her eyes wide with concern, Mrs. MacIntosh's mind raced. She could understand the doctor coming to the house, but why in the world would the police be with her?

TEN

T HIRTY MINUTES LATER, the thud of the front door knocker echoed through the Château. Delphine pulled the heavy oak door open, wincing at the blast of winter air that poured in. A tall, angular woman stood on the wide landing so close to the open door that Delphine took a startled step backward.

The house manager assumed this was Dr. Aubert, the physician who had pronounced Wallace dead. Though her features were pretty, her expression was severe—not quite mean, but warning. Behind her, two men waited on the second step. The taller of the two was aristocratic and elegant, with salt-and-pepper hair and a cleft in his chin. The hem of his open tweed topcoat flapped as the wind gusted up the stairs to the landing. Obviously, he must be the Directeur Général of the hospital in Libourne, where Wallace had been taken. Much to her surprise, Delphine knew the other man.

"Ah, bonjour, Chef Picard," she said, her eyes wide with questions for the local chief of police.

He said nothing, only inclined his head in greeting.

"Entrez." She stood to one side and motioned for the trio to come in. Leaning her shoulder against the polished wood, she shoved the heavy oak door closed against the wind.

"Vos manteaux, s'il vous plaît." She held out her hand. As the guests struggled out of their heavy garb, she took each coat and hung it in an armoire that stood on one wall of the foyer. When she turned back, though they tried to look blasé, the docteur and directeur's eyes were wide with wonder, their heads swiveling back and forth, up and down, taking in the grandeur of the nineteenth-century house.

Watching them, Chef Picard enjoyed a smug smile. Earlier in the year, he had spent time at Château Beaulieu helping to solve a wine-counterfeiting case, so he fancied himself a friend of the family and very much an insider.

Delphine could appreciate how dazzled first-time visitors were by the beauty of the gracious vineyard house and its surroundings. Though she had been the head of the household for many years, she too still marveled at the relaxed grandeur of what she thought of as *her* Château.

She started across the foyer, stopped, and turned to the three visitors. "Par ici, s'il vous plaît," she said, directing them to come with her.

The small parade followed her into the beautiful salon filled with suede camel overstuffed chairs. Large square tables held mounds of books. Vases filled with hydrangeas, rose lilies and tulips were tucked among the volumes. Huge abstract canvases filled the paneled walls and on a massive carved sideboard, a bronze ballerina arched in arabesque toward the ceiling.

Everything about the room spoke to centuries of wealth and tradition, but a love of the modern as well.

Though the day was cold, the sun was brilliant and poured through the wall of French doors on the far side of the sophisticated room. A coffered ceiling and crackling fire on the hearth made the room seem cozy in spite of its vastness.

"Mettez-vous à laise." Delphine motioned for them to be seated and, just as she told them their hosts would join them shortly, Philip strode into the room, looking very much the master of his domain. He moved with an easy elegance, stylish in camel cashmere trousers, a crisp white open-collared dress shirt and shawl-collared navy cardigan. The guests, who had just sat down, popped to their feet.

"Bonjour à tous." Philip crossed the room with an outstretched hand. "Dr. Aubert." He said nothing else, simply shook her hand firmly.

The elegant man to her right stepped forward. "Lord Crosswick, I am Martin Follet, the Directeur Général de l'Hôpital. I appreciate the time you are giving us today. We are here on a very strange mission indeed."

When Philip gripped his hand, he was surprised to find it was damp. *He must be nervous,* he thought, then turned to Chef Picard.

"Frederick, ça va?" Philip greeted him like a friend, much to the policeman's pleasure. "To what do we owe your visit with the hospital staff?" When he saw the officer's serious face, Philip pressed him. "What is it, Frederick?" He motioned for everyone to sit. "What's going on?"

Chef Picard looked over Philip's shoulder and watched Genevieve come into the room, her hand tucked into the crook of Mrs. MacIntosh's elbow.

She looked at each of the guests before moving to Dr. Aubert. "Docteur." She extended her hand, her eyes cool. "I'm sure you remember Mrs. MacIntosh, Mr. Wallace's dear friend."

"Bien sûr." Dr. Aubert shook Genevieve's hand then turned to Bertie. "Bonjour, Madam McIntosh." She proffered her hand but couldn't look Bertie in the eye.

Mrs. MacIntosh said nothing and waited several seconds before accepting the handshake.

Genevieve turned to the man she assumed was the directeur of the hospital. "Monsieur, je suis Genevieve Warwick." She waited for him to offer his name and then introduced Bertie.

That done, she turned her attention to Chef Picard. "Frederick," she said, her voice full of warmth. She liked this man. He had been kind and helpful earlier in the year when they were living through a challenging dilemma with the vineyard. "How wonderful to see you, though I'm not sure why you're here. I don't believe you have met our dear friend Alberta MacIntosh. Mrs. MacIntosh heads our family seat near York and has for many years, with Reginald Wallace, who, as I'm sure you know, died the day before yesterday at Libourne Hospital."

He opened his mouth, then closed it, uncertain what to say.

Genevieve flashed a courteous smile at each guest. "Please, if you would like tea or coffee it's on the sideboard."

When everyone was seated with a drink in hand, Philip said, "So what is this meeting all about? I think I speak for the three of us," he nodded at Genevieve and Bertie, "when I say we're anxious for the hospital to release Mr. Wallace's body." He looked at Frederick. "And I must say, I find it curious that Chef Picard is here."

The docteur, the directeur, and the chef exchanged uncomfortable looks. No one spoke for several seconds until, at last, last Picard said, "We have some very good news we thought should be delivered in person." He did not look like a man with good news. Beads of sweat glistened just below his hairline and he clasped and unclasped his hands.

Genevieve scooted forward on the sofa cushion. "I don't understand, Frederick. What good news could you possibly have?"

"Well." His voice cracked and he started again. "I, um…"

Genevieve looked at Bertie, who had twisted her linen hanky into a tendril and was weaving it in and out of her fingers. Then she looked at Philip, whose eyes were glued to the chief. "Chef Picard, would you please spit it out?" she insisted. "You're making us very nervous."

"Yes, of course, Lady Crosswick. I'm so sorry." His knee bounced like a piston. "I… um, we're very happy to tell you Reginald Wallace did not die." He paused to look at three blank faces, then went on. "He is very much alive."

The room was silent as a grave.

After a long moment, Philip pierced the quiet. "What do you mean he's very much alive? I don't understand."

Dr. Aubert rose, walked to the fireplace and stood with her back to everyone for a moment. When she turned around,

Genevieve was surprised to see her eyes flash with defiance and her lips drew taut. "First, let me say how sorry we are that this mistake was made. But I am certain you can recall how busy the emergency room was on—"

"Excusez-moi, Docteur," Mrs. MacIntosh interrupted Aubert, much to the doctor's surprise. "I believe we're all a bit confused." She turned her narrowed eyes on Chef Picard. "Chef, did you just tell us Reginald Wallace is not dead?"

Chef Picard opened his mouth to speak, but Mrs. MacIntosh held up her hand.

"Chef Picard, you just said Reginald Wallace is very much alive, did you not?" She pushed herself from her chair to stand. "Reg is alive? Alive?" She sobbed the last word.

Unphased, Dr. Aubert started again. "If you will let me explain." Her voice was still full of arrogance. "I am certain you remember how chaotic the emergency room was that night. A man arrived in an ambulance at the same time as Monsieur Wallace. We shall call him Monsieur X. He and Monsieur Wallace were of similar physical profiles and their gurneys were next to each other in the hall for a short while. In all the chaos, the files were swapped." She shrugged. "Imagine how the other family felt when they came in to see their loved one and it was Monsieur Wallace. Then they found out their beloved was dead."

With that, Bertie's sobs erupted and tears poured down her cheeks. In a single move, Genevieve was at her side, her arm around Bertie's shoulders, her own tears soaking the front of her sweater. Bertie turned in Genevieve's arms and buried her face in her employer's chest. "Reg is alive," she said, her sobbing voice muffled by Genevieve's thick cashmere turtleneck.

Watching Mrs. MacIntosh reeling from the shocking news, the full weight of Wallace's mistaken death hit Philip, and he turned his rage on Dr. Aubert. Through gritted teeth, he said, "Thirty-six hours ago you declared our dear friend dead. Why are you now telling us you were mistaken? How in the hell could that possibly have happened?" He held Dr. Aubert in his icy glare. "Why didn't Wallace let you know you had the wrong person? Surely you called him by the wrong name?"

Dr. Aubert shifted in her chair. "Ah, there is, of course, an explanation."

"I would surely hope so," Genevieve said, shooting Aubert a searing glance as she cradled Bertie, whose sobs were subsiding.

"Believing Monsieur Wallace had suffered a serious heart attack, as was indicated by the blood enzymes in Monsieur X's chart, we heavily sedated him, which is protocol and allows for the possibility of the best outcome in such circumstances."

Bertie dropped back into her chair, dabbed her eyes and blew her nose.

Genevieve narrowed her eyes at the two people from the hospital. "So when did you realize Wallace was still very much alive?"

"Excellent question, G." Philip sat on the edge of his seat, waiting.

Aubert took a deep breath before answering. "It was early this morning, when we reduced the sedation. When Monsieur Wallace became lucid, he was very quick to tell us who he was."

Bertie smiled for the first time since the three visitors arrived. "I'm sure he was not well pleased with being called someone else's name. That would get right up his nose."

Directeur Follet straightened in his chair. "I understand how you all must feel," he said.

"Oh, I doubt that very much." Philip's stare was stony.

To his credit, Follet didn't cringe, but went on. "I certainly don't need to tell you, from a legal as well as an ethical perspective, we at the hospital are not standing on strong ground. Mixing up two patients and pronouncing the wrong patient dead was not our finest hour," he said.

"To say the least." Philip spat the words.

"My lord, my lady, Madame MacIntosh, we came today to offer our deepest regrets for everything that has happened." Follet and Dr. Aubert exchanged a nervous glance. She returned to her chair and crossed her long legs. "But there is more."

"Dear god." Bertie wiped her eyes, red from sobbing, with a tissue she had pulled from her sleeve. "How could there be more?"

Though her demeanor was still cool, Dr. Aubert's voice was softer. "When a patient comes into the salle d'urgence, the ER, with an expected heart attack, we check many things. Among the most important is blood enzymes to confirm the patient is, indeed, having a heart attack." She leaned forward, her elbows on her knees, comfortable as she spoke about the medicine.

"And?" Genevieve said.

"Because the files were confused, the blood results were appropriated to the wrong patient." Dr. Aubert pressed her lips together and shook her head.

"I suppose that makes sense," Philip said, trying to tamp his anger. "Please go on."

"When we finally sorted things out earlier today," she continued, "the test results showed digoxin in Monsieur Wallace's blood."

Three blank faces stared back at him. Then Philip said, "I'm not sure what digoxin is. Do you know, G?"

"I've heard of it, but I couldn't tell you what it is."

"Digoxin comes from the plant digitalis purpurea. It is très jolie. A very pretty flower. But very poisonous. One would not take digoxin intentionally. It appears Monsieur Wallace was poisoned by foxglove."

ELEVEN

POISONED.

Genevieve felt the blood drain from her head. All she could think was, in the immortal words of Yogi Berra, "Déjà vu, all over again."

They had been through this experience all too recently. Sir Mark Holmes, one of their estate solicitors, had an unfortunate encounter with poisoned mead at Wilmingrove Hall last year, but unlike Wallace, when he died, he stayed dead.

With her head swimming, Genevieve barely heard Philip's barrage of questions.

"Frederick, what else do you know about this? Do you have any clue how this could have happened? Who would do such a thing?" Philip peppered Picard. "I know about foxglove. When I was a kid, we had a dog who ate foxglove and died. It was terrible. Where in the world would someone have gotten the poisonous flower in the dead of winter?" Philip snorted. "Pardon my use of 'dead'."

Understanding the news he had just delivered was shocking for everyone to hear, Chef Picard waited for Philip to run out of steam. When he stopped to take a breath, Picard said, "I assure you, my lord, we are launching a thorough investigation into this matter with the intention of having answers to your questions and many more. Unfortunately, it is rather late for any clues or evidence that might lead us to the auteur."

"Lead us to the author?" Philip asked, confused.

Picard smiled. "Non, my lord. The perpetrator. The person who somehow gave this poison to Monsieur Wallace."

"Aha, the author of the crime, if you will."

"Ah oui. Exactement," Picard said.

Philip looked at Genevieve who had said nothing since Picard made his announcement. "G, are you all right?"

When she looked at him, the lines around her eyes were tight with anxiety.

"What is it?" Philip pressed.

It was a long moment before she spoke, but finally she said, "I know where the foxglove came from."

Philip and Picard looked at each other, then at Genevieve.

"My lady," Picard said. "How could you possibly know the source of the foxglove?"

Genevieve stared out the French doors, mesmerized by naked rose bushes quivering in their pots in December's frigid gusts. At last she drew her focus back to the salon and to Chef Picard. "Frederick," she said. "I know the source of the foxglove because we grow it here, at Château Beaulieu, in our greenhouse."

TWELVE

MRS. MacIntosh balanced a tray of tea and biscuits with one hand and opened the glass door to the orangerie with the other. She took two quiet steps into the room, closed the door, and turned to look at her friend.

Thanks to years of traversing Wilmingrove Hall's miles of corridors and mountains of stairs, at sixty-one, Wallace was fit and his recovery was coming along well. Three days after his return home, he strolled the Château grounds every afternoon, walking further each day. Bertie was pleased the color was returning to his cheeks, but she was concerned about how quiet he had been since his return to Château Beaulieu. Now, tucked into a cozy corner of the orangerie, he lay with his eyes closed, his face warmed by the sun flooding through the French doors.

As she settled the tray on the table next to his chaise lounge, Wallace opened one eye. She smiled at him and placed a comforting hand on his forehead.

"Bertie," he said. "You didn't need to bring me tea. I can get a cup myself."

"You need to let someone wait on *you* for a change." She patted his shoulder as she sat down in the chair next to him. "You've just been through a series of traumatic events—dying, coming back to life, learning someone tried to poison you." She grinned and squeezed his hand. "You deserve a little rest. And don't worry, Chef Picard will get to the bottom of this."

His eyes sparkled with tears as he looked at her.

"What is it, Reg?"

She poured two cups of tea from the Sadler Tower of London pot she had brought with her from Wilmingrove Hall. Using this little whimsical teapot with its hand-painted Tower characters always made her smile. She added milk and plopped two lumps of sugar into one of the steaming cups, just as Wallace liked it. She offered him a plate of buttery French biscuits with sea salt, then took one herself.

Settling back into the armchair, she took a sip of Earl Grey, enjoying the scent of bergamot wafting from her cup. "Well," she said and offered Wallace an encouraging nod. "What's going on, Reg, my dear friend?"

His cheeks pinked at her endearment. He stared at the caramel-colored liquid in his porcelain cup for a long while before looking into her eyes, their corners etched by years of worry and joy. "Bertie," he began, then stopped.

Not wanting to pressure him, she sat in silence sipping her tea, waiting for him to continue.

He pulled a linen napkin from the tray beside him, wiped his mouth, then began again. "Bertie." When he raised his head, a wan smile sat on his lips. "Something has been niggling me since my mistaken demise." He looked back at his mug, set it on the tray, and dragged his eyes back to Mrs. MacIntosh. "I'm quite certain you'll say I'm barmy, but I have had the distinct feeling since Sir David and Ms. Conway's wedding that Olivia Conway means to do me harm."

A furrow bloomed between her brows. She wasn't sure she had understood him correctly and she studied his face for several seconds. "Reg, you're afraid of Olivia? Is that what you mean?"

As if she'd stuck him with a needle, Wallace sat ramrod straight. "I did not say I was afraid of her, although we all probably should be. I said I think she might want to do me harm. Those are two quite different things."

Mrs. MacIntosh raised her palms in defense. "So sorry, Wallace." Though she kept her lips from smiling, her eyes laughed at the idea that Wallace thought he was in Olivia's crosshairs. "Heavens, man! What did the lass do to make you fash so?" Mrs. MacIntosh prodded in her thick northern Scottish accent.

He flashed her a dark eye and she knew to proceed with caution.

"Wallace." Her voice softened and she laid her hand on his. "Did something happen between you and Olivia?"

"You're going to think I'm a silly old man when I tell you, but you know my instincts rarely fail me."

"True." She nodded. "You are a perceptive man." She patted his hand, then leaned back in her chair.

"You know I saw Olivia when we arrived at the Château the day before the wedding."

"Umm hmm." Mrs. MacIntosh hummed her reply. "And?"

"Though she didn't speak to me, she sent a clear message that I was supposed to keep my distance from her."

"If she didn't speak to you, how did she let you know you were to stay away?"

He smoothed the napkin on his lap, then said, "She gave me a look that would have withered Stonehenge."

Bertie caught a laugh in her throat before it could erupt. "Reg, why in the world would she do that?" She was sympathetic but skeptical. "You've never done anything to her."

Wallace twiddled his thumbs for a moment.

"Wallace?" Mrs. MacIntosh waited.

When he looked up, she saw his eyes flash and was surprised to see secrets dancing there.

"Reginald, what did you do?" She leaned forward, tilting her head.

"Well…" He stopped to clear his throat then went on. "A couple of months after Olivia was admitted to Blain Lodge— you know, the private psychiatric hospital where she's been?"

"Of course I know Blain Lodge." Mrs. MacIntosh couldn't keep the annoyance out of her voice. She had lived through the frightening experience of Olivia terrorizing everyone at Wilmingrove Hall, just as he had. "Go on."

"I went to see her there."

"I remember. You took her a package from her mother."

He nodded. "Ms. Conway—well, now Lady Weatherington, asked me to take some of Olivia's favorite sweets, Harrods Marmalade Biscuits. I was more than happy to do so because I was anxious to give her a piece of my mind. I was still very angry about what chaos and fear she caused Lord and Lady Crosswick, Sir David… and really, everyone at the Hall. She had no right to terrify and disrupt our family."

Mrs. MacIntosh smiled at his tender use of "our family." She too had grown to love the new Earl and Countess, the entire Warwick family, and their friends. They had brought joy and life back to the House of Crosswick and she embraced the new energy that came with them.

She took Wallace's hand. "What exactly did you say to her? What happened to make you think she wishes you ill?"

He pulled his eyes from hers and stared at their interlaced hands.

"Wallace," she said, her voice gentle. She waited a moment. "Wallace," she repeated.

He sighed. His shoulders rose then sagged before he looked up. And still Mrs. MacIntosh waited, refusing to fill the silence between them.

"All right." His voice was husky. "When I went to see Olivia, my intent was to give her the package and a good wigging. I wanted her to understand how she had terrorized the household and devastated her mother."

Mrs. MacIntosh smiled, envisioning Wallace in his well-cut black suit and elegant overcoat, his hat in his lap. She imagined him sitting, stiff and still as a statue, waiting for beautiful, villainous Olivia to join him in the visitors' lounge. She knew her old friend well and was certain he had believed his stern words would touch Olivia's soul and she would dissolve into a pile of regret and repent her actions. But Bertie also knew that would absolutely not happen.

"So, what did you say to her?"

"Bertie, you know I am a man of restraint."

"I do." She bit the inside of her cheek to keep from smiling.

"I fear, though I meant to be firm but not threatening, that is not what happened."

Her eyes widening, she leaned forward. "Go on." She couldn't imagine what Wallace was about to tell her.

He cleared his throat then took a gulp of tea, which had cooled. As he set his cup back on the saucer, he chuckled under his breath. "You will not believe what I did."

Mrs. MacIntosh looked like an inquisitive puppy, her head tilted to one side, waiting for Wallace to continue. "Well?"

His private joke pulled at the corners of his mouth. "The staff brought me a mug of coffee while I waited. When Olivia walked through the door, I don't mind telling you, I felt my breath quicken, and my palms were so damp I wiped them on my trousers. She looked sweet with her blonde curls, rosy cheeks, and you know that perfect bow mouth turned slightly up. But her eyes. Her blue eyes ringed with violet were as icy as the winter sky. When she sat down across from me, my adrenalin surged and I was not as measured as I had planned to be. I was surprised when I heard the harsh edge in my voice."

Leaning forward in her chair, Mrs. MacIntosh could wait no longer. "Reggie, what did you say?" Her tone was insistent.

He inhaled, and an impish smile crossed his lips. "I said, 'Ms. Conway, you are a nasty piece of work and what you have done to my family is unforgivable. I shall make it my mission to see you spend the rest of your life here at Blain Lodge and that you die here knowing what a wretched wench you are.' Then I stood, dumped my coffee in her lap, and I walked out."

THIRTEEN

AT 14:47 THE elegant TGV from Paris glided into Bordeaux, Saint-Jean station and stopped at voie six. Lillie Langdon stood at the door, her tote and purse secured over her shoulder, one suitcase in front of her and one behind, ready to roll off the train. For two hours and fourteen minutes her stomach had churned. It might have been the bag of Oreo Minis she had eaten, but it was more likely the fear of the unknown, soon to be known.

She had been working fifteen hours a day and had traveled thousands of international miles trying to solve a problem that was plaguing the Laney Museum of Fine Arts Foundation, of which she was Executive Director, and its two museums. After six weeks, the problem was not only unsolved, but it seemed to be growing like dough with too much yeast—too fast and out of control. She would have been better off if she had told Lord and Lady Crosswick about what was happening from the beginning. Telling them now was going to be so much worse. In fact, she wouldn't be surprised if they fired her.

She drew in a mighty breath, then exhaled. "Be brave," she said, repeating the words her father had said to her so often as she was growing up. She had never been sacked before and of the few jobs she'd had since completing her master's degree in art history, she loved this position the most.

When the door whisked open, she lifted one case out onto the platform, turned and rolled the other across the narrow gap and onto the concrete quai. Crowds swarmed around her, hurrying to get to their Christmas Eve destinations. Pushed and nudged, she was forced into the rapid stream of people rushing off the platform to the station exit and their loved ones.

When Philip called two weeks ago to invite her for the holidays, Lillie had instantly accepted the invitation. With her parents on their much-anticipated round-the-world cruise, and her sister at her in-laws, she had been feeling quite sorry for herself.

Now, standing just outside the station exit, she smiled as she saw Henri, the Warwicks' driver and the man who reigned supreme over their impressive automobile collection. She threw her hand in the air and waved at Henri, who waved back and started to make his way to her, weaving between the mass of oncoming passengers.

When he arrived at her side his smile was broad. "Joyeux Noël," he said. "Let me take your bags and let us get out of here. Quelle maison de fous!"

Lillie stood on her tiptoes and yelled into Henri's ear so he could hear her over the loudspeaker announcing arrivals and departures. "A madhouse is the perfect word for it."

They made their way toward the exit, where Henri stopped to loop his scarf around his neck, button his black wool jacket, and flip up his collar. "Button your coat. C'est un temps de chien. I am over there." He pointed in the direction of a cluster of waiting cars, then charged out of the station with her cases.

She did as she was told, buttoning, wrapping, and tugging on her gloves. When she walked out into the Bordeaux afternoon, true to Henri's promise of a dog's weather, a blast of frigid air slapped her cheeks and tears blurred her vision. She lowered her head against stinging drops of sleet whipping through the air. Eyes narrowed to slits, she glanced up and saw Henri already putting her luggage in the back of a British racing green Range Rover. He and the car waited for her in the far lane where only VIP cars could idle. She was grateful she didn't have far to walk in the foul weather.

As soon as Lillie had eased herself into the car, Henri closed the door. Tucked into the supple camel leather, she melted in the warmth of the heated seat.

He eased from the curb and joined the river of traffic flowing away from the station.

"Henri, how is everything at Château Beaulieu?" Lillie said, testing the waters.

Her eyes met his in the rearview mirror, but she could read nothing in his glance. "Mon dieu, Mademoiselle Langdon. Tout est mal en point."

Lillie thought she had misheard. "Everything is in bad shape?" she said. "What do you mean? What's going on?" She scooted forward as much as her seatbelt would allow and leaned her forearms on the back of the passenger seat to get a better look at the driver.

"Much has happened since the wedding just a few days ago."

Lillie regretted missing the grand event, but for much of December she had been at Art Basel Miami Beach, where leading galleries from five continents showed significant works by masters of modern and contemporary art, as well as the new generation of emerging stars. She was the featured lecturer on "How Technology Will Change Your View of What Art Is," and one of three experts on a panel entitled, "Is It a Dream or a Nightmare: The Good, the Bad, and the Ugly Sides of Art and Artificial Intelligence," a nightmare she was living at the moment. After her week in Miami Beach, she spent the next two weeks traveling the US, following up with new, exciting artists she had discovered at Art Basel, artists the Laney museums might want to buy. All the while, at every opportunity, she defended the Laney Musée des Beaux-Arts' reputation.

Still straining against her belt, she asked again. "What's going on? Tell me everything."

For the next fifty minutes, Henri shared the details of all the happenings at Château Beaulieu, starting with a recount of the beautiful wedding then moving to Wallace's death, and ending with the miraculous discovery that Wallace was, indeed, still very much alive. "And that's what has been happening at Château Beaulieu," he said as he slowed the car.

Turning left, he drove between two stone monuments that announced Château Beaulieu and onto a long gravel drive that led to a circle in front of the Château. As he stopped the car, the hand-oiled oak door opened just wide enough so Lillie could see Genevieve smiling her welcome. *Let's see if she's still smiling when*

I tell her the disastrous news. She sucked in a breath then exhaled, trying to calm her fluttering heart.

With her anxiety mounting, she threw open her door and swung her feet toward the ground, but when she pushed out of her seat, she was held like a marionette by her seatbelt, her arms flopping and her legs dangling above the pavement while her bottom barely hung on the edge of the seat.

"Lillie!" Genevieve called out, dashing down the wide steps to where Lillie still drooped from her belt, unsure what to do. The sleet was coming down harder and the wind was still blustering.

Just as Genevieve reached the car, a gust whipped her hair straight up as if she were standing on a New York City subway grate. "Whoa!" she said and laughed.

Hearing the commotion, Henri looked around the rear of the car where he was gathering Lillie's cases. "Lady Crosswick, it is freezing out here. Please go back in the house. I shall take care of Mademoiselle Langdon." He dashed around the car and in one smooth motion he lifted Lillie's legs, scooched her bottom further back on the seat, and pivoted her around so her feet were in the footwell. He reached across her, unsnapped her seatbelt and held out his hand.

With as much grace as she could muster—which was little at this point—Lille slipped her hand into Henri's, swung her legs back around, felt for the running board and stood. She took the one small step to the ground then lowered her head, looked up at Genevieve through her thick lashes, and rolled her eyes. "Lady Crosswick," she sighed.

"You're a crazy woman, Lillie." Genevieve gripped Lillie's

slender shoulders and pulled her into a warm hug. "Come on. It's freezing out here. Let's get in the house."

Genevieve put her arm around Lillie, ushering her up the stairs where the door stood wide, allowing the frigid wind and freezing sleet to pour into the foyer and down the grand hall. Following close behind, Henri pulled the luggage into the hall, and, with some effort, pushed the door closed against the howling wind.

Shaking from head to toe and with her teeth chattering, Lillie looked forlorn.

"You poor thing," Genevieve said, and pulled her into the grand salon where she planted the younger woman in front of the crackling fire and cozied Lillie's frigid hands in hers. Lillie's curly hair stood out like a cupie doll. Her cheeks flamed and her nose glowed red from the cold. Taking a shoulder in each hand, Genevieve leaned in to give Lillie a kiss on each cheek.

Without warning, and much to Genevieve's surprise, Lillie burst into tears. She pulled the weeping girl into a firm embrace, and, with Lillie's body heaving in Genvieve's arms, rode the wave of sobs until it subsided.

When Genevieve pulled back, she searched Lillie's ice-blue eyes for a hint of what was happening but could read nothing.

"Genevieve—" Lillie started to cry again, but Genevieve caught her before she could erupt.

"Lillie, stop right there." Holding her hand, she pulled Lillie around the square coffee table and down onto the cushions of the suede sofa. "All right, my darling girl, what's going on?" She stared at Lillie, who was usually so bright and composed, and refused to release her from her gaze.

Face ruddy, nose damp, eyes puffy, Lillie unzipped her large purse and dug deep, looking for a tissue, sniffing every few seconds. At last, she pulled her hand from her satchel like a magician snatching a rabbit out of a top hat.

"Tada." She waved a gauzy tissue, sniffed again, and smiled, her eyes still flooded with tears.

Genevieve waited while Lillie blew her nose and patted her hair, trying to tame the curls that had sprung from her silver clip and were bouncing everywhere. She closed her handbag, put it on the table next to the sofa and said, "I think I'm ready to apologize now."

"Apologize for what? Why would you apologize?" She knitted her brows, confused.

Lillie twisted the frayed tissue in her hand, took a breath to steady her voice and began. "Genevieve, since September, Richard and I have been working on repairing the damage done when Bernard sold two forgeries to La Cité du Vin."

"Yes. Philip and I know all about—"

Lillie put up her hand to stop Genevieve. "Though La Cité has been extraordinarily understanding, a blizzard of rumors fueled by online posts and fake news stories keeps burying us. It simply won't stop. We kill one and another pops up."

As Lillie spoke, her strength revived and, before Genevieve realized it, the dynamic executive director of the Laney Museum of Fine Arts Foundation was back in full force and pacing in front of the fireplace. "I'm sure you remember after Richard Durand took over as Directeur of Laney Musée des Beaux Arts, he discovered Bernard Reine's art fraud while *he* was Directeur of the LMBA.

"Of course I do." Genevieve nodded. "Very clever and very criminal."

Lillie stopped and stood in front of Genevieve. "That was the beginning. That's when the fake news articles and social media posts started showing up. It was just a few stupid things at first, but recently the rumors are really flying. I should have told you and Philip about all of this immediately." She looked down at her clasped hands. "But I honestly thought I could manage the situation." When she looked up at Genevieve, Lillie's eyes ached with regret and worry.

Staring at the earnest beauty, Genevieve leaned back into the sofa cushions. She crossed her arms and studied the smart, competent young woman standing in front of her, the glow of the fire creating a halo behind her.

Finally, Genevieve said, "The posts that are popping up, what are they about? I thought we had an agreement with Cité du Vin that the incident would stay between our two organizations. That's why we *donated* two equally important works to their collection. So that we could contain the damage."

Lillie shook her head. "I have no idea who might have leaked the information but the first couple of stories were true. They were about Bernard selling fake art. After that, everything that's been published is just insane, faux news."

"Like what?" Genevieve pressed.

Lillie grimaced and looked at the ceiling before she answered. Genevieve could see her jaw clenching. When Lillie looked down again, Genevieve saw strength and determination blazing in the fiery young woman's eyes.

"The most recent posts have accused the museum of owning many paintings looted by Nazis."

Genevieve's left eyebrow arched. "Really," she said. "And do these," she paused, "news articles," she paused again, "offer any source?"

"Of course not," Lillie spat. "They don't need to. They're popping up on X, Facebook, and a blog called *Art's Underbelly*."

"*Art's Underbelly*? Really? Sounds…" Genevieve searched for the right word.

"Smutty?" Lillie offered.

"That works. Has this blog been around long?"

"I'm quite certain you won't be surprised to hear volume one, issue one was an article entitled, 'Are the Laney Musée des Beaux-Arts Walls Hung With Nazi Loot?'"

Processing everything Lillie had just told her, Genevieve waited several seconds before seething under her breath, "Merde! Merde! Merde! Damn it, Lillie. What made you think you could handle an online campaign to discredit this family and our museums alone? What in the fuck were you thinking?"

"Whoa! It seems we've just missed Lady Crosswick at her finest, Finn."

At the sound of Philip's voice, Genevieve clamped her hand over her mouth and winced with embarrassment.

Philip relaxed against the door jamb. Next to him stood a man who was two inches shorter than Philip's six-foot-one frame. His ruddy complexion said he was either a sportsman or spent his days working outside. But regardless of how he came by his healthy color, his well-tailored, dark-green blazer, black-worsted pants and black-suede Crockett and Jones loafers said he was a man of means.

"Do you often come across beautiful women in the throes of swearing like sailors in your home, Philip?" When he spoke, it was with a posh public-school accent, probably Eton and Cambridge; but rather than seeming stuffy, he emitted a jolly energy.

"Finn!" Genevieve clapped her hands, jumped to her feet, and dashed to throw her arms around the newcomer's neck. In return he gave her a mighty squeeze, lifting her off her feet. When he set her down, she planted a kiss on his cheek, and then remembering she was in France, she kissed him on the other cheek as well. "When did you get here?"

"I just got here, lovely lady. I've been in Geneva finishing some negotiations we wanted to complete before the end of the year. I flew into Bordeaux and your man Émile was kind enough to pick me up at the airport." He let Genevieve ease out of his arms.

"Ahem." Philip cleared his throat. "Did you forget someone over here?"

Genevieve turned to her husband. "I could never forget you." She caressed the back of his neck with her palm and eased into his arms. "You, my sweet, were the clever one who invited this darling boy to Château Beaulieu for the holidays; a lovely idea on its own, but after what Lillie just told me, it turns out to be timely as well."

"What do you mean?" Philip said, brows drawn together.

"Later. I'll fill you in later. But for your brilliance, you deserve a kiss." A smile flooded into her eyes and her lips landed on his with a loud smack.

"Not a very romantic kiss," he said, and, slipping an arm around her slim waist, pulled her close. "Another, please." A knowing look electrified the air between them.

Holding his gaze, she gave him another quick peck on the lips with the promise of more to come.

With a swat on her bottom, he let her go and threw his arms wide. He walked to where Lillie stood in front of the fireplace and gave her hug then la bise. "Lillie, I want you to meet Finnegan Mountbatten. Finn, this is the famous Lillie Langdon I've been telling you about."

Finnegan strode to Lillie, extended his hand, and offered her a smile that made her stomach flutter.

"How lovely to meet you, Finnegan." She cocked her head. "Am I to assume you are related to the *royal* Mountbattens?"

"Isn't everyone?"

He was flip and charming, and Lillie liked him instantly. "If I am indeed the famous Lillie Langdon, I'm guessing you know all about me. Why don't I know about you?"

"Ah," he said, tenting his hands and rocking back on his heels. "Perhaps Philip and Genevieve thought you would flee if you knew they'd invited me to Château Beaulieu for Christmas so we could meet."

"Finn!" Genevieve rolled her eyes. "You were supposed to be more subtle than that." She let out a puff of air. "Men!"

Lillie's brows arched toward the curls wisping on her forehead. "Indeed?" she said, and her cheeks dimpled. "So what you're saying, Finnegan, is that this Christmas holiday is going to be one long chat up."

"I think you've hit the proverbial nail on the head." His toothy grin disarmed her.

Energy radiated from this compelling man. Though he didn't have classic good looks—his face was too square, his cheeks a bit sharp, his nose had a bump at the bridge, and his eyes might have been too close together—when all his features were put together, he was striking.

As Finnegan and Lillie walked together to the sofa in front of the fire, Genevieve caught Philip's eye, her smile wide and brows raised. Knowing he was responsible for this inspiration, he returned her look with a smug nod.

"And how do you know the Warwicks?" Lillie asked.

"Ah." His face clouded. "It's a rather dark story, but since we're doomed to be partnered for the next few days, I should bare my soul sooner rather than later."

"Excuse us for a moment while we go organize some refreshments." Genevieve jerked her head at Philip and turned to leave. When he didn't follow but started to sit instead, she loudly cleared her throat and called over her shoulder, "Philip, I need your help."

Finally realizing Genevieve wanted to leave Finnegan and Lillie alone, he stopped himself mid-sit and pretended he had been squatting to pull a log from the copper wood box. He tossed it on the dwindling flames and sparks flew up the chimney.

"Of course. Of course," he said, and followed behind his chuckling wife.

FOURTEEN

With Philip and Genevieve's departure, an awkward silence hung in the room until Lillie said, "So, Finnegan, you were about to bare your soul."

She sat facing Finn with one leg under her and her arm resting on the back of the sofa. With curls falling around her face, he thought she looked like Leonardo da Vinci's unfinished *La Scapigliata, The Lady with Disheveled Hair.* He could imagine the great Leonardo, brush in hand, forming her heavy-lidded eyes, thick black lashes, delicate nose, and high cheekbones. When Genevieve had described Lillie, she did not exaggerate her classic Renaissance beauty. But her sparkling exuberance was twenty-first century. He was already dazzled.

"Ah, yes. Bare my soul I must." He crossed his legs and settled his shoulders into the down sofa cushion. "My tale begins when I was fourteen and my parents moved from London to Washington, D.C. My mother, who was in Her Majesty's Diplomatic Service, accepted a posting as Deputy Head of Mission at the British Embassy in Washington, D.C., a plum job. I'd only been at Eton for a year, so was happy enough to go to D.C. The first day I was in my new school, I met Duncan and we instantly became best mates." When he glanced over Lillie's shoulder, he spied bottles of wine on the sideboard against the far wall. "Glass of wine?" he said and walked to the buffet as if he owned the Château.

"Fast forward three years," he continued, as he ran the opener blade around the foil capsule, "and my mother was offered the Ambassadorship to the Netherlands. There was no question she would take the position. By then I was seventeen. I had one year left in school and I was not going to leave Washington, full stop."

He pulled the cork out of the bottle of Château Beaulieu Grand Cru with a gratifying pop and splashed the ruby wine into long-stemmed goblets. Returning to the sofa, he handed a glass to Lillie and tapped her glass with his. "Cheers. There's nothing better than a Château Beaulieu cab, is there?" Before he sat, he took a noisy slurp of wine, swished it for a moment then swallowed with a gratifying smile.

For several seconds, Finn stared into his goblet. When he finally spoke, his voice was thick. "I shall never be able to repay Philip, Genevieve, and Duncan for what they did for me." His eyes clouded and his voice cracked.

Sensing he was grappling with his emotions, Lillie waited patiently for him to compose himself. She swirled the ruby cabernet in her glass, held it to her nose and breathed deeply of the plum, blackcurrant, and warm spices. As she drank, she closed her eyes and felt liquid velvet hit her tongue. When she opened her eyes, Finn was smiling at her and heat rose into her cheeks. "Are you going to tell me the rest of the story?" she said, diverting attention from her embarrassment.

Pulling his gaze from her, he nodded. "What I'm about to share with you is humiliating. I'm not sure why I'm telling you my sad tale, but it's too late to turn back now." He drank the last of his wine and set the goblet on the coffee table in front of him. "My parents and I rowed repeatedly about me leaving Washington, but my mother couldn't decline the new post and my father, who is an international security specialist and worked all over the world, always followed my mother. Obviously, now I understand what a ridiculous demand I was making on my parents, just so I could stay in Washington for another nine months. But to my adolescent brain, it seemed selfish and cruel that they wouldn't put their lives on hold for me. More than once I went to Duncan and had a moan about my unreasonable parents. Much to my surprise, my best mate told his parents about my misery. When they heard the story, Philip and Genevieve called my parents and invited me to live with them for my last year of school." He bit his lower lip. "Those Warwicks are really something, aren't they?"

"Mmm," Lillie said. "They are." She reached over and put her hand on Finn's and arched her brows. "But where is the humiliating part of the story?"

"Ah, yes. My personal opprobrium. More wine, I think." He ambled to the sideboard, grabbed the bottle by the neck, and sighed comically as he trudged back to the sofa. Though Lillie still had two fingers of wine in her glass, he offered more. She declined. He gave himself a generous pour and set the bottle on the table.

After taking a long swig, he said, "Imagine, Lillie, my parents are a third of the way around the world and have just left me in the care of generous friends who have agreed to supervise me for a year. Wouldn't you think I would be the most grateful boy and the model of obedience? I wasn't."

Little beads of perspiration glistened on his upper lip and he swiped at them with the back of his hand. "Overnight, the charming, well-behaved young man the Warwicks agreed to host," he jerked his thumb at himself, "became an entitled brat. I was reckless. I was thoughtless. I would come home drunk, come in late. I was a swine. I kept my room like a pigsty. But that wasn't the worst. I fell in love with weed. That was long before it was legal in D.C. Of course, like any self-respecting stoner, I kept a stash in my car."

"This is getting interesting," Lillie said. She had kicked off her shoes and sat cross-legged, her elbows on her knees.

Finn held up a finger. "Ah, but it gets better." He rolled his shoulder. "One day the battery on Philip's car was dead. He was late for a meeting and my car was in the driveway, so he borrowed it." He looked at his hands in his lap and Lillie thought she heard him sniff.

Lillie shivered. Realizing she was getting chilly, she shoved off the couch, plucked a thick throw from an ottoman, draped it over her lap, and cozied back into the cushions. She tilted her head. "And? Was there a problem with your car?"

"Sort of."

"Sort of?" She wrinkled her nose. "That's an odd thing to say. What kind of car was it? Was it a banger?"

"Certainly not." Finn was indignant. "It was a red vintage XKE." He laughed a hearty laugh. "Vintage Jags don't often run, but they always look splendid. Unfortunately for me, it ran that day."

"Why unfortunately?"

Finn held up his hand. "Just wait. Philip was driving down Foxhall Road—" He interrupted himself. "Do you know the road?"

"I do. I was at a residence on Foxhall for a dinner party last year. The people had a fabulous art collection."

"Most people on Foxhall have art collections worth seeing. But we digress."

Lillie waved her hand. "Sorry."

"Quite all right. So as I was saying, Philip was driving down Foxhall Road and saw lights flashing behind him. Foxhall is a narrow road so he had to find a place to pull over. The cop took forever to run the plate and Philip was getting later and later for his meeting. When at last the copper came to the car, he wanted to see Philip's driver's license and the car reg. Philip leaned over, popped the glovebox open, and out fell two nickel bags of weed."

Having just taken a drink, she gulped it down so it wouldn't spray all over Finn. "No, Finn! You can't be serious!"

He felt a flutter of warmth at her first use of his nickname. "Oh, Lillie, I assure you, I am."

"What happened?" She leaned forward so she was only inches away from him, but he could barely hear her whispered question.

"Nothing," he whispered back.

"Nothing?" She slumped back into the sofa.

"The Jag is very low to the ground so the cop didn't see what fell out of the glovebox. Philip is a pretty composed guy. He handed over his driver's license and reg and chatted up the policeman. The cop told Philip he had stopped him because one of the taillights was out, asked him to get it fixed as soon as possible, and sent him on his way."

Except for the crackling of the fire, the room was silent. Eyes wide and mouth open, Lillie was speechless.

"Good story, isn't it?" Finn drank half the wine in his glass and waited for Lillie to speak.

At last, Lillie composed her thoughts. "I assume Lord and Lady Crosswick immediately put you on a plane to the Netherlands?"

"They did not. They should have, but they did not." Love flooded Finn's face. "Duncan and I had a soccer game, you know, a football match, after school. When we got home and I took my books to my room, there in the middle of my unmade bed were the two nickel bags. I have never felt so sick in my life." He glared at his lap where his hands clutched his wine glass so tightly his knuckles were white.

Lillie saw a drop of water—a tear, she assumed—plop onto his trousers.

When he raised his head, his eyes were damp and his lips pulled into a sweet, sad smile. "It's a terrible thing to disappoint people you love."

"Oh, I know what you mean." Feelings from Genevieve's earlier tongue-lashing flooded through her and she returned his gloomy grin. "Believe me, I know what you mean. What did they say to you?"

"That evening at dinner, the conversation was the normal chatter about everyone's day. Duncan talked about the football match, Genevieve talked about a huge client they had just landed, and I couldn't say a word." Finn's voice cracked and he cleared his throat. "Then Philip said, 'Oh, Finn. When I borrowed your car today, I was stopped by the police.' The blood was rushing in my ears and I could barely hear what he was saying. 'You have a taillight out. You better get that fixed.'"

He hung his head for several seconds then raised it, his eyes misty again. "That was it. I would die for this family."

⁘ ❖◦❄◦❖ ⁘

Having pulled Philip from the salon into the study, Genevieve sat opposite her husband. With his head tilted to one side, Philip waited.

Genevieve sat on the edge of the cushion with her elbows on her knees, her fingers interlaced. "Here's the story behind my torrent of expletives," she began, then laid out everything Lillie had told her, leaving out no detail.

While he listened to Genevieve, Philip relaxed against the cushion of the loveseat.

After ten minutes, she ended with, "I'd say having Finn here for the holidays is a godsend, wouldn't you?"

He scowled, then spoke for the first time since she pulled him into the study. "I don't think there's any question. It sounds as if these cyber-attacks—or whatever they are—are taking on a life of their own, and one well beyond Lillie's skillset. We need someone who knows what the hell they're doing to get this situation under control."

"And that's Finn, right?" Genevieve's green eyes flashed.

Philip gave a sharp nod. "Absolutely. He's the one who can do it."

FIFTEEN

After yesterday's busy preparations for Christmas Eve and Christmas Day, Genevieve stood in the middle of the dining room, enjoying the fruits of their labor. Her eyes closed, she inhaled the aromas of the holidays: pine, clove, cinnamon, chocolate, orange, ginger. A smile graced her lips and when she opened her eyes, her smile grew broader. Delphine had executed Genevieve's vision to perfection. Tonight they would celebrate a very French Christmas Eve, and tomorrow they would honor English and American Christmas traditions.

"Tutu," Ella called from the foyer.

"I'm in here, darling."

The seven-year-old bounced into the room as if she had springs in her feet. "Tutu, everything is so beautiful!" she said, her voice hushed in awe.

"You know you're not supposed to be in here until this evening."

Ella's eyes, round as silver dollars, reflected the hundreds of fairy lights on the soaring tree in the corner and her grin stretched from ear to ear. "I know." She wandered around the table, touching a linen napkin, admiring the faceted crystal. "Tutu, look. The Christmas crackers have each person's name on them. Oh! Here's mine." Squealing with delight, she picked up her Christmas cracker and looked at the pretty handwriting that spelled out her name.

"This has to be our secret, darling girl." She put a finger to her lips. "We mustn't tell anyone you've been in here." In her black-velvet skirt and her metallic-gold cable-knit sweater, Genevieve looked like a model in a spread for Ralph Lauren. To Ella, her grandmother was a beautiful queen from a fairytale.

"I promise I won't tell anyone," Ella said, her cherubic face serious. Then she brightened. "Tutu, do you like my dress?" She spun like a ballerina, her long ringlets lifting off her shoulders and her hunter-green velvet dress billowing as she twirled for her grandmother.

When she stopped, Genevieve squatted and her skirt mushroomed around her. "Your dress is almost as beautiful as you are." She threw her arms wide. "Come here, I need a hug."

Ella barreled into Genevieve, almost bowling her over. "Whoa! You have to be careful with your old granny."

"Tutu, you're not old."

"Right you are," Philip said from the doorway where he'd been watching the two beauties. "Tutu is a hottie."

"What's a hottie, Bumpa?"

Genevieve shot him a warning glance.

He strode across the dining room, bent down, and snatched Ella up onto his hip. He gave her a noisy kiss on her pink cheek and said, "Ella, my sweet, a hottie is a beautiful woman who loves her grandchildren." He winked over Ella's head at Genevieve. "I've come to kidnap you. We only have an hour to practice our duet one more time before we perform it at the Christmas Eve Musicale. You need to show me that dance step I keep messing up."

"I know, Bumpa. You still get it wrong." She shimmied down Philip's leg till her feet hit the floor. She yanked the front of her dress down, smoothed it, then grabbed his hand and tugged. "Come on. Let's go practice. I don't want you to embarrass me."

As Philip and Genevieve exchanged smiles, Genevieve knew she would remember this moment for a very long time.

For over thirty years, the Warwick Christmas Eve had been an elegant black-tie evening with everyone—even the children—dressed in their shiny best. It was an evening filled with performances by every guest, followed by a sumptuous dinner. The meal's climax was the discovery of *the almond* buried in someone's dessert, which won them a prize. And then, accompanied by sleighbells and a booming "ho ho ho", Santa's arrival brought almost more excitement than one could bear. This year it would be Père Noël who would bring the gifts.

Even after their huge inheritance, Philip and Genevieve made certain the tradition carried on. Last year, they incorporated their Christmas Eve ritual into Wilmingrove Hall's traditions, offering their own addition to the Laney heritage.

This year, though they would change nothing about the Musicale, they would be resurrecting Château Beaulieu's Christmas Eve dinner that Delphine and Genevieve had discovered. In the late fall, while pouring through boxes of journals, notes, and letters, yellowed from centuries spent in the oppressive heat and frigid cold of the attic, the two explorers had found a handwritten shopping list for le réveillon de Noël, Christmas Eve celebration, from December 14, 1824.

Now, two months after their historical discovery, the music festival, feasting, and fun were about to begin.

SIXTEEN

A T THE STROKE of six o'clock, the tinkling chime of the Morbier rang through the Château, calling guests to gather in the grand salon. Not wanting to miss a moment of the special evening, everyone was there. Back from their brief honeymoon, Becca and David were sun kissed from their few days on the white sand beaches of Tenerife. With Bertie by his side, Wallace was reveling in his recovery from his recent death. Waiting for the Musicale to start, Olivia entertained Alex and Ella by pulling coins from behind their ears.

The pop of Champagne bottles announced that the evening had begun. Duncan poured glass after glass, handing them to Finn to distribute, until everyone, including the children with their sparkling cider, held a crystal flute.

Stepping to the center of the room, Philip held out his hand to Genevieve. She left Mrs. MacIntosh and Wallace where the three had been laughing at a joke Wallace had told, glided into Philip's outstretched arm, and kissed his lips with a loud smack.

"Merry Christmas, darling," she said.

He closed his arm around her waist and pulled her into him

for another lingering kiss. "An early Christmas present, G," he said as he relaxed his hold on her. "And that's only the stocking stuffer!" He swept a smile around the room at his friends and family, then raised his glass. "And now, a toast."

"Wait a minute," Finn said. "Where's Lillie?"

"I'm here! I'm here." With a fistful of burgundy satin in each hand, Lillie charged through the doorway of the grand salon. As she stopped abruptly, a few curls that had escaped from the messy bun atop her head bounced around her face. She looked down at her décolletage to make certain the bodice of her strapless dress was still in place. When she saw everything was where it should be, she breathed a sigh of relief. "I'm so sorry," she said, breathless from her dash down the stairs. "I've been on the phone with an art blogger."

"Good news?" Philip asked.

"Not really." She frowned. "But it can wait."

Genevieve and Philip caught each other's eye and shook their heads almost imperceptibly.

Finn took the glass Duncan had just filled and made a beeline for Lillie, who forced a grin and presented him with a kiss on the cheek.

Philip held her gaze until she gave him a nod, then said. "Now that you're here, the party can begin." He raised his glass and the guests followed suit. "Nothing could be better than for G and me to have all of you, our family, here tonight to enjoy one of our most cherished celebrations. For thirty-three Christmas Eves, we have enjoyed this tradition of family performances, fine food, conversation, lots of laughter, spectacular company, and always excellent Champagne. As this is their first Musicale, let's raise our glasses and toast Lillie Langdon and Olivia Conway."

"To Lillie and Olivia!" The room was noisy with cheers and then silent as everyone drank. Drifting to chairs and sofas around the room, guests found a comfortable seat with a good view of the performance area in front of the fireplace. Because there would be dance numbers, the massive carpet had been rolled toward the audience, creating a demarcation for the stage.

"Lillie, Olivia, which one of you would like to kick off the Warwick Christmas Eve Musicale extravaganza?"

"I'll do it!" Lillie stepped forward, her hand waving in the air. "If I go first, I can enjoy the rest of the performances without worrying about my own!"

"Drat you, you clever girl!" Olivia snarled in mock annoyance, and the two giggled as Lillie rose and walked to center stage.

She fought to calm the butterflies fluttering in her stomach. Mustering her poise, she took a deep breath and took a moment to look at each person in her audience. When she came to Finnegan, she lingered a moment. Her mouth bloomed into a smile and her cheeks hinted at dimples. She pulled a piece of paper from her skirt pocket, unfolded it, and began to read.

> *"It's Christmas for Alex and Ella.*
> *They know Santa's quite the fella.*
> *He'll land overhead*
> *while they're asleep in their bed,*
> *and snoozing with their heads on their pilla."*

Everyone laughed and started to applaud, but Lillie held up her hand. "Wait, wait. There's more," she said.

> *"When Alex and Ella awake,*
> *I bet their presents they'll take*
> *from under the tree*
> *with so very much glee,*
> *and then, they'll eat Christmas cake."*

Lillie pulled two huge, chocolate lollipops in the shape of snowmen from her pockets and tossed them to Alex and Ella. "Merry Christmas, everyone!" she said.

With hoots of appreciation, people jumped to their feet and applauded as Lillie, offering the queen's wave, exited the makeshift stage and sat down by Finn, who had been patting the cushion beside him.

With everyone still clapping, Philip stood. When the crowd had quieted, he shook his head and said, "Lillie! Way to set the bar high." He searched the eager faces looking back at him. "I think it's only fair since Lillie went first, Olivia should go next. Olivia, you're on."

Without hesitation, Olivia sashayed to the piano in a form-fitting velvet gown that perfectly matched her violet eyes, her straight blonde hair swinging as she walked. Before she sat, she turned and addressed the audience. "I'm delighted to play a little ditty I wrote especially for this evening. It expresses my feelings for all of you," she said, and smiled warmly before settling at the keyboard.

Sitting next to the makeshift stage in an overstuffed chair, Wallace kept a laser focus on Olivia. As she began her song, he was sure each word had a double meaning. After the first verse, his eyes darted around the room looking for signs that others were detecting a threat in her Musicale offering. He was surprised to see everyone smiling and laughing at the clever lyrics. He had to admit she had written a charming melody, but what did she mean when she sang: "Each of you will get what you deserve for Christmas. Ella wants a pretty foal, but she might get a lump of coal." Even though she winked and smiled at Ella, the words were still ominous. His neck dampened from dread.

On the final chorus, everyone chimed in and the room was filled with the sound of her lively composition. "Let's all raise our glasses high, Christmas Eve is coming nigh. To the House of Crosswick sing. Who knows what tomorrow will bring? Tra la la la la tr la la la."

Olivia finished the tune with three grand chords and a glissando. Everyone stood, cheers roaring and applause filling the room. Finn's whistle of appreciation cut through the air. Ella rushed to the piano, hugged Olivia, and gave her a kiss on her cheek. The clapping went on while Olivia swept into a bow, as everyone smiled at the radiant performer. Everyone but Wallace. Reaching into the inside pocket of his tuxedo for his handkerchief, he felt the edge of a notecard and a chill rippled down his spine.

While the crowd was lost in the excitement of Olivia's performance, Wallace remained rigid in his chair, with his hand inside his jacket. His heart raced and the words written on the card flooded his mind: *"Vengeance is justice and it's time for mine!"*

Until this moment, he had completely forgotten the notecard and Rolex attached to it. With all that had gone on over the last several days, he was certain Bertie had not thought about it either, and he was certain the Rolex was still tucked in her evening bag.

He stared at the young woman he believed had written those threatening words. When her eyes met his, the smile drained from her face. She froze him in her glare for several seconds then pulled away and took one last, deep bow before returning to her seat next to her mother.

"Who's next?" Philip said, rubbing his hands together.

Waving her hand in the air, Ella jumped to her feet. "Bumpa, Bumpa! Pick me."

"Not yet, Ella. We'll go after the next act and I think that will be," he waved his pointed finger back and forth building the suspense of who would be next, "Wallace and Mrs. MacIntosh."

Bertie MacIntosh's hand flew to her mouth, stifling an, "Oh no!"

When Wallace heard his name, it took a moment for him to realize what was happening. He took a deep breath, pushed himself from his chair, and held out his hand. "Come on, Bertie," he said. "Let's give them a show. Lady Crosswick, I believe you are going to accompany us on the piano?"

As she walked to her place at the keyboard, Genevieve ran her hand along the Pleyel's polished wood, then settled on the petit point-covered bench. She rested her hands on the keys and waited while Wallace and Bertie took center stage. Mrs. MacIntosh stood as tall as her sturdy frame would allow, looking serious in a long black wool dress, the collar and front placard trimmed with her clan tartan. She clasped her hands in a rigid grip in front of her.

Never one to go against tradition, Wallace was the perfect complement in his conservative tuxedo, pleated shirt studded in onyx, and black cummerbund snug around his middle. Still not fully recovered from his hospital mishap, Bertie had put a tiny swipe of blush on his cheeks. Together, they looked like stately version of Grant Wood's *American Gothic*. They exchanged glances, Wallace nodded at Genevieve, she gave them a trill, and the sedate Mrs. MacIntosh started.

"I don't want a lot for Christmas, there is just one thing I need." Her pure alto rang through the salon and everyone in the room sat forward, surprised.

With a voice reminiscent of Tony Bennet, Wallace crooned. "I don't care about the presents underneath the Christmas tree."

No one could believe their ears. Bertie and Wallace were spectacular.

Bertie finished the introduction with, "All I want for Christmas is you", and fluttered her lashes at Wallace. Genevieve hit the first driving chords, the audience hollered and clapped, and the couple was off and running, delivering the rest of the song as if they were professionals at Radio City Music Hall. Genevieve kept the melody driving while Wallace and Bertie moved and swayed to the beat until the final notes began to slow. They took each other's hands and looked into each other's eyes and sang. The piano tinkled the last notes and everyone stood and cheered an ovation. Wallace swept his arm toward Bertie. She blushed, bowed, and cocked her head toward Wallace. He nodded and bent at the waist. When that was done, he took Mrs. MacIntosh's hand and led her back to their chairs.

Delphine had been watching from the doorway, jealousy bubbling under her congenial surface. She had a wonderful voice. She could sing a carol or two, but here she was serving hors d'oeuvres to everyone. It wasn't fair. She began to pass the appetizers while Duncan refilled Champagne glasses. When she got to Wallace and Bertie, she leaned over and offered them the tray and a brittle smile. "You two really think you are something, don't you?" she said, her tone more than her words leaving an uncomfortable chill between them.

"I beg your pardon?" Mrs. MacIntosh said, unsure she had heard Delphine correctly.

Delphine gave them a searing look before flashing a dazzling smile at Lillie and Finnegan and offering them the tray, leaving Bertie and Wallace confused by what she had just said to them.

With everyone replenished, Philip took the floor again. "Now, lords and ladies, ladies and gentlemen, it is my great pleasure to introduce the next act in the Warwick Christmas Eve Musicale. It is none other than our very own Ella Laney Warwick, soon, I'm sure, to be a performer of great renown in London's West End and on Broadway."

Brimming with confidence, the rosy-cheeked seven-year-old walked to the front of the room and took over. "Performing with me this evening is my Bumpa. He has been working very hard on this number so please be encouraging. He will do his best not to make any mistakes. Bumpa?" Ella held out her hand and

Philip joined her. "Daddy," she said to Duncan. "Music, please."

Duncan hit "play" on the remote for the sound system and the brass introduction to "Sleighride" blasted through the speakers. Ella twirled into an elegant bow, then she and Philip began the dance Ella had choreographed. It was part ballet, part hip hop, a little bit jazz, with a step or two of tap thrown in. Ella had it mastered, flowing from step to step, the beat from the trumpets guiding her. Philip did his best, but in the end he was more of a prop than a partner, and the one step he had practiced over and over with Ella was nowhere to be found. When the trombones played their last notes, Ella and Philip bent forward, huddled together. Then they reared back, mimed the last, long neighing of the trumpet and the song was over. Philip lifted Ella to his shoulder as applause thundered and they basked in the glow of a performance well done, at least for Ella.

Next, David played the guitar while he and Becca sang "Silent Night", he in English, she in German. Last year Becca had sung the elegant carol at the Wilmingrove Hall celebration as a solo. This new rendition as a duet was a beautiful intermezzo among the fun and frivolity of the other performances.

Back by popular demand, Duncan reprised his wacky version of "Twelve Days of Christmas", adding Julia as his co-conspirator. With twelve days, each person had a role to play. It was wild and silly and a crowd-pleaser.

And, at last, it was time for the finale. Alex carried his snare drum, Finnegan extended his hand to Genevieve, and the three of them settled onto center stage.

"It gives me great pleasure," Philip said, "to introduce the final act of this year's Warwick Christmas Eve Musicale. May I present our three Christmas elves: Alex, Finnegan, and Genevieve, singing 'Little Drummer Boy'. Take it away."

The three grinned at each other, ready to go. Alex held his drumsticks overhead, tapped them together four slow beats and Finnegan sang the first haunting notes.

"Come, they told me, pa rum pum pum pum," Genevieve's pure soprano began. "Our newborn king to see, pa rum pum pum pum."

With each verse the music swelled, and Finnegan began to double-time his vocal drum.

Alex played his snare drum faster and louder.

Genevieve filled the salon and crescendoed with, "I played my drum for him, pa rum pum pum pum! I played my best for him, pa rum pump um pum, rum pa pa pum, rum pa pa pum."

For four beats there was silence. Then the trio almost whispered, "Then he smiled at me, pa rum pump um pum, me and my drum."

For several seconds, the only sound in the room was the crackling fire, then the audience erupted, jumping to their feet, cheering, clapping.

"Bravo! Brava!" The salon rang with praise and the guests crowded around the trio.

Mrs. MacIntosh and Wallace hugged Alex and asked him to play a short lick.

Lillie tucked her arm through Finnegan's, stood on her toes, and kissed his cheek. "You're just full of surprises, aren't you?"

He leaned close to her ear. "Just you wait," he whispered.

"There are more to come."

"Magnificent!" Becca threw her arms around Genevieve. "You were magnificent!"

Philip caught Genevieve's eye as she looked over Becca's shoulder. He put his hand over his heart, patted it, and saw her eyes mist. She offered him a smile. He threw her a kiss. Then out of the corner of his eye, he saw Delphine standing in the doorway, looking very much like an outsider. When he looked her way, she turned and left.

With everyone still showering the trio with compliments, the room was noisy so Philip grabbed a cheese knife from the sideboard and rapped it against his glass. A tinkle rang out but did nothing to quiet the laughter and chatter in the room. He pulled his bottom lip over his teeth and curled his tongue. When a piercing whistle cut through the din, the crowd silenced.

He grinned and held his head at a rakish angle. "Lords and ladies, ladies and gentlemen, I believe dinner is served. Shall we?" He extended his arm, indicating everyone should wander toward the dining room.

Genevieve drifted to his side, took his arm, and kissed his ear. "That was fun. You and Ella were wonderful. I particularly liked your adlib when you couldn't remember any of the steps." A snicker gurgled in her throat.

He grinned. "You know, with Ella, the only thing you have to do is stand there. I was nothing but a prop. But, sweet girl, you three were as Becca said: magnificent. I almost teared up."

"Come on, cute boy. We have guests to host."

They sauntered across the hall where Delphine and Lizette

were waiting to throw the doors wide. "Lord Crosswick, sommes-nous prêt?" Delphine said.

"We're *almost* ready," he said in response, then turned to find his grandson in the crowd. "Alex, are you ready to play us in?"

Alex pulled his harmonica from his trouser pocket and waved it in the air. "I'm ready, Bumpa," he said, weaving his way to the front of the crowd. He put his lips on the mouthpiece and blew, playing glissandos up and down the instrument. "Can you all hear me?"

The crowd cheered.

"Now, Delphine, we are indeed ready."

Delphine and Lizette pushed the heavy, paneled pocket doors into their wall casings and a hush fell over the group.

Ella had been true to her word. She had told no one how beautiful the dining room was. She caught her Tutu's eye, smiled, and mimed zipping her lip.

As Genevieve winked at Ella and blew her a kiss, she smelled the faint fragrance of Rose Otto. She smiled to herself and whispered, "I'm so glad you're here, Charlotte."

Alex began to play "We Wish You a Merry Christmas" and led the parade into the dazzling room. When he finished, he acknowledged the polite applause with a smile, took a brief bow, and shoved his harmonica back into his pocket.

Entirely lit by candles and fairy lights, the room was something out of a dream. In the far corner of the dining room, a noble fir tree soared sixteen feet, the star on top almost touching the ceiling. Two thousand lights wove in and out of every branch, making the tree glimmer from top to bottom. Cookies, nuts, red papier-mâché apples hung from red ribbons, and pheasant feathers poked out from between branches.

Set for thirteen diners, the table was a work of art. Thirty-six candles blazed on three tall candelabras. Pomegranates, nuts, and pinecones spilled over an evergreen tapestry that ran the length of the table, and dozens of crimson-edged coral roses peeked out from fir sprigs. Red ribbon wove through branches nestled on the table. Echoing the tree, pheasant feathers were tucked here and there, a regal homage to nature.

On the massive sideboard, all the traditional réveillon desserts waited to be devoured: a croquembouche, its choux pastry puffs stacked high into a cone shape and spun with threads of caramel; a two-foot-long bûche de Noël, a rolled sponge cake filled with buttercream and decorated with ganache to resemble a log; and silver trays piled with cookies and chocolates. And then there were the boissons, the drinks to accompany every course: endless wines. Champagne for dessert and cognacs for digesting.

As French Christmas carols wafted through the dining room speakers, guests bustled around the table in search of a cracker with their names written in calligraphy. When they found their places, they stood behind their chairs, waiting.

With Philip and Genevieve at the head and foot of the table, Philip picked up his Champagne glass, ready to offer a toast. "Looking around this table," he said, his eyes sweeping over everyone, "I am—"

"Wait, wait, wait," Genevieve broke in. She looked at Wallace, who was sitting between Mrs. MacIntosh and Lillie. "Before Philip begins, I just want to say Wallace, we love you and we are so happy you're here with us, healthy and oh-so handsome." She smiled broadly, then looked down the long table at Philip. "I'm sorry, darling. That just had to be said. I'll try not to interrupt again."

"Of course you will," he said, rolling his eyes. He raised his glass again. "As I was saying when I was so rudely interrupted…" A chuckle bounced around the table. "G and I love every one of you. You enrich our lives and bring us joy. There is nothing we wouldn't do for you and we cherish the love we feel in return. Thank you all for your exceptional performances tonight. I hope each of you is already planning what you'll do for next year's Christmas Eve Musicale… not that we're competitive, but I'd get on it if I were you." He looked down the long table at Genevieve and winked. "In the meantime, let's remember yesterday fondly, enjoy today, and look forward to tomorrow's surprises. Merry Christmas to us all."

There was a resounding "Merry Christmas". Diners clinked glasses with those closest to them and the din of an exuberant evening began to build as everyone sat. Everyone but Genevieve, who remained standing. She tapped her empty wine goblet with her knife and the room silenced. "You all know I can never let Philip have the last word." She shot him a flirtatious glance. "Last year we were at Wilmingrove Hall to celebrate the Christmas holiday, and it was gloriously English. This year, because we've been living a French life, we are celebrating la veille de Noël, a French Christmas Eve with a French menu, French wines, of course, and later a visit from le Père Noël." She pointed at Alex, then Ella. "But don't worry, you two, Santa will be coming later tonight so you will eventually need to get to bed."

"And Santa's bringing me a pony," Ella squealed.

At Ella's declaration, Philip and Genevieve rolled their eyes at each other, then Genevieve continued. "As I was about to say, there is one English custom that was invented by the French. Though the French have long since abandoned this delightful tradition, we aren't willing to give it up. What is it? Christmas crackers. How could we set a Christmas Eve table without crackers? Well, we just couldn't. So, Delphine was kind enough to secure Christmas crackers and included them in our beautiful French table setting. That said, before we pop our crackers and the meal begins, I want to offer the Christmas toast that has been our family's wish for almost forty years."

She raised her glass and said:

"On this happy Christmas tide,
Gathered round our table here
Are those we love and hold so dear.
To you, we wish good Christmas cheer."

A noisy "Cheers!" rang out, accompanied by the tinkling of clinking crystal.

Genevieve sat, then held up her tapestry-covered Christmas cracker. "Everyone, grab an end with your partner and pull."

Too excited to find a partner, Alex pulled his cracker apart and whooped at the satisfying pop. Everybody paired off, wrapping a fist around the end of a festive tube then snapping, and popping, and laughing.

Philip and Mrs. MacIntosh grabbed each other's end wrapper and tugged. "Blast it!" Bertie said, disappointed when there was no tiny explosion, just the sound of tearing paper.

"It's okay, Mrs. MacIntosh. We still have our prizes." Philip unfolded his tissue paper crown, put it on his head, and waved a regal wave to Genevieve at the other end of the table.

Wallace and Lillie were the only two left who hadn't popped their crackers, so they had the attention of the entire table.

"Let's go, you two." Duncan started clapping and chanting, "Pull, pull, pull!"

Wallace was ready, firmly holding his end, when Lillie insisted on a countdown.

"All right, Wallace. We'll pull on one. Okay? Five, four, three, two—"

"Excuse me, Ms. Langdon," Wallace interrupted. "Will you pull on one or after you say one?"

"I'll say one and then we'll pull." Lillie rolled her eyes and started her countdown again. "Five, four, three, two—"

"You're certain it's *after* one?" He teased her with a grin.

"Wallace! Just give me the bloody cracker!" she laughed. In one motion, she snatched the cracker from Wallace and stood. As she yanked both ends with a mighty tug, a flash of fire and a thundering boom exploded through the room and Lillie was thrown against the wall.

SEVENTEEN

S CREAMS ECHOED OFF the ceiling and the walls as clouds of smoke billowed through the room. Paintings were askew and the dining room was thick with the smell of sulfur. On pure instinct, Julia had thrown her arms around Alex and was now lying on top of him under the table. Out of the corner of her eye, she saw Duncan at the other end of the table, covering Ella with his body.

"Mom, I can't breathe," Alex gasped. Julia rolled to the side and scanned him quickly to see if blood oozed from anywhere. Seeing none, she checked for broken bones. Finding none, she looked across the carpet to where Duncan still laid on top of Ella.

"Duncan, is Ella all right?" she shouted under the table.

"I think so."

Julia could see him checking her skull, her arms, her legs, more relieved every time he confirmed an unharmed body part.

"If you think Ella's okay, could you go get my medical bag? It's in the clo—"

"I know where it is." He kissed Ella on top of the head. He could hear his father shouting orders and his mother calling to people, asking if they were all right. "Ella, crawl over there to Mommy. I need to go get her bag so she can help anyone who's hurt."

Ella's sweet face was twisted in fear. "What happened, Daddy?" she sobbed.

"I don't know, darling. But I promise everything is going to be all right." *But is it?* Duncan asked himself. "Crawl over there to Mommy and I'll be right back."

Tears streamed down Ella's cheeks as she inchwormed her way across the floor to Julia and Alex. Duncan pushed himself out from under the table and off the floor, ran through the foyer and up the stairs, taking two at a time.

Having no idea what had just happened, Julia hugged her children in a vice grip. "Listen, you two. I want you to stay right here under the table until Daddy or I come to get you. Do not move from here. Do you understand?"

"I'll take care of Ella, Mom." Alex stuck out his lower lip and set his jaw.

Her throat thick with emotion, Julia could only nod at her brave boy. She kissed them both and crawled backwards out from under the table, straight into Duncan's legs. She looked up into his face, his eyes dark with concern, his jaw set in a rigid line.

"Here's your bag," he said as he offered his hand and pulled her to her feet.

Everyone was crowded at the far end of the table around Wallace and Lillie.

"Call an ambulance!" somebody shouted.

Philip was already on his phone dialing.

"Let me through." Julia wedged her shoulder between Mrs. MacIntosh and David, pulled Becca out of the way, and saw Wallace, still seated at the table with his soot-covered face in his hands. There was no blood.

"Wallace, are you hurt?"

Julia watched as he shook his head, then she saw Lillie crumpled on the floor, half sitting against her broken chair that had smashed against the wall as she was blown away from the table. She was relieved to see Lillie's chest rise and fall with steady breath and was pleased to feel a strong pulse beating in Lillie's carotid artery.

"Lillie," she said. No response. She put her cold stethoscope just above Lillie's strapless top on her bare skin.

Lille shivered, then moaned.

Julia listened until she was satisfied Lillie's heart sounded as it should.

"Lillie," she said again. After a moment, Lillie's lids crept up until her eyes were open. Julia shined her penlight into each and was satisfied with the reaction of Lillie's pupils.

"Follow the light with your eyes," Julia directed, and Lillie obeyed.

"Lillie, do you have pain anywhere?" Julia was in full doctor mode.

"My back." Lillie winced as she tried to sit straighter.

"Don't move, Lillie," Julia said, just as Olivia squatted next to her.

"How can I help?" Olivia asked, her voice strong and eager.

"And I'm here," Finn said. He dropped to his knees and took

Lillie's hand. "What the hell, Lillie? I have big plans for us. If you think you're going to get away from me by blowing yourself up, you're wrong."

Lillie's smile was weak, but Finn was grateful for any reaction.

"I need to check Lillie's back. Help me ease her onto her side, then we'll roll her to her stomach. Lillie," Julia said softly, "let us know if this hurts and we'll stop."

Julia directed the task as the three of them shifted her onto her side. They moved slowly, a constant moan rolling from Lillie's throat until her shoulder was on the ground and they could stretch her legs out straight. Ever so gently they guided her onto her stomach.

"Oh my god!" Olivia shouted.

"Get back," Julia said, as everyone crowded to see why Olivia had yelled. "Where is the emergency team?"

"What's going on? What's the matter?" Lillie's voice was remarkably strong. "Something's stinging me."

Sticking out of Lillie's back, just below her shoulder blade, was a rung from the back of her chair that had snapped off and turned into a dagger.

EIGHTEEN

"What in the hell just happened?" Finn said to Philip. With Julia racing ahead, they trotted on either side of the emergency team rushing Lillie's gurney to the ambulance. "One minute Lillie and Wallace were pulling their cracker, and the next minute, boom!"

"You don't think for one second that explosion was caused by a cracker, do you?" Philip stopped, surprised at Finn. The EMS team kept going. "Finn, that's impossible." They stood three feet apart, staring at each other.

"I don't understand." Philip could almost see the wheels in Finn's mind spinning. "Are you suggesting what just happened wasn't an accident?"

"I don't see how it could be. That was too big an explosion to be caused by a little Christmas cracker. I'm going to call Chef Picard, our friend at the Saint-Émilion Police Department. Julia's riding in the ambulance to the hospital. After what happened with Wallace, we're not leaving Lillie alone with this medical staff."

Philip looked down the driveway and wasn't surprised to see Henri running toward them.

"Que se passe-t-il?" Henri hollered while he was still at some distance.

"Finn, go with Henri. He'll get you a car so you can follow the ambulance."

Finn didn't need to be told twice. He intercepted Henri and filled him in on what had just happened before they turned and ran toward the garage. By the time Lillie was loaded into the medical van, the garage door was lumbering open. An Aston Martin Vantage pulled into view and paused. Philip heard the throaty growl as Finn revved the engine, before rolling onto the gravel drive. The racing green sports car eased toward the front of the house, pulled just behind the ambulance, then stopped.

"You look good behind the wheel of an Aston Martin," Philip said, bending down and putting his elbows on the edge of the window.

"It's not an XKE, but it isn't bad."

Finn's cheeky remark brought a smile to Philip's serious face, then he sobered again. "Listen, Finn. Lillie was very lucky. That chair rung could have done so much more damage. The EMS folks said though it caused her some real pain, a few stitches should be all she'll need."

Philip saw relief flood into Finn's eyes. "I've never believed in love at first sight, but I think Lillie might have changed my mind." Finn's lopsided smile said everything.

The slam of the ambulance doors cut their conversation short. Philip slapped Finnegan on the shoulder, stepped back from the sleek convertible, and said, "Keep her safe, Finn, and bring her back home. Tomorrow's Christmas."

Four hours later, Finn was back at Château Beaulieu, helping Lillie up the stairs, tucking her into bed, and thanking the good-luck gods that Lillie hadn't been more seriously injured.

NINETEEN

PHILIP AND GENEVIEVE heard whispers from their bedroom doorway.

"Bumpa, Tutu, are you awake?"

"Brace yourself," Philip said to Genevieve, linen sheets and the duvet pulled over his head. They heard claws tap on the hardwood floor before four furry feet hit the carpet, then Cooper sailed like a flying squirrel onto their bed, followed immediately by two whooping children screaming, "Merry Christmas." And the morning began.

The day was a whirlwind of too many gifts and too much food. With the dining room now a crime scene, a table had been set in the orangerie. The rules of the day were to keep it simple, keep it casual, and keep it cheerful. There was plenty of conversation, plenty of laughter, arguments and makeups between Alex and Ella, and finally a royal decree from Philip that everyone put on warm clothes for a walk before Christmas dinner. The chaos of finding mittens, gloves, boots, hats, and scarves was exhausting, but at last everyone was ready.

Delphine, who had returned just an hour ago from spending Christmas Eve at her sister's, stood in the middle of the foyer laughing at the mayhem.

"Delphine, we'll be back," Philip bellowed. "Now, everyone out!" He threw open the door and as the frigid air rushed in, he waved his arms, shooing the group onto the wide front stoop as if he were driving chickens from a coop.

Delphine closed the door against the cold.

"Where are we going, Bumpa?" Alex was ready to lead the way.

"Let's walk around back, down toward the stables." He caught Genevieve's eye and winked. She smiled back, feeling the thrill of conspiracy.

"Bumpa!" Ella caught up with her grandfather and grabbed his hand. "Isn't this a beautiful Christmas Day?"

He snatched her under her arms, swung her around twice, then planted a kiss on her cold, pink cheek. "Ella, it couldn't be a more beautiful day." When he set her down, she bolted ahead and caught up to Alex.

The sun was low in the sky, painting the clouds with red and orange streaks. The smell of woodsmoke wafted through the air, making the cold evening seem cozy.

"Alex, go into the barn and we'll get warm for a minute." Philip pointed down the hill to the stone-and-shake stables.

"Okay, Bumpa," Alex yelled back as he headed toward the archway connecting the two wings of the écuries. Philip watched his two grandchildren disappear through the door into the warmth of the barn.

Genevieve caught up to Philip and slipped her arm through his. When he looked at her, her eyes were misty. He stopped walking. "You okay?" he asked.

She wiped a lone tear from her cheek. "After everything that's happened in the last few days, I'm a mass of conflicted emotion."

Philip kissed the top of her head. "And?" he said, encouraging her to continue.

"I'm fearful, happy, nervous, excited. I'm angry. I'm grateful. I'm overwhelmed. I think about what happened to Wallace and the explosion last night and I'm terrified. Then, in the light of day," she swept her hand across the horizon, "I think of all we have. It couldn't be more beautiful. And look at that." She looked behind at the chattering, laughing group following them. "They couldn't be more wonderful."

"And you, my darling G, are the most spectacular of all."

Genevieve rolled her eyes and Philip kissed the tip of her nose.

"We'll get to the bottom of what's been happening, I promise. But let's enjoy today. Alex and Ella deserve a wonderful Christmas Day. Hell, we *all* deserve a wonderful Christmas Day."

She put her hand to the side of his face, drew him in, and met his lips. They lingered there, enjoying each other's warmth, until Ella's blood-curdling scream split them apart.

TWENTY

"**E**LLA!" DUNCAN BLEW by his father and streaked the last few yards to the barn, with Julia matching him stride for stride. They were through the door before anyone else realized what was happening. "Ella," they bellowed.

"Daddy, Mommy!" At the far end of the stables, in the middle of the well-lighted aisle, Ella jumped up and down clapping her hands, and shrieked, "Bumpa bought me a pony! Bumpa bought me a pony!"

Expecting the worst, the rest of the group crowded through the door and everyone was relieved to see darling Ella unharmed.

"Dad, Mom." Duncan narrowed his eyes at his parents. "Did you really buy Ella a pony?"

Sensing a family discussion about to ensue, the rest of the group quietly left the barn and headed back to the safety of the house. As he left, David waved and said, "We'll meet you back at the Château," then eased himself out the door.

Genevieve stepped to the side, distancing herself from Philip. "He did it," she said, pointing a finger at her husband.

Chest out and jaw set, Philip was ready to defend his decision.

"I've been promising Ella a pony since before she understood what a pony was. She's seven now and everyone says seven is the perfect time for a child to have a pony."

"And who is everyone?" Duncan challenged his father.

"Articles. You know, Google. The internet," Philip said, flatly.

"Right, Dad." Duncan dismissed his father's response.

"I think it's wonderful, Philip." Julia stretched to kiss her father-in-law's cheek. "Duncan, it's time for Ella to learn some responsibility. She will be responsible for feeding and exercising her pony and can participate in…" She looked at Philip, "His, her?"

"Her. She's a filly, just like Ella."

"She can help train her. It will be a good experience."

Duncan's frown began to dissolve. "Tell me about the horse, Dad."

Philip's shoulders relaxed. "Ah, she is an eleven-year-old Selle Français, French Saddle pony. Henri helped decide what would be the best horse for Ella. Actually, he insisted the Selle Français was the only horse for Ella. I'm sure you won't argue that Henri is our expert regarding horses, both in the stables and under the hood of a car."

"Well, Dad. I have to say, I feel a lot better knowing Henri was involved." Duncan patted his father on the back as he headed down the aisle toward his wiggling daughter.

Ella danced up and down the aisle, rollicking back and forth between the horse's stall and the adults. "Daddy, come see." Unable to contain her excitement, she tugged on her father's hand, pulling him toward her new best pal. Then she had a thought. "Bumpa, does she have a name or do I get to name her?"

"She has a name. It's Jolie Fille. What do you think that means?"

She jumped in place. "I know what it means! I know what it means! It means pretty girl." She grinned broadly at the adults, who seemed impressed. "That's what Delphine calls me."

Philip squatted in front of Ella and took her hands in his. "Do you want to give her a different name or do you think Jolie Fille suits her?"

She thought for several seconds. "Bumpa, if I went to live in a new place, I would miss all of you." She turned her enormous brown eyes on her family. "It would be hard enough to live with new people, but if they changed my name, it would be the worst. Jolie Fille is a beautiful name and that's what I'm going to call her." She threw her arms around Philip and hugged him fiercely. "Thank you, Bumpa. I love you."

"I love you too, Ella. I know you and Jolie Fille are going to be best friends for a long time."

"No, Bumpa. We're going to be BFFs. Best friends forever!"

For the last few minutes, Genevieve had been watching Alex. He was standing alone and when she edged over to him and put an arm around his shoulders, his back and arms tensed. She pulled his rigid body to her and kissed the top of his head. "Quite a day for Ella, isn't it?"

She felt his head nod. "You know you're going to have to be her coach. You've been riding forever and you know all about horses. How long have you had Commander?"

"Three years."

"You were a little younger than Ella when you got him, weren't you?"

"Mm-hmm."

"Do you think you'll be able to teach her how to saddle and curry her horse?"

He looked at his Tutu with a crooked smile. "Maybe, if she'll listen to me. You know she doesn't always listen."

A lump rose in Genevieve's throat. This young man was wise beyond his years and one of the loveliest people she had ever known. She dug her fingers into his puffy jacket, trying to find a rib to tickle, and knew she had struck gold when he began to squirm and giggle.

"Okay, darling boy. Let's get these people back to the house and have dinner."

TWENTY-ONE

Though it was only eight thirty, Alex and Ella were already tucked in their beds, deep asleep. Fresh air, a sumptuous Christmas meal, and two days of non-stop excitement had played a role in the two children falling asleep in front of the fire immediately after dinner. Their parents hauled them upstairs like two sacks of flour and neither child stirred even when their clothes were pulled off and their pajamas tugged on.

When Julia and Duncan returned to the salon, each looked as if they could have crawled into bed with their children.

"Cognac, my lord?" Wallace said, offering Duncan a wide-bottomed glass with two fingers of ruby-brown liquor. After dinner, Wallace had taken over the role of host and seemed delighted to be in control.

"Yes please, Wallace." Duncan accepted the snifter, slipping the stem between his fingers and warming the liquid in his palm before drinking.

"And, my lady?"

"That would be lovely, Wallace. Thank you." Julia collapsed next to Genevieve on the sofa facing the fire. "Well, we made it through the day." Scanning the room, she said to everyone, "Thank you for salvaging Christmas for Alex and Ella."

"It was really a marvelous day, wasn't it?" Lillie laughed. "In spite of… well." She shrugged her shoulders, then winced at the pull of the butterfly stitches on her back. "Well, you know."

"We're just grateful you're going to be okay." Genevieve bit her lower lip. "What a calamity!"

"That was lucky, wasn't it?" Olivia chimed in, smiling sympathetically at Lillie.

Genevieve shook her head. "I hate to think how much worse it could have been," she said, and noticed Finn holding Lillie's hand. Given what Lillie had been through last night, Genevieve was surprised at her pink cheeks and the sparkle in her eyes. *Love's amazing,* she thought, then watched Philip walk to the wood box and toss a log onto the flaming pile. He stood in front of the crackling fire, swirled the amber liquid in his snifter, and her heart fluttered as he took a sip then ran his tongue over his lips. *Love's amazing,* she thought again.

Around the room, everyone was settled on a sofa or in an overstuffed chair. Bertie sat next to Wallace, cozy with a lap robe pulled up to her shoulders. Becca and David were next to each other on a loveseat holding hands and Olivia sat on the floor next to her mother, her legs curled under her and her arm draped over her mother's lap.

Duncan slumped in his chair with his elbows on the padded arms and his brandy glass cradled in his hands. He seemed mesmerized by the flames devouring the logs on the hearth and flinched when Genevieve reached out and touched his knee. "Duncan, are you all right?"

He sat up straighter and shook his head at his mother. "I'm fine, Mom." He coughed a laugh. "It's been a wild few days, hasn't it?"

"It has, but it's going to get better," Philip said from across the room. "Frederick Picard will be here first thing tomorrow with a team. He's going to get to the bottom of these two incidents."

"And if he can't?" Duncan said.

"If he can't, we'll get someone in here who can," Philip said with conviction.

"Ah, my lord." All eyes focused on Wallace. "I'm afraid I have something to add to the mystery."

"Do you, Wallace?" Philip couldn't imagine what Wallace was about to share.

"I'm afraid I discovered something several days ago, during Sir David and Lady Weatherington's wedding. With my death," he looked at everyone with a wry smile, "it seems to have slipped my mind until now. After Mrs. MacIntosh and I were seated for the ceremony, Cooper lay down next to me." He glanced down to where Cooper was again curled up beside him and patted the sleeping dog on the head. "Very much like this. When I reached down to scratch behind his ear, I found these." With a small flourish, Bertie handed him the Rolex and Wallace pulled the notecard from the pocket of his tweed jacket.

"What do you have there?" Genevieve leaned forward and squinted.

Wallace captured Olivia in his glare as he said, "It's a note. And a Rolex watch was tied to the blue ribbons Cooper wore for the wedding."

"Hey! Is that my watch?" Duncan pushed out of his chair and was across the room in three strides. Wallace handed him the timepiece and he ran his finger around the edge of the crystal. "This is mine," he said, holding it for everyone to see. Then he looked at his parents. "You gave it to me when I graduated from high school. The crystal's been chipped since the day I got it." He pointed at Finn. "Remember? You smacked my wrist with your damn signet ring when we were horsing around. Thank you, Wallace." He slipped the watch on his wrist and snapped the metal clasp. "I've been looking everywhere for this since the day of the wedding. I thought it was lost forever." Then, like a lightning bolt, it occurred to him to ask, "Hey, wait a minute. Why was my watch tied inside Cooper's bow?"

"A very good question, my lord. Perhaps this will explain. This was tied with your Rolex." He handed the note to Duncan, who read it then gave it to Philip.

"What does it say?" Genevieve pressed.

"Read the note!" Julia and David said in unison.

"Tell us what it says!" Olivia stretched forward trying to see what was written on the card.

Philip held up his hand to quiet the crowd and read. "Vengeance is justice and it's time for mine!"

"What?" Genevieve tilted her head, confused.

He read it again.

The room filled with the buzz of many voices. Everyone talked at once; everyone had something to say.

"What does that mean?" David said.

"It sounds like a threat?" Olivia's eyes were wide.

"Vengeance is a pretty dramatic word," Julia said. "It sounds like the title of an Agatha Christie mystery."

Mrs. MacIntosh, who had been quiet to this point, said, "I'm not certain what the message means, but I don't think it was a very nice wedding wish."

With his elbows digging into his knees, Wallace cradled his head in his hands.

"Are you all right, mate?" David said. "Can I get you something? Water?"

When Wallace lifted his head, though he was pale, he surprised David with a smile. "A refill of cognac would be perfect," he said, offering his glass.

David took the snifter, gave Wallace a generous pour, and returned the goblet to his outstretched hand.

Wallace took a long, slow sip of the cognac, inhaling as he did so. "That's the ticket," he said, his color returning. "I'm fine, everyone," he said. "Just fine." He set his glass on his side table. "The thing that struck me as odd is anyone at the wedding could have discovered this note. Cooper and I just happen to have a rather special relationship. Don't we, boy?" He reached down and stroked Cooper's golden head.

Philip waved the card in the air. "No doubt Chef Picard will find this very interesting," he said. "And when he adds it to the other mysteries, I'm sure he'll have some thoughts."

"I'm sure you're right, my darling." Genevieve flashed Philip a smile. 'I know this is unnerving and we all probably have worries and theories—not all of them pleasant—but Wallace found this note the day of the wedding and nothing has happened, yet. Let's reconvene with our speculations in the morning. But for now, we need to bring this Christmas Day to a close and send these lovely people to bed before everyone falls asleep right here."

David pushed out of his chair and held out his hand for Becca. Before she took it, she leaned over, kissed the top of Olivia's head, and squeezed her shoulder. "Good night, mia bella," Becca said, using the name she had called Olivia from the time she was only a few days old. David pulled Becca to her feet and she threw tired kisses to the room.

The rest of the group stood, offered good nights, la bise, and Merry Christmas wishes, then drifted from the salon. Philip took the bottle of cognac back to the credenza then walked around the room gathering paper cocktail napkins that had been left on the side tables. When he threw them in the fireplace, the dwindling coals sparked to life then died back to a glow as blackened bits of paper floated up the chimney. Genevieve moved from chair to sofa to chair, fluffing pillows and smoothing fabric on the cushions where people had been sitting for a while.

The only people lingering in the room were Bertie and Wallace. With narrowed eyes, Wallace watched Olivia, Lillie, and Finnegan giggle and saunter out of the room, Olivia holding Lillie's elbow to steady her as they made their way into the foyer. When he was confident they were heading up the grand staircase, he said, "Lord and Lady Crosswick, if you don't mind, I'd like to ask you to stay for a moment."

Philip and Genevieve looked at Wallace, then at each other. Desperately tired, Philip said, "Of course, Wallace," and plopped into the chair next to the fireplace where he had been sitting the entire evening.

With her arms wrapped around a throw pillow, Genevieve mustered an exhausted smile and eased herself back onto the sofa.

Before either Philip or Genevieve could ask any questions, Wallace launched into what he wanted to say, but his voice was so quiet, Philip barely heard him.

"What did you say, Wallace?"

He cleared his throat. "I have something to add about the note and watch," he said, his voice stronger this time.

"Really?" Genevieve hugged her pillow a little closer.

"Yes, my lady. I do. The night of the wedding, I had an encounter with Ms. Conway."

"What kind of encounter, Wallace?"

Wallace looked at Bertie. When she nodded encouragement, he told them about going to the kitchen to get Champagne and seeing Olivia squatting by Cooper and rearranging his bow. "I can't say I actually saw her put the card and watch on Cooper's bow. But it's possible she could have done it. I could be very wrong, but I thought my encounter with Ms. Conway was worth mentioning."

"Wallace, I can't imagine Olivia was responsible for the note. She's doing so well. She's happy and engaged, hardly the frightening young lady who created such chaos at Wilmingrove Hall."

"It's certainly worth mentioning to Chef Picard. I know he'll be interested to hear what you have to say."

"And there is one more thing I think I should share with you. I have told no one about this but Ms. MacIntosh." He looked at Bertie. "But it has a bearing on the events we are discussing."

Genevieve shivered. She pulled a pashmina from the back of the sofa and wrapped it around her shoulders. "I'll brace myself, Wallace," she said.

"There's no need to be nervous, my lady. I actually think what I am about to tell you will give you a chuckle. I hope you understand I would never have done this if I didn't care deeply about the Warwick family." He then told about his visit the previous year to Blain Lodge to deliver Becca's package and give Olivia a good talking to. His voice intensified as he described how angry he had been that Olivia had caused such mayhem to everyone in the family.

"As I stood to leave, I said, 'Ms. Conway, I shall make it my mission to see you spend the rest of your life here at Blain Lodge and that you regret what a wretched being you are.'" He and Bertie exchanged a conspiratorial grin and he went on. "Then, I stood and dumped my coffee in her lap as I walked out."

Philip smiled at Wallace and shook his head before saying, "Well, well, well. I have to admit, that was unexpected."

"My goodness, Wallace. You do surprise me." Genevieve's lips twisted in amusement then drew into a tight line. "Are you concerned Olivia is angry about what you did?"

"I think that is a reasonable assumption, Lady Crosswick, but according to everyone, she has made great strides in her therapy. So much so that she's able to stay here through the New Year. When I see her so happy and spirited, I wonder if I have misjudged her."

After a long silence, Philip looked at his watch and stood. "I think we all need to get to bed. Thank you, Wallace, for sharing this. Chef Picard will appreciate having as much detail as you can remember about seeing Olivia in the hall with Cooper. And as for your encounter at Blain Lodge, well, that's a story worth telling." He walked to Genevieve and extended his hand. "Come on, cute girl. It's past our bedtime."

Genevieve took his hand and he pulled her to stand. "Good night, you two. Sleep well." They walked hand in hand into the foyer.

"Do you think Wallace is right?" Genevieve's voice was laced with fatigue.

"Which part? That Olivia's up to some dirty tricks or that she's making great progress in her therapy?"

"The making great progress part."

"If I had to guess, I'd say she's making real progress. What do you think?"

Genevieve slipped her hand through the crook in his arm. "I think you're probably right. I also think before she and David leave in the morning, I need to tell Becca about Wallace's encounter with Olivia."

Philip stopped and looked down at Genevieve. "Why would you do that?"

"I just think she should know. Don't you?"

"I don't think there's anything to tell, but it's up to you." He shrugged his shoulders.

They stood at the base of the staircase that loomed in front of them and looked up to the top.

"I don't know if I can make it up the stairs. How about you?"

Philip sighed and his shoulders sagged. "I was counting on you carrying me."

"You clearly miscalculated, my friend," Genevieve said, grabbing the wrought iron handrail and pulling herself onto the first tread.

<hr>

With Philip's study door ajar, it was easy to watch Lord and Lady Crosswick as they made their way up the stairs. It was good news that they thought Olivia was on the road to recovery. Very good news, indeed.

TWENTY-TWO

"**P**HILIP, TURN OFF your alarm." She nudged his bottom with her foot. He didn't move but offered a groan. She rolled over and touched the small of his back with her cold hand.

"Yikes! What are you doing?" He reached his arm around and grabbed her wrist. "Get your freezing hand off me, you mad woman."

"Philip, turn off your alarm."

He heard the persistent sound of "Les Marseillaise", his chosen ringtone. "That's not my alarm. Somebody's calling." He squinted at his watch. Ten past eight. "Who in the hell is calling this early?"

"If you let it ring much longer, they'll leave a message."

"Good point," he said as he stretched to pick up his cell phone, which was singing and vibrating on his nightstand. He glanced at the screen: Frederick Picard. He punched the green button. "Picard, bonjour. Qu'est-ce qu'il y a?"

"Whatever's happening better be important," Genevieve mumbled, burrowed into Philip, and rested her head on the left side of his chest. He draped his arm over her shoulders and pulled her closer. Genevieve could hear Chef Picard's muffled voice at the other end of the phone but couldn't make out any words. Philip's periodic "Um hm," gave her no clue what they were talking about and soon she found herself drifting back to sleep.

"That sounds like a good plan, Frederick." Deep in conversation, Philip sat up and Genevieve's head slid off his chest onto the bed. "You want to interview the entire staff at Château Beaulieu?" He flopped back against what he thought was his pillow, but when he looked behind him, Genevieve's head was wedged between his back and the headboard. Before he could sit forward, she pushed on his side and pulled her head out from behind him, gasping for air.

"Oui, Frederick. We'll make sure everyone is here. See you at nine o'clock." He finished the call, looked down at her and bellowed a laugh. She looked like Medusa on a bad hair day. Philip tapped the camera icon on his phone, switched to selfie mode and turned the phone around so Genevieve could see the wild image that filled the screen.

"I can see why you love me," she said. "After all these years, I still have my looks." She made a face like Edvard Munch's *The Scream* and pressed the button. "I want to show this to Alex and Ella. They'll love it." She looked at the photo and growled a laugh. "Perfect," she said, then asked, "What did Frederick want? I thought he was coming this afternoon but it sounds as if he's coming this morning."

"He is. At nine o'clock. He's anxious to get started and is bringing a forensic team from Libourne and the few officers he has. He wants to interview everyone on staff."

"So, darling boy, I guess we'd better get up and get going."

Philip put his phone back on the nightstand and scooched back under the covers. He rolled toward her and smoothed her hair as best he could. "Right now," he said, his voice husky and his eyes sultry. "Right now, G, there's only one thing getting up." He wrapped his arm around her waist and pulled her to him so they were body to body.

"Well, my love, time's a wastin'." She wiggled her brows. "Since you're up, we'd better get going." She giggled and pulled the covers over their heads.

TWENTY-THREE

For the next three days, pieces were slowly uncovered, put into place, and the puzzle began to take shape. At this point, the police had no idea if all the events were connected, but they would gather the evidence and follow where it led. They interviewed everyone at Château Beaulieu from the top to the bottom: from Lord and Lady Crosswick to the vineyard workers. They clarified and confirmed every detail of each incident that might be related to the attempt on Wallace's life: the note on Cooper's bow, Wallace's encounter with Olivia in the foyer, his poisoning at the wedding, the explosion in the dining room, and the barrage of destructive rumors about the Laney Musée des Beaux-Arts.

It had been just over a week since the beginning of the foul play, except for the rumors, which had begun trickling onto the internet several months earlier. Though by now much of the evidence had been contaminated or obscured, Picard and his two-man team rooted through the Château like terriers hunting rodents.

Sitting across from Chef Picard in Philip's study, Émile de Laudre fidgeted in a straight-backed chair. This was not their first encounter. Picard liked the attractive young man. He had matured in the months since they had last seen each other. His shoulders had broadened, his beard had turned from fuzz to stubble, and his face was more chiseled. Though it was almost January, his bronzed skin said he spent his time on ski slopes or working in the vineyard. Picard knew, though he came from wealth, he was at Château Beaulieu as a form of penance and working hard in the vines to make amends to the Warwicks.

Picard set a small recorder on the table between them. "Émile, if you have no objections, I will be recording our conversation."

The boy shrugged.

Chef Picard clicked the recorder on and proceeded. "I understand, Émile, that you have settled into Château Beaulieu and are becoming a valuable part of the Château family. Quite a turnaround, young man." The chef was pleased to be able to offer the mischievous Parisian a genuine compliment.

Émile pinked at Picard's kind remarks.

"I have also been told you and Olivia Conway were quite friendly during the Weatherington's wedding festivities.

At that, Émile squirmed under Picard's laser stare, and he felt his armpits moisten. "Oui, chef. Olivia and I met the day she arrived for her mother's wedding. We have become friends."

"You know she has a troubled history with this famille, n'est pas?"

"Oui. She told me what she did last year and how she is working hard to get well."

"And you believed her?"

"Mais oui." He looked surprised at the question. "She is

charming, funny, smart. She told me how distressed she is to have caused so much upset to Lord and Lady Crosswick and to her mother. I believe she is on her way to being well." He leaned toward Picard and the chef was struck by how young and earnest he looked. "I hope she continues to get well because I want us to be better friends. You know," he looked down at his twiddling thumbs, "like, maybe become her boyfriend."

Picard tried to keep the corners of his mouth from pulling up, but didn't succeed.

"Ah, you think me a petit garçon idiot." Hurt flashed in his eyes.

"Non, I do not think you are a silly little boy. I think you are a young man whose heart has been stolen by a beautiful girl. It happens to us all." He smiled kindly at Émile. "My only concern is perhaps she persuaded you to do some favors for her, some favors that might have been criminal."

Émile's eyes flew wide. "What do you mean, criminal? What do you think she asked me to do?"

Picard sat back in Philip's chair on the other side of the desk. "Émile," he said, keeping the pressure on the lad. "We suspect Olivia was causing difficulties for the Warwicks while she was at Blain Lodge and continues to be behind some not-so-good deeds while she has been here. If she is behind these events, it would be easier for her if she had an accomplice. I am wondering if that accomplice is you."

Picard watched the blood drain from Émile's face until he was a ghost of himself and heard his breathing turn to a rasp. *He is either innocent, a good actor, or had no idea what he was doing when he did Olivia's bidding.* The thoughts ran swiftly through his mind as he planned his next move.

Adopting an avuncular tone, Picard said, "Émile, can you tell me about the time you spent with Olivia? What you did, what she said, and how she acted toward you?" His voice was soothing as he went on. "I'm sure anything you can tell me would be helpful."

Picard watched the boy as his color returned and his breathing calmed. After several seconds he inhaled a huge, quivering breath and let it slide slowly out. "Chef Picard." He leveled his gaze. "I shall tell you anything I can to help you and your team get to the bottom of this, but I can't imagine I know anything that would be helpful."

For a moment, Picard thought Émile was going to burst into tears and was grateful when he didn't. "Don't worry, mon ami. I'll ask the questions. All you have to do is answer them truthfully. Can you do that?"

"Mais oui, chef. If I have an answer, I shall give it to you, I promise."

Picard reached for a bottle of Badoit sparkling water sitting in a chiller on the table between them. "L'eau?"

"S'il vous plaît." Émile took the bottle, unscrewed the cap and took a long drink.

"Bon. Why don't you start at the beginning? When did you meet?"

Émile took another long drink, set the bottle carefully down on a coaster, then began. "Olivia arrived two days before the wedding. I was helping Henri, who takes care of the Warwicks' car collection and helps Delphine with many things. I guess you could call him the chauffeur/butler but he is much more than that. I showed guests to their rooms and carried their luggage, you know, all the jobs requiring big muscles." He looked up at Picard through his thick lashes and smiled an impish smile.

"And that is how you met Ms. Conway?"

"Oui. She arrived at the Château in the Crosswick helicopter. I took a golf cart down to the helipad to pick her up. I had to make two trips. One for her and one for all her luggage. I remember wondering why someone would have so much luggage for just a few days. Then I thought back to before I came here to Château Beaulieu, when I was a rich, spoiled brat. I used to take three bags to spend one night at a friend's villa in Nice." He smirked. "It takes a lot of clothes to be a party boy. What a useless snob I was."

Picard jotted a few lines in his notebook. Though he was recording the conversation, he took periodic notes when he wanted to remember a gesture or facial expression that might prove important later. He laid his pen on the desk and studied Émile for a moment. "Is that when she seemed to take an interest in you?"

He frowned in thought and hummed. "It was not when I showed her to her room but when I came back with her valises. She was extremely impressed I could bring them all at once."

"What did she say?"

"It was not so much what she said, but what she did that made me think she wanted to get to know me." Under his tan, crimson crept up Émile's neck. He shifted in his seat, embarrassed at what he was about to tell Picard.

"And?" The officer waited.

"She felt my bicep and said 'Oohlala'." He rolled his eyes. "And then she tucked a €50 note in the waistband of my jeans. Of course I gave the money back to her." He threw up both his hands. "Sacrebleu! I don't need her money. I have a trust fund! I told her Château Beaulieu was not a hotel and I am not le groom, a bellhop."

"Was she angry you refused her tip?"

"Non. Not at all. She laughed and said there were other ways she could thank me later." He tilted his head and arched one brow. "Chef Picard, I have had many girlfriends—enough to know when a woman is coming on to me—and Olivia was coming on to me."

Picard choked back a chuckle at this young buck sharing a man-to-man moment.

Émile continued. "I have to say, I liked that she was flirting with me. Olivia is very beautiful. Since I came to Château Beaulieu, I have not had une copine. Not a single girlfriend for a year. I have done nothing but work. I am not complaining, but," he shook his hand in front of him as if he burned it, "roohlala. I would not recommend such a thing to any man."

Picard picked up his pen and hovered it just above his pad. "So you thought this might be an opportunity?"

"No, chef. I thought only one thing. I would like… you know." He made two thrusting motions with his fist.

"Ah. I see. You really were not thinking with your mind at all."

Picard watched Émile shake his head and saw his embarrassed smile and a lusty gleam in his eyes. "No, chef. I was not."

"It sounds as if you might have done anything Olivia asked of you, so you could get into her…" Picard paused for effect, "into her good graces," he finished, smiling.

Laughing out loud, Émile nodded. "Oui, chef. I wanted to get into her… good graces," he said, embracing the joke.

Picard sobered. "So… did you?"

"Get into her good graces?" Émile asked, now confused.

"Non, Émile. Did you do everything she asked? Like, perhaps, put foxglove in Monsieur Wallace's Champagne glass?"

"Non, non, non! Non, Chef Picard. I did not do such a thing or anything else that would cause harm to anyone. I have learned my lesson and have worked hard here to make Lord and Lady Crosswick proud of me. I would never do anything to hurt them or anyone here at the Château. This has become my home and everyone here is my family." He had lost his color again and his fingers laced and unlaced in his lap. He took another swig of his water, hoping to moisten his dry mouth.

"Is there nothing you can tell me about Olivia that might help me figure out if she was involved in the attempt on Monsieur Wallace's life?"

Émile chewed his lips trying to think of something he could offer the chef. Finally he brightened. "The night of the wedding, I did see Olivia talking—well, really whispering—with Delphine just outside the kitchen."

"Really?" Picard's interest piqued. "Tell me about that."

Relaxing back into his chair, Émile cleared his throat. "Olivia and I had been dancing to every song. She is a good dancer." He smiled and, for a moment, was far away, thinking about Olivia's wiggling hips and sexy moves.

"Émile," Picard barked.

He jumped at Picard's shout and was startled back to the present. "Ah, oui. When the band took a break, Olivia said she had to go to the toilette. She left and after a few minutes, I decided I would go out to the terrace and have a smoke. That's when I saw her and Delphine in the hall."

"Did you hear what they were saying?"

"Non."

"Did you notice anything? Anything at all?"

As he thought, he ran his tongue back and forth across his lower lip then stopped. "I think Delphine gave Olivia a card or a note that she slipped into her pocket… maybe."

Picard tapped his pen on his bottom lip as he reviewed his notes. He flipped through the pages with his thumb, humming "La Mer" under his breath. When he looked up at Émile, the lad was riveted to the screen on his phone, reading. "Something interesting?" he asked.

Émile turned his screen toward Picard. The officer squinted at the email. The type was too small for him to see, so he reached across the desk and brought the phone closer. He looked for the sender's name but there was none. He read the message aloud. "If you tell the police anything, you'll find yourself back in Paris in prison" He looked up at Émile's crumpled face. "Olivia?"

"Je ne sais pas. I don't know," the frightened boy said. "As you can see, it says 'Sender unknown'. It could be anyone who knows about the little art prank I pulled on the Warwicks."

Chef Picard studied Émile for a moment then narrowed his eyes. "Who knows about the Warwicks keeping you out of prison?" He said each word slowly.

Surprised by the question, Émile shot up straighter in his

chair. He squinted at the ceiling. "Hmmm." He thought a moment before answering. Then, looking back at Chef Picard, he began listing names. "Alors. There is Olivia. And, of course, the Warwick family. Wallace and Mrs. MacIntosh. Sir David and Lady Weatherington. Lillie Langdon." He paused and thought again. "Ah. I almost forgot." He bit his lower lip. "Delphine knows."

TWENTY-FOUR

Though the wipers slapped back and forth at top speed, they couldn't keep the windshield clear. Becca leaned forward, white knuckling the steering wheel and squinting, trying to see between the sheets of rain. The dual carriageway winding from York to Blain Lodge was charming and quaint, with hedgerows looming on both sides, but, with standing water and the fear of hydroplaning, Becca longed for a motorway—modern, safe, and wide. From the moment Genevieve called her with the news that Picard and his team were at the Château interviewing everyone and that Olivia was of particular interest, Becca was hell-bent on meeting with Dr. Morgan, Olivia's primary psychiatrist. Only he could reassure her that her brilliant, tricky daughter was not the architect of the assault on Wallace and the troubles plaguing the House of Crosswick.

BBC News droned on about the effects of El Niño and the violent changes in weather patterns. Becca laughed at the irony and kept her eyes glued to the road. After an hour and a half of treacherous country lane driving, she slowed and turned left between two naked and shivering oak trees onto the entry road that led to the elegant private hospital. She stopped in front of the grand wrought iron gates that sported a brass *"BL"* on each panel and gazed out the side window at the security keypad. Rain sheeted the windows so everything outside the car looked like an Impressionist watercolor. Knowing she was about to get a good soaking, she blew a puff of air from her cheeks as she tapped the button and the window slid down. A gust of wind blasted spray into the car and she winced. She steeled herself, stuck her hand out and pressed the call button on the stand.

A voice crackled through the speaker. "Yes. How may I help you?"

"Rebecca Weatherington here to see Dr. Morgan." She heard a buzz, then a click, and the gates lumbered open.

By the time she got the window up, the damage had been done. Her hand and arm were soaked and her face and hair had been well-spritzed.

She pulled up to the building, parked, and opened the car door. She turned in her seat and stepped out of the car into a puddle that covered her Nomasei loafers and soaked her socks and the cuffs of her camel trousers. "Damn it!" she said. Just as she raised her umbrella, a gust of wind yanked it inside out. "I give up!" she yelled, and shook her fist at the sky while the rain washed over her face. She dashed to the front door, dumping the useless umbrella in the tidy green rubbish bin at the side of the walk.

She pulled open the heavy glass door and walked into the lobby, dripping and squishing all the way to the reception desk.

"Oh my goodness. Lady Weatherington?" The middle-aged

woman behind the desk couldn't hide her surprise at Becca's appearance. She had pulled up the list of approved visitors and Olivia's mother, with her new name, was last on the alphabetized list, just below Reginald Wallace. A photograph of a beautiful, perfectly coiffed woman looked out at her from her computer screen. She looked at the image then looked at Becca, mascara running down her cheeks, strands of wet hair plastered to her head. She glanced back at her computer. "It's pouring buckets out there, isn't it?" She shoved her wheeled desk chair back and stood. "You're here to meet with Dr. Morgan, aren't you?"

Becca sniffed then nodded. "I am."

"I'm Mrs. Powell," she said as she walked around her desk to stand in front of Becca. "Let's get you sorted out, shall we? Give me your coat. It's soaking."

Becca nodded again and felt like weeping. She bit the inside of her cheek to stem the tide of tears she knew could flow at any moment and gave the kind woman a pathetic attempt at a smile. As she wiggled out of her dripping Burberry, she started to speak, but her voice cracked so she faked a cough instead. "Mrs. Powell, you're very kind," was all she could squeak out.

"Oh, bosh." The receptionist waved away the compliment. She took the coat and held it away from her. "Come with me." She led the way down a short corridor and through a door into a cozy lounge, leaving a trail of water dripping off the hem of the coat. She picked up the handset on the wall phone and punched in a number. "George," she said. "Would you bring a robe, a pair of slippers, and several towels to the family lounge, please?" She smiled into the receiver. "Yes, I would appreciate that." She hung up and turned to Becca. "We'll get your shoes, socks, and trousers dry and you can blowdry your hair in the lavatory. There should be everything you need, but just press 'reception' on the phone if you need my help. I'll let Dr. Morgan know you're running a smidge late."

There was a knock and Mrs. Powell said, "Come in." When the door opened, a curly-headed man entered the room. His smile flashed a set of blindingly white teeth and, when he handed Becca the towels, slippers, and robe she couldn't help but notice his biceps straining through his snug t-shirt.

"George, could you please see that Mrs. Weatherington's things are dried? She needs them as quickly as possible." She turned to Becca. "Just put them on the chair outside the door."

"Madam," he said to Becca with a nod, and threw a wink at Mrs. Powell. Looking back at Becca, he said, "I'll be waiting just outside. If you need any help, I'm your bloke."

When he had gone, Becca arched her brows and the receptionist rolled her eyes. "I know," she said, and shrugged her shoulders. "He's a bit much, but the residents love him, especially the women." Mrs. Powell headed to the door. "I'll leave you to it."

"Give me fifteen minutes. If my things are back that's all the time I need."

"Just come back to me when you're ready and I'll take you to Dr. Morgan."

Becca gave her a warm smile. "Thank you, Mrs. Powell. You're wonderful."

"I'm happy to be of help, Lady Weatherington."

Half an hour later, Becca was repaired and waiting for Dr. Henry Morgan in his office, a cup of coffee in her hand and slightly damp socks on her feet.

Dr. Morgan, the clinical head of Blain Lodge, had been in charge of Olivia's care since her arrival just over a year ago.

By all reports, Olivia had been working hard and making remarkable progress. Each time Becca had visited her daughter she was warmer, more relaxed, and forthcoming. At her mother's wedding, she had appeared to be a well-adjusted, fun-loving young lady who was having a great time. But Becca had been here before. Many times over the years, just when she thought her daughter was on the road to recovery, everything fell apart. This time she was holding her breath, but the news that Olivia was under suspicion of trying to murder Wallace and might be the instigator of other dirty tricks eroded Becca's confidence that Olivia would one day be well.

Deep in thought, Becca didn't hear Dr. Morgan come into the room and flinched when he touched her shoulder. "Dr. Morgan!" she said, laughing. "Obviously, I didn't hear you come in."

They shook hands, then he walked to the other side of his desk and sat in his burnished brown leather chair. "I understand you and Mother Nature had a bit of a tussle." Though his face was plain and undistinguished, there was a comforting warmth about him.

Becca blew air from her lips and they vibrated. "She and I had a pretty heated exchange and, in the end, I lost. Lesson learned—don't mess with the Grande Dame."

"So tell me, Lady Weatherington. To what do we owe this pleasure?" Dr. Morgan leaned back in his chair. "I trust you enjoyed having Olivia at your wedding. Best wishes, by the way."

"Thank you." Becca's smile was radiant. "We had a wonderful celebration. I can't tell you how important it was to have Olivia there, for both of us."

"It's critical for her treatment plan to be a part of family gatherings. As her therapy progresses, I would like you to include her in more family festivities." He smiled easily. "When I talked to her on the phone the day after the wedding, she was in excellent spirits. She even mentioned a lad she'd met and enjoyed."

"Yes." Becca leaned forward. "He's a charming French boy who is working through some issues of his own at the vineyard." Her brows drew together. "That's really the reason I'm here, Dr. Morgan. There was an unfortunate incident during our wedding celebration and there is concern Olivia might have had something to do with it. I came to confirm that she didn't."

The surprise on the psychiatrist's face was gratifying and the taut muscles in Becca's neck relaxed just a bit as she shared what had happened at Château Beaulieu.

"I find that hard to believe." He shook his head. "Olivia has been a model resident and has been making extraordinary progress. I'm even presenting her case at a conference in Geneva next month."

Hope gave Becca's heart a little jolt. "That's wonderful news. As far as I know, they have no hard evidence that Olivia was involved, just speculation. The police are talking to everyone at Château Beaulieu but seem to be focusing on Olivia. Maybe they're going down the wrong path."

"That would be my guess. But given her history, it's not surprising Olivia would be a person of interest. Have you had a conversation with her?"

Gazing out of the window, Becca was mesmerized by the sun slashing through a split in the clouds. "No," she said, dragging her gaze back to Dr. Morgan. "I wanted to see you and hear what you thought before I did anything."

"That was probably wise. My biggest concern is how she might deal with a police interview." He tapped his pen on his receding chin and the room was quiet until the *brrrrr, brrrr* of Dr. Morgan's phone shattered the silence.

"Excuse me." He held up a finger at Becca as he put the handset to his ear. "I asked you not to disturb me," he said, then listened for several seconds. "No." The furrow between his brows deepened. "No, absolutely not. Did you check the computer room?" His pleasant expression from a moment before had been replaced by a professional facade. He stood as he hung up the phone. "If you'll excuse me, Lady Weatherington, I'll be back in just a moment."

"Of course, doctor. Please take your time."

Becca walked to the window and looked out at the grey landscape. She glanced at her watch then back at the trees dripping from the recent deluge. Though the conversation with Dr. Morgan had been reassuring, Becca could feel tension creeping back into her shoulders and up her neck. She strolled around the room, read his diplomas: Oxford, Cambridge. She looked at her watch again. Eleven long minutes had passed since Dr. Morgan rushed out of his office.

"Becca, this is a waste of your time," she said aloud. A quick search of Olivia's room would be much more productive, she thought, as a plan formulated in her head. *It might reveal nothing. It might confirm my daughter is on the right path. Or I might discover something that would tell me she is up to her old tricks.*

"Lady Weatherington." Mrs. Powell stuck her head in the door. "Dr. Morgan is going to be longer than he had anticipated. Can I get you another coffee or cup of tea?"

The pulse in Becca's neck picked up speed. "Thank you, Mrs. Powell, but I'm running short on time. Dr. Morgan answered my questions and put my concerns to rest. I do need to collect some things from Olivia's room, however. She asked me to pick up a couple of her favorite sweaters and send them to her. It's colder in Bordeaux than she had anticipated." The lie made her armpits dampen. "I assume that won't be a problem."

"Of course not. Let me find George and he can unlock Ms. Conway's door for you. It won't be a minute."

Matching George stride for stride, Becca didn't know if her shallow breath was because of their brisk pace or because she was about to search her daughter's room. That search might confirm Olivia's improvement or reveal she had tricked everyone into believing she was on a healthy path. She hoped it would be the former but what would Becca do if it were the latter? She had no idea.

George stopped at a thick walnut door with a brass number ten centered in the top panel.

"Here we are," he said, slipping the key into the lock. It turned easily and he pushed the door wide, holding it there for Becca to enter.

"Just let Mrs. Powell know when you're finished."

"Thank you, George." Becca heard her voice quiver as she handed George a ten pound note for his assistance. He slipped it into his pocket and smiled.

"You are ever so welcome, Lady Weatherington." He leaned against the door jamb, in no hurry to leave. "Is there anything else I can do to be of service?"

"Thank you, no." Becca was sure he could hear her heart thumping in her chest. "I'll just gather the things Olivia asked me to send and I'll be on my way." With her hand on the handle, she edged the door closed, forcing George to push away from the frame. Reluctantly he headed back down the hall, looking over his shoulder once to find Olivia's door firmly closed.

TWENTY-FIVE

B ECCA COLLAPSED AGAINST the door and tried to steady her breath. She was not at all confident she should be invading her daughter's privacy, but here she was. She glanced at her watch and gave herself five minutes to search for any clue that Olivia was either well on the road to mental health or just the opposite.

She inhaled deeply and was surprised to notice the light scent of Rose Otto hanging in the air, Charlotte Chaubert's fragrance. Across the room, a pink-faceted glass jar caught her attention. She pushed away from the door and walked across the room to the chest where the container sat. The candle had been burned to a thin layer of wax and a stub of wick. Becca smiled thinking how—between the ruby ring and the Rose Otto—Charlotte's specter was an active part of all their lives a hundred and fifty years after her death.

She turned slowly, taking in the details of her daughter's tidy room. Nothing seemed out of place or gave her any clue that Olivia was anything but a young lady with broad interests and many talents. On the walls hung several paintings filled with vibrant color and whimsy—their signature read *Olivia H. Conway.* Becca studied each piece, delighting in the light and composition. She hadn't seen Olivia's artwork since her daughter was a little girl slapping angry slashes of black across her paper during therapy sessions. The images in front of her now were full of happiness and energy.

Becca walked slowly around the room, noting the meticulous organization. Each drawer she pulled out was flawlessly arranged: underwear sharply folded, t-shirts rolled and grouped by color, sweaters sorted by fiber—cashmere, cotton, wool—each in a separate drawer. Each hanger in the closet was separated by half an inch and the clothes were arranged from white on the left, graduating through every hue to navy and then black on the far right. Something unnerved Becca about the ruthless precision everywhere she looked. Nothing was out of place. No dust bunnies floated from under the bed, which was covered by a taut linen duvet and shammed pillows, perfectly arranged.

From somewhere in the building, a clock chimed three times. Becca looked at her watch and couldn't believe she had been in Olivia's room for fifteen minutes. Someone was going to come looking for her soon. She needed to finish her search and leave. So far she had been mesmerized, absorbing her daughter's life; a life Becca knew nothing about. Now she needed to get down to business.

She walked toward a bookcase filled with an array of volumes and one caught her eye: *How I Killed My Daddy,* a novel by Olivia H. Conway. She hadn't seen this book since last year when the police used it to prevent a tragic end to a terrifying story. Becca pulled the hardback from between Machiavelli's *The Prince* and Michael Brown's *Death in the Garden: Poisonous Plants and their Use Throughout History.* She opened the cover, cringing at the black dust jacket splashed with blood-red ink. She thumbed the fly leaf over and a surprised cough caught in her throat. Like something out of a spy novel, a reservoir had been created inside the book. Hidden in the well, was a small, leather-bound journal. Becca pried the notebook from its hiding place and let *How I Killed My Daddy* clatter to the floor.

With her pulse beating in her ears, Becca riffled through the pages of the journal, periodically stopping to scan for any telltale words. She glanced at her watch one last time, snatched the book from the floor, and shoved it back into the bookcase, empty. She dropped the journal into her Louis Vuitton handbag and zipped it closed. She grabbed her coat and looked around the room to make certain she was leaving everything as it had been when she arrived. Satisfied, she opened the door just wide enough to peek into the hall, then eased into the empty corridor. She strode to the elevator and pressed the button several times, tapping her foot while she waited for the door to open. When the car arrived, she hustled in, held the "G" button, and the doors closed. She shut her eyes until the elevator slowed to a stop and the doors opened. Anxious to get out of the building, she intended to barrel past Mrs. Powell's desk and straight out the door, but when the receptionist called her name, Becca stopped and mustered a bright smile through her frazzled nerves.

"Lady Weatherington." Mrs. Powell popped up and dashed from behind her desk. "It appears you didn't find what you were looking for."

"Uh," Becca said in response. She could offer nothing but a blank look.

"You didn't find the sweaters for Ms. Conway?"

She had forgotten the lie she had told to get into Olivia's room, but quickly recovered. "Sadly, no," she said, shaking her head. "But that's all right. I'm sure she won't mind going on a little shopping spree." She set her purse on a chair and thrust her arms into her coat. "Thank you for all your help, Mrs. Powell," she said, and turned toward the door. "I'll see you on my next visit when Olivia returns."

Becca was nearly out the door when Mrs. Powell called to her again.

"Jeeze. What now?" Becca said under her breath. She turned to find Mrs. Powell holding out her handbag she had left on the chair. "Oh my! Thank you. I'd be in trouble without that, wouldn't I?"

"Have a safe journey, Lady Weatherington," Mrs. Powell said, and walked back to her desk as the door closed.

Becca couldn't get to her car fast enough. She sat clutching the steering wheel with both hands, her heart pounding in her ears. She was overwhelmed with relief that she had not been caught searching Olivia's room, but terrified what the journal might reveal when she was finally able to read it.

She started the car, backed out of the parking space, then steered around the circle and down the long driveway. She approached the end of the lane and stopped to wait as the gates trudged open. As soon as they were wide enough, she eased between them and stopped at the main road. When she was sure no cars were coming, she accelerated and crossed over to her lane on the dual carriageway and gunned the engine, calling on all the raging horsepower under the hood of the Mercedes SL63 roadster, to get home to Swiss Cottage as quickly as possible.

TWENTY-SIX

R AIN HAD CROSSED the Channel and was washing Château Beaulieu's sleeping vines with furious torrents. In Genevieve's bedroom, she and Ella cuddled on an oversized, overstuffed chair. Though the day was raw, they were comfy with a fire crackling and a cashmere throw wrapped around them. The two had planned to spend the morning in the riding ring working on Ella's riding skills. When they woke to a cold, rainy day, though the ring was indoors, they couldn't resist a cozy day snuggling together. There was always tomorrow.

Immersed in a photo album with a green, cut-velvet cover spread across both their laps, they leafed through page after page of black-and-white portraits of elegant people in elegant clothes staring back at them.

As Ella turned a heavy cardboard page, a stunning beauty of about thirty-five looked out at her. She stood in a fashionable wide-brimmed hat next to a smaller version of herself. It was unmistakable that they were mother and daughter. The mother's arm draped around her daughter and her hand hung over the little girl's shoulder.

When Ella saw her, she bounced up and down next to Genevieve. "Tutu! Tutu!"

Genevieve glanced at her excited granddaughter and saw a smile stretching across the little girl's face. "What is it? Why are you smiling?"

"That lady is wearing Aunt Becca's pretty ring. I love that ring. It almost fits me." The moment she spoke, Ella slapped her hand over her mouth.

Genevieve studied her a moment before she said, "Ella, how do you know Becca's ring almost fits you?"

Ella's hand fell from her mouth into her lap and her eyes slid from Genevieve's, searching for somewhere else to look, anywhere but at her grandmother.

"Ella?" Genevieve waited. "Do you have something to tell me? Did Aunt Becca let you try on her very expensive, very precious ruby ring?"

Genevieve saw tears plop into Ella's lap. She reached down to tip the perfect young face up to hers. "You need to tell me the truth. How do you know the ring almost fits you? You know when Becca got back to London, she couldn't find her ring."

Ella's face had clouded and her eyes shone with tears ready to pour down her cheeks.

Genevieve held up her finger. "No, no, no," she said, trying to be stern. Where Ella and Alex were concerned, it was difficult for her to be anything but warm, loving, and fun. "You tell me what you know about how the ruby ring wound up in my jewelry box. Then you can cry. You can cry all you want."

Ella's face crinkled like a wadded linen hanky as she tried to hold back her tears.

Genevieve waited, her heart breaking as she watched the precious child. She wanted to take Ella in her arms and comfort her, but she resisted.

Trying to keep her sobs at bay, Ella struggled to keep her jagged breaths under control. There was nothing she could do about the fat tears that poured over her lower lids so she simply let them fall and began her tale, her voice jerky as she gasped between words. "W-w-when w-w-we were g-g-getting ready…" Ella choked out the words and Genevieve couldn't help but squeeze her hand.

"Just take a big breath, sweetheart. You know I love you and you can tell me anything."

"But, Tutu, what I d-d-did was terribly naughty."

Genevieve's eyes rounded. "My goodness. I can hardly wait to hear the terrible tale." She kissed Ella on the top of her head and smoothed her hair. "Go on, darling."

Ella's breathing began to calm and her sobs almost disappeared.

"Okay. Let's start again," Genevieve encouraged.

She wiped her cheeks with the back of her hand and took a mighty breath. As the air whished out, she offered a shy smile. "Okay," she said, and gave a sharp nod. "I'm ready. We were in Bumpa's study just before the wedding started and Olivia gave me the ring and asked me to run to Aunt Becca's room."

Genevieve thought she had misheard or Ella had misspoken. "You said Olivia? Do you mean Auntie Becca asked you to do that?"

"No, Tutu. Olivia asked me to do it and she said it would be fine if I tried the ring on before I put it away in the jewelry roll."

She sniffed and ran her hand under her nose.

Genevieve plucked a Kleenex from the square holder on the table next to her and handed it to Ella, unnerved that Olivia had lied to her mother and to her.

Ella blew mightily, then gave the tissue back to Genevieve who stifled a smile, wadded the used tissue, and tossed it onto the table.

Ella looked up at her Tutu and bit her lower lip. "I know I should have just put the ring right in the jewelry roll, but Olivia said it would be all right if I tried it on, so I did. It was too big for my other fingers so I put it on my thumb." Her eyes widened and she barely took a breath. "Just as I got it on, I heard someone in the hall. Delphine was calling my name." The story was coming so fast, the words were tumbling over themselves.

"I tugged and tugged but the ring wouldn't come off. So I stuck my thumb in my mouth and just as Delphine came through the door it came off. She was very stern and said everyone was waiting for me. She grabbed my hand and we raced back to Bumpa's study. I spit the ring out of my mouth into my hand and stuck it in the pocket of my dress. I thought it would be safe there until I could put it back, but the wedding was so exciting I forgot about it." Ella blew out an exhausted breath. "By the time I remembered the ring was in my pocket, Auntie Becca and Uncle David had gone back to England." The words had slowed and the tears started welling again. "Then I didn't know what to do, so I came up here and put it in your case. That one over there." She pointed to the Italian leather jewel box where Genevieve had found Becca's treasured ruby ring.

Exhausted from guilt and her big confession, Ella snuggled closer to Genevieve and leaned her head against her Tutu's shoulder. She started to put her thumb in her mouth, thought better of it, and laced her fingers through her grandmother's.

Feeling the need to use the ordeal as a teaching moment, Genevieve said, "Well, my darling, Ella, what did you learn from this event?"

Without missing a beat, Ella said, "I learned I should never look at old pictures. They can get you into real trouble." She turned to look up at Genevieve, her mouth somber, but her eyes dancing with humor.

"Well, my darling girl, it's not the lesson I hoped you would learn, but I guess it's better than no lesson at all."

TWENTY-SEVEN

A T THE PERFECT moment, Delphine walked through the bedroom door carrying a small tray with two cups of hot chocolate and a plate of buttery galette with little bits of sea salt sprinkled across the top—Genevieve and Ella's favorite.

"I thought you two might need a petite collation. There is nothing better than hot chocolate and cookies for a snack, eh?"

"Ah, merci, Delphine. You read our minds. Right, Ella?"

"Oui, Delphine. Merci beaucoup. J'aime les galettes." Ella's French improved daily. Genevieve was pleased that Ella and Alex often spoke to each other in French rather than English, trying to help each other master their second language.

Delphine beamed at her young protégé and rattled off a rapid phrase. "Quand tu auras fini, viens à la cuisine et nous préparerons des cookies ensemble."

Ella slapped her hands to her cheeks. "Yikes! Delphine that's too fast! I understood cookies, but that's all."

A chuckle rolled from Delphine's throat. "When you are finished here, come to the kitchen and we'll make cookies together. Eh bien?"

Ella's wild grin was a perfect response and Delphine couldn't resist pinching her cheek. "À bientôt," she said, and walked down the hall whistling.

As they drank their chocolate, they turned back to the photo album.

"Tutu, who's that little girl on the horse?" Ella pointed to a photograph and squinted into the face of a pretty child about her age. "I like her curls and I think she looks very fancy in her riding coat. But why isn't she wearing a helmet? She might get hurt." A frown tugged her seven-year-old brows together and she looked disapprovingly at the girl. "Didn't her mommy and daddy know she should wear a riding helmet?"

Genevieve smiled down at her granddaughter. "Do you know how proud I am of you? You're so smart and sensible." She pulled the photo from the rigid cardboard frame. When she turned it over, the girl's name, the location, and the date were written in elegant script on the back. Genevieve read out loud:

Château Beaulieu, August 19, 1880
Katherine Victoria Laney, 7 years old,
with Lightning, her beloved pony

"So, this young lady was the daughter of Charlotte Chaubert, our resident ghost. And her horse's name was Lightning," Genevieve said.

Ella sparkled. "I remember Charlotte from Wilmingrove Hall! Do you think Katherine lived here?"

Genevieve loved that Ella was chronically curious, asked

endless questions, and never ran out of theories.

"I know that Charlotte's family, the Chauberts, owned our house in Paris as well as this vineyard. When Charlotte and the 9th Earl of Crosswick married, Charlotte's parents gave them the vineyard as a wedding gift. Much later, Jonathon Laney, Bumpa's cousin, repurchased the Paris house, which they had sold, and brought it back into the family. We're very grateful for that, aren't we?" She kissed Ella on the nose and they exchanged Eskimo kisses.

"You know what I think, Tutu?" Ella wiggled closer to Genevieve, took her grandmother's arm, and draped it behind her neck so she was tucked into her Tutu's side. "I think Katherine is my cousin and Lightning is Jolie Fille's brother." Still fixated on the fact that Katherine was not wearing a helmet, she asked Genevieve, "Did you wear a helmet when you were a little girl, Tutu?"

"I did, Ella. I always wore a helmet, even as a child."

Ella looked relieved. "That's good, Tutu."

"But hold on to your hat, my sweet," she continued, about to tell her that she hadn't worn a helmet to ski when she was a child.

Ella tilted her head, baffled. "I'm not wearing a hat," she said, and patted her head to confirm it was bare.

Genevieve leaned away from Ella and looked down at her with narrowed eyes. "What are you talking about? You're wearing a perfectly lovely hat with pink flowers in the band," she teased. Then, she raised her hands over her head like Frankenstein, wiggled her fingers, and thrust them into Ella's ribs, tickling her until the screeching child cried for mercy.

"Stop, Tutu! Stop," she gasped. "You'll knock my hat off!"

"What's going on here?" The boom of his voice matched the sternness of his brow and Ella and Genevieve's eyes flashed wide. "How dare you have all of this fun without me!" he said as he plucked Ella off the chair by her waist and threw her over his shoulder.

"Bumpa!"

Philip winced as Ella screamed her delight directly into his ear.

Genevieve stuck out her lower lip and blew out a stream of air that ruffled wisps of hair on her forehead.

She sensed a new presence, and, when she looked at the entry to the bedroom, Duncan filled the doorway.

"Just in time to catch your daughter," Philip said as he heaved Ella into her father's arms.

"Whoa!" Duncan said as he caught her. "Jeeze, Ella, you're getting heavy. I hope I don't drop you." And he feigned loosening his hold on his little girl.

"Daddy!" Ella shrieked.

Duncan smiled and set her on the floor. "All right, cute girl. Lizette has lunch ready for you and Mom is waiting for you in the petit salon. We'll be right down. I just need to talk to Bumpa and Tutu for a minute." He smacked Ella's bottom as she ran to the door.

He sat opposite his mother on the other side of the fireplace. "Dad, why don't you sit down?" He pointed to where his mother was seated in the double chair. Philip wiggled in beside her and she scooched her bottom over to give him a bit more room.

"What's going on, Duncan? Something's wrong, isn't it?" She leaned forward, her brow crinkled. "What is it?"

Philip laid his hand on her back. "If you give him a minute I bet he'll tell us, G?"

Genevieve rolled her eyes.

"Listen, guys," Duncan started. "I just got off the phone with David. He tried to call you, Dad, but it went straight to voicemail so he called me."

Philip pulled out his phone. "Ah, yup," he said, hitting the airplane mode switch. "Ella was looking at my videos earlier this morning and must have silenced my phone. What did David want?"

"Is everything okay in London?"

"Everything is fine in London, but not so good in Yorkshire."

"What?" Genevieve's antennae were immediately on high alert. "Is something wrong at Wilmingrove Hall? Why was David calling? Why didn't they...?"

"Mom," Duncan interrupted. "Would you just let me tell you why David called?"

"Sorry, sorry." She made a motion to zip her lips and put her hand over her mouth.

Philip nodded for Duncan to proceed. "Yesterday, after she heard about Olivia being under suspicion, Becca went to Blain Lodge to talk to Dr. Morgan. With Picard focusing the investigation on her, Becca wanted Morgan's opinion on whether or not Olivia could be behind any of this."

Genevieve took her hand away from her mouth. "And what did he say?"

"He thought there was little likelihood Olivia was involved." He brightened just a bit as he interrupted himself. "You remember they moved her from a secure wing at Blain Lodge to an open residential wing three months after she arrived?"

His parents nodded. "That's the reason she was able to come to the wedding and stay until after the New Year," Genevieve said. "She's been doing really well."

"That's what everyone seems to think." Duncan's brows drew together.

"What do you mean?" Genevieve felt the muscles in her neck tighten.

"While Becca was with Dr. Morgan he was called out of his office. After waiting a few minutes, Becca decided she wanted to search Olivia's room to see if she could find anything incriminating."

Philip leaned forward, putting his elbows on his knees and his chin on his fisted hands. "What horrible thing did she find?" he mumbled.

"What did you say, Dad?"

He looked up. "I said, what did she find?"

"Olivia's journal," Duncan said. "She found Olivia's journal. She'll be back here the day after tomorrow to talk to Olivia with what she's found. She said she's taken pictures of a few pages that she's going to email to us. We're not to let Olivia know she's coming because she wants to surprise her."

TWENTY-EIGHT

"**W**HAT DO YOU mean you heard it from a reliable source?" Lillie almost screamed into the phone. "Peter, you tell me who the reliable source is and I'll tell you why they are *not* reliable."

The reporter on the other end of the phone was calm but insistent. The more emphatic Lillie got, the firmer Peter Fletcher became in his assertion that the Laney Musée des Beaux-Arts and the Warwick family were under investigation for selling forged paintings. Lillie was a favorite of *The Times*' arts writers. She always had a glamorous event to talk about or an interesting art-world tale to tell, but no reporter was going to let the whiff of gossip go without sniffing it out, just because they liked the foundation's director.

Since the New Year started two weeks ago, the rumor campaign to create havoc for the Laney museums and the House of Crosswick had gone from last year's serious annoyance to something that needed full-blown damage control.

Lillie suddenly felt exhausted. "Peter, if your newspaper prints one malicious word about the Laney museums, the foundation, or the House of Crosswick, I assure you there will be a lawsuit sitting on the editor-in-chief's desk ten minutes after the story hits your website." She rubbed her neck, trying to keep the headache that was lodged there from creeping into her temples. "*The Times* isn't a gossip rag. Leave that rubbish to *The Sun*. The story you should be looking into is who's trying to discredit us and why."

She picked up a cream-colored envelope and fanned her face. "If you want to investigate, I'll give you all the help you want." She looked down at the blinking light on her desk phone. "Peter, I have to take another call. Why don't you ring me tomorrow and let's see if we can figure out what the real story is. Would that work for you? Call me tomorrow."

She pressed the blinking hold button. "Lillie Langdon."

"Lillie Langdon, Finnegan Mountbatten." Finn's voice sang through the line like a sweet song.

"Oh my god, Finn. You have no idea how wonderful it is to hear your voice." Lillie swung her chair around so she could look out the window across Rue Scribe at one of her favorite buildings in Paris, Le Palais Garnier, the opera house made famous by *The Phantom of the Opera*. "Where are you, Finn?"

"Actually, I'm right behind you."

She spun around like a top, shot out of her chair, threw her phone on her desk, and flung herself at Finn, clutching him in a vice grip, much to his surprise. Though they hadn't seen each other since they met at Château Beaulieu over Christmas, they had spent hours on FaceTime nearly every evening since then. Lillie had never been attracted to anyone so quickly or so deeply—ever.

"Well, well, well," he said. She loosened her hug and tilted back in his arms so he could look at her. When he saw her clouded face, he knew something was wrong. "What is it, Lillie? What's the matter?"

Without saying a word, she burrowed her face into his chest. The scratch of his Harris tweed topcoat on her cheek was oddly comforting. It felt sturdy and strong; just what she needed to remind her of her own strength, which had suffered blow after blow over the last two weeks.

He said nothing, just held her.

After a long moment, she leaned back. "I'm so glad you're here," she said, tears misting her eyes.

He led her to a chair in front of her desk and gently pushed her to sit. He slipped off his overcoat, tossed it on Lillie's desk, then dragged the matching chair to her so they sat knee to knee. "Okay, pet. Tell me everything."

She drew in a breath and her voice wavered as she began. "Remember when we were at Château Beaulieu and I told you about the onslaught of internet rumors smearing Laney Musée des Beaux-Arts?"

"Of course. You said people were even asking you about the gossip when you were at Art Basel Miami Beach."

Her lips tilted up. "So you do listen when I talk. I'm delighted and not just a little surprised."

Finn leaned forward and kissed her on the nose. "Though you are a fascinating woman, I'm pretty sure I have an ulterior motive." He grinned an impish grin. "But, my darling, we digress. Tell me more about this rumor mill that keeps churning."

Her strength revived, Lillie's voice was full and firm. "Since the New Year, the slander and libel have increased dramatically. Richard… ah, you haven't met Richard. Richard Durand is the Directeur of the museum. He replaced Bernard Reines last year." She shifted in her chair. "At any rate, Richard and I have been doing what we can to contain the worst stories, but it's gotten out of hand."

Finn settled back and crossed his legs. "Actually, Lillie, that's why I'm here."

"What do you mean?" She scowled. "You didn't just come to see me?"

"Well, of course I did. When Philip asked me to give you a hand with this barrage of negative rumors, I couldn't say yes fast enough. I couldn't wait to see you and help you get to the bottom of this smear campaign. Tell me everything. I find when we're analyzing a security issue, it helps to have fresh eyes and ears assess the situation."

"Security issue?" Lillie's brows flew up. "What makes you think this is a security issue?"

Finn tented his hands. "In this day and age, Lillie, almost everything is a security issue. I'm only suggesting if you tell me the story from the beginning maybe I can provide some insights you hadn't considered." He cocked his head. "Does that make sense?"

"Of course it does." She tossed him a chuckle. "In the short time we've known each other, you seem to make sense most of the time. It's annoying."

He looked around the room. "Is there coffee?"

She pointed to a sideboard where a silver thermos sat surrounded by porcelain mugs with Impressionist paintings printed on them.

"Excellent. Can I get you a cup?"

She shook her head.

"Go ahead, start at the beginning."

As Lillie started telling the saga, he sauntered across the room, poured himself a coffee and came back to sit. For the next hour, she talked and he listened, occasionally asking a question.

As she finished recounting the series of events, her confidence surged back. "You know, Finn, you're right."

He leaned toward her. "I'm sorry, what did you say?" He tilted his ear in her direction. "I didn't quite hear that."

"Ha!" she said. "There's nothing wrong with your hearing. I feel better just telling you about the problem."

"There's truth in 'A problem shared is a problem halved.' Having said that, it's my job now, as a savvy cyber security savant, to come up with insights and solutions."

"Nice alliteration," Lillie said, as her phone vibrated on her desk. She looked at the screen and Philip's face stared at her. "It's Philip," she said to Finn as she answered the call, her voice bright. "Finn's here. I've been going over the details of the rumors and the damage they're doing. He's going to come up with some ideas on how we can find out where they're coming from and then, of course, he'll have to figure out how to combat them. Thank you, Philip, for sending him to the rescue. I can't tell you how relieved I am to have someone with Finn's skills looking at what's happening. It's been so—"

Philip interrupted her on the other end of the phone. The smile melted from her face and was replaced with worried eyes and a furrowed brow.

"What is it?" Finn mouthed.

Lillie shook her head.

Finn wrote on a pad, "Is something wrong with the family?"

"Philip, I'm going to put you on speaker. Finn's going crazy wondering what's going on."

"Is everything all right?" Finn watched the phone as if Philip might jump through it any moment.

"Actually, there have been a couple of developments," Philip said, his voice brittle. "I've had two calls from big donors today."

"Oh my god, Philip!" Blood drained from Lillie's face. "Who called you?"

"The first call was from Michel Beaufoy."

"No, no, no, not Michel." She turned to Finn. "Monsieur Beaufoy and three of his friends pledged a million euros a year for the next five years to support the foundation's education fund. If they pull their funding, it will be disastrous."

"Don't jump to conclusions, Lillie. Michel was very understanding. He went through something similar last year with his bank, Credit Alliance. He wanted to give me the name of the company that got to the bottom of their problem, but I assured him we have an excellent firm working on our behalf."

Lillie eased out a long breath and mustered her courage before asking, "Who was the other call from?"

There was a pause at Philip's end of the phone before he said, "René Moulard."

"Of course," she moaned.

"Who's René Moulard?" Finn didn't know the name.

Lillie rolled her eyes to the ceiling. "He's the Ministre de l'Éducation Nationale et de la Jeunesse, Minister of National Education and Youth. For two years, we've been working to create a joint project with them and we're about to finalize the details. Their support will mean the world to the foundation's children's program. If they back out, well…" She couldn't finish the sentence.

"Don't panic yet, Lillie. I assured René that everything he's seeing on the internet is false. I told him we've brought in an international cyber specialist—that's you, Finn—to get to the bottom of these attacks."

"Philip, I don't—"

"We're meeting with him next week, Lillie," Philip interrupted. "Let's hope you have something for us by then, Finn."

Lillie sensed Philip was ready to move on. "You said there had been a couple of developments. What's the other one?"

"I'm just full of good news." Philip took a drink at the other end of the line before he answered. "Becca is coming back to Château Beaulieu tomorrow to share something she found in Olivia's journal. She was going to email some pages but I haven't seen them. I've been so busy with this other issue, I might have missed them. She'll fill us in when she gets here."

Lillie's face clouded. "She didn't tell you *anything* over the phone?"

"I didn't talk to her. She gave Duncan the message. Becca wanted to wait until she arrived to tell us about it." Philip sighed into the phone. "I doubt it's anything good. Poor Becca. She's been thrilled at Olivia's progress. Well, we all have."

"What are you talking about?" Finn looked confused. "I haven't spent much time with her, but the little I have spent has been delightful."

Lillie nodded.

"Finn, you're right. Since she's been at Château Beaulieu, she's been charming and lovely—hell, she's been a lot of fun. But her history…" Lillie and Finn could hear Philip exhale at the other end of the phone. "There's no way I can tell you what this young woman is capable of. But, if I were to try, I would say think of the cleverest person you've ever known, add to that guile, cunning, and a talent for disguise and mimicry and you'd begin to build an image of Olivia Conway before she went to Blain Lodge, before her recovery. She is brilliant and *was* treacherous. Becca has told us that Dr. Morgan, her psychiatrist, assures her Olivia's been a model patient, making excellent progress." He cleared his throat. "Let's hope she hasn't reverted. Let's hope she's not a clever patient perpetrating a big, fat scam."

As Philip spoke, a text pinged on Lillie's phone. She glanced at it as Philip continued, but then he stopped.

"Lillie," Philip said. "Did you just get a text?"

"Yes, I did. Did you?"

"I did," Philip said, his voice frigid. "Read it to me."

Lillie tapped her text icon. Her voice cracked as she read, "I'm coming for all of you.'"

"Yup. That's what mine says."

"Give me your mobile, Lillie." Finn took the phone and tapped a few keys. "They've used a VoIP, a voice over protocol. There's no easy way to identify the sender."

"Damn it! Damn it!" Philip seethed, more to himself than Lillie and Finnegan. "Finn, could the same bastard who's sending threatening messages be responsible for the smear campaign?"

Finn coughed a laugh. "You don't have to be a cyber security specialist to know that if you're a clever clogs anything's possible on the internet.

TWENTY-NINE

GENEVIEVE LAUGHED AND jogged to keep up with Ella as she danced, skipped, hopped, ran, then danced again along the path to the stables. She was making up a song about Jolie Fille and belted it louder and louder with each step. Excitement oozed from every young pore and there was no question, she was a little girl besotted by her horse. She was the first to the barn door, well ahead of her grandmother, and pushed it open with a mighty shove.

"Jolie Fille, Jolie Fille," Ella called, her little-girl voice full of love.

Genevieve stepped through the door and closed it behind her. She stood for a moment, letting her eyes adjust to the dimness, and smiled at the comforting noises of horses blowing raspberries, nickering, snorting, and the gentle swishing of tails. They were perfectly punctuated by the sweet sound of Ella cooing Jolie Fille's name, her lowcut riding boots tapping on the worn brick floor as she raced down the aisle. Genevieve watched her granddaughter stop in front of her pony's cubicle and rise on her tiptoes, trying to look over the paddock door. She looked at Genevieve, who still stood at the entryway.

"Tutu, Jolie Fille isn't in her stall." She looked in the enclosure next door where Alex's beautiful stallion could usually be found. "Commander's here but Jolie Fille isn't. Where is she?"

Genevieve looked at her watch: 7:14. It was quite early in the morning, but not too early for the horses to have been fed. Maybe Jolie Fille had been turned out into the field. The morning was cold but sunny, and a graze in the pasture would be a lovely treat after yesterday's rainy day. She pulled her phone from the pocket of her barn jacket and dialed Henri's number.

He answered on the second ring. "Lady Crosswick, bonjour."

"Henri, bonjour. Ella and I are in the stables, but Jolie Fille isn't here. I was going to give her a riding lesson but—"

"What do you mean Jolie Fille isn't there?" Henri sounded skeptical, as if Genevieve had overlooked her granddaughter's horse.

"I mean," Genevieve was emphatic, "Jolie Fille is not here!"

Silence.

"Henri, are you still there?"

"Oui, my lady. I'll be right there. Give me ten minutes."

Genevieve looked around and spied a blackboard where the stable staff kept track of feedings and left messages for each other. There, in the tray on the lower edge, was a fat piece of chalk.

While they waited they played hopscotch, and Ella was beating her grandmother badly. As she waited for Ella to toss her small stone into a square, Rose Otto wafted into Genevieve's nostrils. She inhaled deeply. Exhaled. She did it again, confirming the air was filled with Charlotte's fragrance, overwhelming the stable's usual smells of oats and hay.

"Charlotte, are you here?" she whispered. She stood stone-still. Only her eyes moved, sweeping from side to side, searching the barn for any clue that the beautiful ghost was here.

"Tutu, it's your turn." Ella stood on one foot then the other.

Just as she was about to take her hopscotch turn, Genevieve felt an icy caress on her cheek. "Charlotte," she said again, and closed her eyes.

A sharp bang of wood on wood made Genevieve's heart drop to her feet. Her eyes flew open, expecting to see Charlotte in her full Victorian glory. Instead, she saw Henri, hair tousled, shirt misbuttoned and fly only halfway zipped, his arm holding the stable door open.

He slammed the door behind him and charged down the aisle, cursing as he strode toward Genevieve and Ella.

When he arrived at the far end of the stables, Ella looked up at him, smiling. "Bonjour, Henri," she said in her tinkling, little girl voice. "I'm beating Tutu. You can play me in the next game."

"Ah, bon, ma chérie." He squatted beside Ella, decked out in her thick navy sweater and tan riding breeches. Her new paddock boots were already scuffed from helping muck the stalls several times in the last two weeks. Henri licked his thumb and ran it back and forth over the toe of Ella's boot, polishing away some of the grime. "I need to show you how to polish these." He looked up into her velvet-brown eyes. "You always want to take good care of the things that are important to you. If you respect them and treat them well, they will serve you well forever. Or so I have always believed."

Genevieve watched the charming interaction and knew Henri was not talking about boots and tackle.

The door opened again and Émile jogged toward them. "Bonjour. Que se passe-t-il?"

Henri rose from his squat and laid his hand on Émile's shoulder. "Something very strange," he said. "*That* is what is going on." As he spoke, Henri clenched and unclenched his grip, causing the young man to grimace. "Émile, do you know where Jolie Fille is? Were you not in charge of caring for the horses this morning?"

Émile's confusion was obvious. "En fait, non. Last night, I received a text from you." He began to thumb through his text messages. "Aha. Ç'est ici."

He handed his phone to Henri. He read the message, looked at Émile, then read the text again. "I did not write this," Henri said.

"But it says it is from you. It is your mobile number."

"I can see that, but I assure you I did not send a message telling you to shirk your responsibilities and sleep in this morning. Does that sound like me, Émile?"

"To be honest, non, but I thought… you know, we were setting smudge pots in the vines until very late." He looked down at the floor. When looked back up at Henri, Émile's face was filled with chagrin. "I thought it was very kind of you to tell me someone else would care for the horses this morning. You know, Henri, I would never neglect them." He smiled at Ella, who was staring at him with enormous eyes, wondering what was going on.

"Ella." Émile took her hands in his and squatted to look at her eye to eye. "Ella, I will always take good care of Jolie Fille."

Ella stepped closer to the young man she thought of as her friend. "Émile, where is Jolie Fille? Is she in the field getting some sun?"

He popped to his feet. "Let's find out, shall we?" He took Ella's hand and started back up the aisle toward the barn door as Henri's phone vibrated.

"Hallo," Henri answered. "Monsieur Wang. Good morning." He looked at Genevieve and shrugged his shoulders as he listened to Kim Wang, the owner of Clos Peyra, the Château next to them.

Genevieve checked her watch again. It was not yet 7:35. There was a lot of activity for so early in the morning.

"Moment, s'il vous plaît." He tapped the speaker icon and put the phone on the gatepost of Jolie Fille's stall. "I have put you on speaker so Lady Crosswick can hear."

"Good morning, Kim," Genevieve said, leaning toward Henri's mobile. "You're calling bright and early."

"Oui, Genevieve, I am." Normally warm, Kim's voice was taut. "I'm calling to ask if Ella's pony is in her stall."

Before Henri could respond, Genevieve interrupted. "Kim, could you hold on just a minute?" she said, and gave Henri a cautionary look. She turned toward Émile and Ella, who were loitering at the other end of the stables. "Émile." She raised her voice so they could hear her. "Ella, why don't you and Émile go back to the Château and have pancakes?"

Ella licked her lips. "Chocolate chip pancakes?" A grin splashed across her face.

"If it doesn't have chocolate chips, is it really a pancake?" Genevieve said.

"No, Tutu. It isn't." Ella shook her head and her curls bounced. "Come on, Émile." She tugged on his hand and Émile nodded his understanding that his task was to divert Ella's attention while the mystery of Jolie Fille was unraveled.

The moment the stable door closed, they turned back to the mobile and Genevieve resumed the conversation. "Why do you ask, Kim?"

"About an hour ago I was driving back from the boulangerie and a rider galloped past me. It wasn't until later, when I sat down with my café et croissant, that I realized the horse looked very much like Jolie Fille."

Genevieve and Henri looked at each other, then back at the phone.

"Kim, did you see who the rider was?" Genevieve held her breath as she waited for the answer.

"Non, I did not. It was still quite dark and the rider was dressed in black from head to toe. I could not even tell if it was a man or a woman. Was the horse Jolie Fille?"

Putting her hand on the stall gate, Genevieve steadied herself.

Henri picked up the phone and looked at Genevieve, who stood with her fists clenched, then said to Kim, "We've just discovered Ella's horse is gone. So I'd say yes, it's quite possible it was Jolie Fille. It appears Ella's pony has been stolen."

"We'll call Chef Picard as soon as we're off the phone. Thank you, Kim. I'm sure Picard will want to talk to you."

"You know, Genevieve, je suis toujours á votre service."

Anxious to get off the phone, Genevieve said, "You're a wonderful neighbor, Kim. There's no question, you are always at our service. We'll see you tonight when you come for dinner. Now we need to call Chef Picard. Au revoir." The line went dead.

"Henri, what about security footage?" Genevieve said.

"Remember, Lady Crosswick, our entire security system has

been offline for the last two days while we update the equipment and software."

She smacked her forehead with her palm. "Of course. How convenient for the horse thief. That's a little too coincidental, don't you think?"

"Ah, oui." Henri massaged his temples. "And the fact someone sent Émile a text telling him not to be in the stables this morning. That conveniently cleared the way for someone to ride off into the sunrise with Ella's pony."

"Who knew the system was down?" Genevieve's mind raced.

"Everyone at Château Beaulieu, except perhaps some of the vandangers, the grape pickers." Henri looked at his phone and tapped in the number for the Saint-Émilion police department.

"Of course everyone knew," she said under her breath. "Henri, I need to run up to the Château," Genevieve said as he waited for someone to answer. He nodded, but she was already sprinting up the aisle.

She ran up the hill to the house and by the time she mounted the last three stairs to the Château's back terrace, her lungs were on fire. She bent over, put her hands on her knees, and tried to get her breath under control. When she was no longer gasping for air, she opened the kitchen door and slipped in. For a moment she stood in the mudroom where coats hung on hooks and boots stood at attention. A beautiful blue paisley scarf hung over a tweedy coat, Barbour wax jackets were at the ready alongside a puffy black coat and some small versions of Barbour country wear, waiting for their young owners to snatch them off their hooks and take them for an adventure outside. As she walked into the bustling kitchen, she smelled pancakes and melting chocolate and her mouth watered. Ella sat at the huge island, chocolate rimming her lips, chatting with Lizette, Sophie, and Émile in Frenglish, a clever blend of French and English everyone seemed to understand.

"Tutu! Are you going to have chocolate chip pancakes with me?"

Genevieve swept by her granddaughter, kissing the top of the curly head. "No, darling. I have to run upstairs to check on something. You and Émile enjoy your breakfast."

She dashed out of the kitchen and raced down the hall. She put her hand on the wrought iron railing and charged up the stairs, stopping at the top to catch her breath once again. She was thankful for the thick Aubusson carpet that ran the length of the hall: she didn't want to alert anyone as she tiptoed to the far end of the corridor. She stopped at the last door, took a deep, silent breath, gripped the door handle, and slowly pressed it down. As she eased the heavy oak slab inward the hinges creaked and she froze. Hoping to lighten the weight she lifted the handle and pushed again. This time there was only silence. When the door was open just enough, she slipped inside the dark room, where the heavy curtains were pulled against the rising sun.

She blinked several times, trying to adjust her eyes to the dimness. When she could see well enough, she stole across the room. A duvet was mounded in the middle of the bed and a mass of blonde hair splayed across the pillow. She listened to the slow, rhythmic breathing then surveyed the room and found nothing out of place: no black riding clothes flung over a chair, no riding boots scattered on the floor.

The mound groaned and shifted in the bed. Genevieve went rigid. She stood with her eyes closed until the deep breathing resumed. Rising on the balls of her feet, she tiptoed back to the door, sidled through the narrow opening, and pulled the slab of oak closed. For several seconds she stood rigid in the hall until relief eased her tingling nerves. There was no way Olivia could have been the one Kim saw riding Jolie Fille and now be in her bed sound asleep. Thank god Olivia hadn't been the one who stole Ella's pony.

THIRTY

ALWAYS THE BUSIEST room in the Château, the energy in the kitchen was even more frenetic than usual. These days, whenever Delphine was in the room, tension wasn't far behind.

Tonight, Kim and Jing Wang were coming to dinner as well as Lian Shou from Château Pitique.

Rapid French whipped around the kitchen like a blizzard. Everyone needed a small piece of Lizette: an answer, an opinion, a recipe, a confirmation. She bit her tongue each time Delphine thrust unsolicited advice on her. Now, just two hours before the dinner party, she had too many details to worry about to avoid stepping on Delphine's toes. The entire afternoon, Delphine had been sticking her nose everywhere it should not have been, and Lizette had done her best to avoid smacking her on that nose.

But the last straw finally came as Lizette carried a large pot of warm water from the sink to the stove, with Delphine so close to her she was nearly stepping on her heels. When Delphine said, "Lizette, are you certain the scallops are fresh? They smell a bit fishy to me," red flashed before the head cook's eyes. She felt as if she were moving in slow motion. Her arms strained as she raised the heavy pot shoulder high, spun around and dumped the water over Delphine's head.

Delphine stood dripping, staring at Lizette, her mouth open, but wordless. She blinked, trying to keep drops from falling from her lashes into her eyes. Not missing a beat, Lizette put the pot back in the sink, turned the water on to refill it and tossed a towel to Delphine. "Sophie, would you mind getting the mop? I seem to have spilled a bit of water on the floor."

While the young kitchen helper mopped furiously, careful to avoid eye contact with Delphine, Lizette carried the pot back to the stove, turned on the gas below it, and went about her business. Without saying another word, Delphine turned on her heels and stormed through the door, which she slammed so hard against the wall it sounded as if it cracked. The moment the door swung closed, the entire kitchen staff stopped what they were doing and applauded their boss's bold action.

"Alons, alons." Lizette clapped her hands twice and everyone got back to work.

Fury pulsed through Delphine's veins as she stormed toward her cottage, her fists clenched at her sides. For years she and Lizette had been the closest of friends, working together at Château Beaulieu, maintaining the beautiful house and creating stunning events that showed the vineyard's wines to the best advantage.

All the years Daniel LaGrande reigned as Managing Directeur, the three of them had loved Château Beaulieu as if it were their own. Now she was furious all the time—angry with everyone. Since the Warwicks inherited the vineyard, nothing was the same. She stopped at her front door, put her hand on the round iron knob, and was about to turn the handle when someone called her name.

"Delphine!" The voice was distinctly Edouard Comte, the vigneron who took over when Daniel LaGrande died.

Delphine swiped a damp curl from her eyes and raised her hand in greeting. Though he was young, Edouard had already gained a wide and well-deserved reputation for understanding the art of winemaking. He was talented and Delphine liked his brash personality.

"Hallo, Edouard." Delphine smiled as he walked up the hill toward her.

"What happened to you?" He looked into the cloudless sky then back at Delphine. He held up a strand of her wet hair and let it drop.

"It's a long story," she said, and opened her periwinkle-blue front door. "Did you need to see me?" She stood to the side, motioned for him to come in, and toed off her shoes before she followed him into her charming cottage.

"I did. I wanted to talk to you about the wines for tonight. Lizette gave me the menu yesterday so I'm set with everything, but I wanted to ask what you thought about serving La Vie Douce for the dessert wine."

No light of recognition showed in Delphine's eyes.

"Remember," Edouard said. "It is the dessert wine Hank Shou created at Château Pitique. Lord Crosswick, Duncan, and I want to work out a deal to produce it here at Château Beaulieu. That's the reason Lian Shou is coming tonight. We have several cases in the cellar since last year. I brought a bottle." He held up a long, slender, octagonal bottle. On the label La Vie Douce was written in gold, with Château Pitique's burgundy logo just above it.

Finally, Delphine remembered hearing about the wine. After producing mediocre products for several years, Hank Shou finally created something very special. Though she had never sampled the sweet wine, Lord Crosswick had raved about it.

She brightened at the thought of a late afternoon wine tasting. "Give me a few minutes to repair the damage, and we'll see just how good this wine is." She ran her hands through her hair—which was wild with curls—then turned and walked to her bedroom, tracks from her wet stockings following as she went.

"Trust me, it's delicious," Edouard called after her. Knowing his way around Delphine's cottage, he opened the door of a carved pine cabinet standing between sets of French doors and took two glasses from the breakfront. He held up the tulip bowls sitting atop long stems to examine them and smiled when they passed inspection. Not a water mark, not a streak. What would he expect from Delphine except perfection? He placed the glasses on the coffee table next to the bottle of La Vie Douce, the liquid glowing like amber as the late afternoon sun slanted through the bottle.

When Delphine emerged, wrapped in a black wool robe with her initials monogrammed in cream on the breast pocket, her glossy curls corkscrewed from her head at every angle, boinging here, boinging there. Her cheeks were pink from her hot shower and the rich, sweet smell of jasmine lotion floated around the room in wispy clouds.

She went to her small pantry, picked out a walnut cheese board, and collected a paper-wrapped package. She unfolded the paper, set the wedge of Roquefort on a porcelain plate, set the plate on the tray, and added three perfect strawberries to the side. She pulled the cutlery drawer halfway out, selected a bone-handled cheese knife, and laid it beside the cheese on the tray. Tapping her chin with her forefinger, she tried to remember what was missing. "Ah, la baguette!" She clapped her hands once, slapped a slender loaf, fresh that morning, on the cutting board, and sliced perfect half-inch slices as if she had done it all her life—which she had. She certainly knew her way around a knife. She tossed the pieces in a hand-woven basket lined with a blue and white napkin, popped it on the tray, and she was ready.

"Voilà," she said to Edouard as she brought the tray to the coffee table.

"Parfaite," he said, patting the cushion beside him.

"All in the name of finding the perfect dessert wine for the Warwicks' dinner party. We live but to serve," she said, her tone laced with sarcasm. She sat on the sofa and tugged on her robe to cover her knees.

"While you were fiddling with the Roquefort, I opened the wine." Edouard handed one tulip glass to Delphine and held the other high, examining its rich color. "It really is quite beautiful, isn't it?"

"Lovely," Delphine said, anxious to get to the tasting.

They tapped rims. "Santé," they said, and sipped the syrupy liquid.

Delphine ran her tongue over her lips then took another sip, larger this time. She sucked on her lower lip. "This is delicious."

"It is, isn't it? It's quite special. It was lucky Château Beaulieu ordered several cases last year for that big party they had for La Cité du Vin, otherwise we would have none. I am not certain what happened to the other cases. I need to ask Frederick Picard." He drained his glass and poured another. "So, Delphine. Do you think this will be a nice accompaniment to the chocolate soufflés tonight?"

"I can't think of anything lovelier." She helped herself to another glass and refilled Edouard's as well.

"Merci," he said, and raised his glass in her direction. "Changing subjects, are you ever going to tell me why you were soaking wet when I arrived at your door?"

Delphine had burrowed herself comfortably into her down-filled sofa and was resting her feet on the coffee table. She looked up at Edouard's cute, young face through her thick lashes. "You really want to know?" she asked.

"Oui, I really want to know. It's not every day one finds Château Beaulieu's house manager standing outside her cottage on a cloudless day, dripping with water."

She studied her cuticles for a moment. When she looked up at him, she shook her head. "Lizette and I had a bit of a contretemps," she said. "Since the Warwicks arrived here last winter, we've been having a lot of those."

"Quoi?" Edouard scowled and sipped his wine. "What do you mean?"

She sniffed. "Never mind. It's nothing."

"I don't believe you."

She said nothing, just rolled her glass between her hands and stared at the golden liquid.

"Come on, Delphine. You know you can talk to me."

Finally she looked up at Edouard. "When Lord and Lady Crosswick came to the Château last winter, I felt I needed to show them how valuable I am to the Château. I think I was worried they might replace me. In all the years I've been here, no one has come to check on Château Beaulieu or the staff. As long as the wine continued to be top class and as long as the expenses were kept under control, the 12th Earl and his trustees were happy."

Edouard patted Delphine's hand, which rested on a needlepoint pillow between them. "Go on," he said.

"And then all of a sudden they were here. There were people here all the time, every day. Watching how I do things, how I manage the Château. It has made me so worried and angry. I started micromanaging everyone in the house, from the housemaids to Lizette." She chuckled under her breath. "I even tried to tell Henri how to reorganize the garage."

"You didn't!" Edouard's eyes widened and he clapped his hand over his mouth in mock horror.

"I did. But just once. As you can imagine, he wasn't having it."

They laughed together and finished the last swallow of wine in their glasses. Edouard held up the bottle of La Vie Douce and brought it close to his eyes, then looked at Delphine.

"Merde!" he said, and licked the last drops from the mouth of the bottle. "That didn't take us very long, did it?"

"It never takes long to drink a good bottle of wine."

"So finish your story, mon amie."

"Ah, oui. Apparently today was la goutte qui fait déborder le vase. I think in English they say, 'The straw that broke the camel's back.'"

Delphine told Edouard the details of the events in the kitchen and how she had criticized everything Lizette did. "Of course, Lizette is a magnificent head cook. I know that, but I couldn't seem to help myself. Finally, after nearly a year of my incessant interference, today she'd had enough and dumped a pot of water over my head."

Edouard's face twisted and Delphine thought he was going to sneeze, but instead he bellowed a laugh. "Baahh, oui?" He howled.

"But that's not the worst! I'm certain I heard all the kitchen staff applaud as I left. That's how terrible I have been… to everyone. But I can't help myself. I am so very angry all the time." She picked up her glass, looked at its empty bowl, and set it back on the table.

"What are you angry about?"

"I am furious at the Warwicks and Wallace and Mrs. MacIntosh for being here at my Château." She cut a piece of Roquefort, put it on a slice of baguette, and popped it into her mouth. She wished she had more wine. Then she turned to Edouard. "Am I the only one angry about this? Are you happy here?"

"I am. I like the Warwicks very much and I appreciate they trusted me enough to let me take over Daniel's position as vineyard manager. I know I am very, very lucky." He watched tiny bits of dust dance in the rays of afternoon sun pouring through the window. "But, I am young and ambitious and I do not always want to be in Daniel's shadow." He looked back at Delphine and shrugged. "So who knows what is in my future? Maybe I shall stay. Maybe I shall go to another vineyard to make my mark."

"You had better be careful, my friend. As you said, you are very lucky. There are few vineyards as fine as Château Beaulieu. Perhaps you can make your mark with La Vie Douce." She stood, swaying from the wine and loomed over Edouard. She pointed a finger down at him and steadied herself on a ladderback chair sitting next to the coffee table. "On n'est jamais content de son sort. No one is ever content with what they have," she said.

As she tried to stop her head from spinning, her phone vibrated and she pulled it from the pocket of her robe.

"Bonjour, my lady. Oui. Edouard and I were just talking about the dessert wine. We tried it and it will be perfect with the soufflés." Smiling at Edouard like a naughty child she tried to keep from slurring her words. She listened for a moment then said, "I am just finishing getting dressed and will be there in fifteen minutes. Oui. Merci." She ended the call and inhaled, hoping Lady Crosswick hadn't noticed she was a bit drunk.

Delphine shoved the sleeve of her robe back and glanced at her watch. "Mon dieu! How did it get to be so late? You need to go, Edouard." She flapped her hands at him to shoo him out the door.

He rose from the sofa but didn't hurry to make a move. "Delphine, before I go I need to tell you something."

"Edouard, you need to leave." Delphine turned to go to her room to dress, but he seemed rooted to the floor. "Edouard, go back to the Château," she said again, annoyed he wasn't leaving.

"Um, Delphine, I, um. I don't know how to say this." He twisted his napkin into a knot, desperation in his voice.

"What? What is it? Just say it." As each second ticked by, Delphine became more agitated.

Finally he drew in an enormous breath, held it then as he released the air the words tumbled out. "The day of the wedding, I saw you coming out of the greenhouse with foxglove."

THIRTY-ONE

T HERE WAS NOTHING Genevieve liked better than interesting people gathered around a beautiful table, although the dinner party she had planned two days ago would not be the jolly evening she had anticipated. Though the police had found some clues in the stables they hoped would help them find Jolie Fille, at this point they were uncertain where the evidence would lead them. They had decided to tell Ella that Jolie Fille had been taken to the veterinarian's farm for a few days so the little girl wouldn't be upset.

By the time the Wangs and Lian Shou arrived, the beautiful day had soured to a chilly drizzle. All the better for roaring fires and plenty of excellent wine.

Philip and Genevieve liked Kim and Jing Wang. They were fine neighbors and were becoming good friends. Closer to Duncan and Julia's age than Philip and Genevieve's, the six of them had spent some lively evenings together over the last year. They rarely saw Lian but hoped she would feel comfortable this evening as part of the lovely group.

When Genevieve extended the invitation she had insisted the evening be casual, and though the Wangs had honored Genevieve's dictum, when they walked through the door they still looked like a high-fashion spread in *Vogue*. Jing's thick black hair was pulled taut into a high ponytail. Despite the severity of the style, she looked as sassy and spirited as she was. Her emerald-green cashmere sweater and trousers draped over her lanky frame, accentuating her long ballerina limbs. From ten years old she had trained at the Beijing Dance Academy. Now in her early forties, she still moved with the elegance of a prima ballerina. Emerald stones at her ears and a gold Piaget watch were her only adornments. The rest was natural beauty.

Kim was her perfect match. Thick black hair with an unexpected natural curl flopped onto his forehead just to the tops of his round tortoiseshell glasses. His lips were full and his jaw was chiseled, but the thing that saved him from Ken-doll looks was his wit. He was handsome and hilarious—a deadly combination.

By contrast, Lian did not possess a sparkling persona. Delicate and pale, her shy demeanor matched her appearance. Where the other women in attendance filled the room with their personalities, Lian preferred to quietly observe. Though she was expensively dressed, she had chosen to wear a beige sweater and trousers that seemed to blend with her complexion. Her jet-black spikey hair and red lipstick were the only nods to style.

Philip, Genevieve, Duncan, Julia, and Olivia—all looking livelier than they felt—rounded out the party. Though they had been invited, Wallace and Mrs. MacIntosh preferred a light dinner and early night.

With all the chaos swirling around them, Genevieve had wanted to cancel the dinner, but Philip and Duncan insisted they rise to the occasion. It was time to broach the topic of the dessert wine with Lian Shou and see if they could entice her into a partnership.

To start the evening, drinks in Philip's study were just the ticket. With a flute of Champagne in each person's hand, Philip raised his glass. "To Lian, Kim and Jing. To wonderful neighbors."

"Santé." The exchange of toasts was accompanied by the sound of clinking glasses and people began to sit.

But Kim held up his closed fist. "I come bearing gifts." When he opened his hand, a flash drive was nestled in his palm. "Philip, put this in your television and let's take a look."

"What do I have here, Kim?" Philip said as he took the flash drive.

"Just put it in. It's from our security cameras just outside our gate."

"Really?" Genevieve was on her feet. "Is this from this morning? Does it show who stole Jolie Fille?"

Philip put his hand on Genevieve's shoulder. "Shall we turn on the television and see?"

"Sorry, sorry. I'm just excited your cameras were able to pick up something. It's unbelievable that our system was in the process of being updated."

Philip turned on the TV, clicked the icon indicating the correct input, and the display went black for several seconds before the image appeared of the road in front of Clos Peyra, the Wang's château.

People leaned forward in their seats, straining to see the television. Lian stood behind Olivia's wingback chair and Kim stood next to the television.

"You see, here's the time stamp at the bottom." He pointed to numbers that ran like a stopwatch as time passed. The only sound in the room was the fire sizzling in the grate and the ticking of a carriage clock on the mantle. No one even breathed as they watched the image of the empty road.

Just as Kim said, "Be patient. The rider is coming soon," a figure in black from hood to boots galloped into the frame. The rider leaned close to the horse's neck and within seconds rode off the screen.

Philip hit pause and the room was silent for several seconds until Duncan said, "That's absolutely Jolie Fille but am I the only one who can't tell if the rider is a man or a woman?"

"Absolutely not," Julia said.

Philip shook his head. "I couldn't."

"No, it's impossible," Jing agreed.

"I looked at the footage three times trying to detect something that would give the thief away, but I couldn't find anything."

"I think it looked like a man." Every head in the room turned to Lian, still standing behind Olivia.

"What makes you say that, Lian?" Genevieve was anxious to know what gave the rider away.

"The boots. They look like a man's riding boots," Lian said with confidence.

Philip rewound the video and they watched again.

"I think you're right," Olivia said. "The sole looks thicker than a woman's boot."

"I still don't see it," Genevieve said, frustrated she still couldn't tell what sex the rider was.

Opinions began to fly and the room filled with excited voices offering theories based on nothing.

When Delphine came to the study door to announce, "Le diner est servi," no one heard her and she had to raise her voice and make the announcement a second time. The guests and their hosts continued the lively speculation about the rider as they walked to the small dining room.

Cozy and inviting, the petit salon was a perfect spot for a winter dinner. Eight chatting diners sitting at the round table, talking over each other, trying to solve the stolen horse mystery was just what the evening required.

As Delphine poured the aromatic Viognier Edouard had selected for their first course, in front of each diner Lizette placed a white porcelain plate with the Château Beaulieu coat of arms and a thick gold band encircling the lip. In the well of the plate, a portion of lobster thermidor sat with a lemon rosette at the side.

The lobster dish was one of Genevieve's favorites and the first fancy meal, as she called it, she prepared after she and Philip were married.

Before picking up her fork so everyone could begin, she looked around the table at her friends, at her son and daughter-in-law, and at Olivia, for whom she had great hopes. No matter how big their bank account grew, she would give it all up if she had to choose between their inherited fortune and those she loved. She was glad she didn't have to make that choice, but she would do it if she had to, she thought, and a smile lifted the corners of her mouth.

Philip raised his glass. "Thank you, Lian, Kim, and Jing for lending your technology and your energy to help with the mystery of the stolen horse. You're the best. Santé."

Genevieve picked up her fork and the meal began. When she finished chewing the small bite she had just put in her mouth, she dabbed at her lips before she said, "So the question remains. Who stole Jolie Fille? And why did they decide on Ella's pony? Alex's horse, Commander, is much more valuable. Why wouldn't they steal him?"

"That's a very good question," Duncan said. "The mysteries keep piling up. I'd say we're at the point that they need to be solved or..." He left the sentence hanging in the air.

Kim looked at Jing and she shrugged her shoulders. "I am sure it is none of our business, but what mysteries are you talking about?"

Duncan looked at Philip and his dad nodded for him to go ahead and share the string of incidents. "Of course, you'd have no reason to know about what's been going on. Except what happened to Wallace, of course." Duncan pushed his chair back, sauntered to the sideboard, and picked up the bottle of Viognier. While he walked around the table refilling glasses, he told Lian and the Wangs about the string of events. When he finished, Kim sat back in his chair, puckered his lips and sucked in a long, low whistle.

"That's a lot of shit going down," he said.

"Kim!" Jing shot him a sharp look. "Forgive my husband's inelegant vocabulary."

He threw up his hands with his palms forward. "Sorry, ladies. It just popped out."

"Not a problem," Genevieve said, and dismissed his apology with a flip of her wrist.

"Don't think a thing about it, Kim," Philip said. "You should hear G when she gets going."

Genevieve looked indignant. "What the hell are you talking about, Philip?" Everyone laughed but Genevieve couldn't help but think Kim would be hearing more about his use of the word shit when he and Jing got home. She didn't envy him.

"That was absolutely delicious," Jing said as she picked the last bite of thermidor out of the lobster shell. "I think this is only the second time I've had lobster prepared this way. I have to remember how much I love it."

"I'm so glad you enjoyed it," Genevieve said as Sophie whisked away the used plates, empty except for a lobster shell, each one picked clean with a twisted lemon rind at its side. Clearly, no one's appetite had been dulled by the stressful events at Château Beaulieu.

Lizette and Sophie brought the next course, which looked almost too pretty to eat. The porc au cassis was both beautiful and aromatic: a perfect winter entrée. The deep purple of the currants and their sauce spilled over the delicate pale pork and fingerling potatoes. Though everyone had devoured the lobster, forks were poised to enjoy the next tasty treat.

"Kim, you've gone very quiet." Julia nudged his elbow that was resting on the arm of his chair next to her.

He squinted at her. "Something is hazy in the back of my mind and I can't seem to get it into focus."

"Do you have any idea what it's about?" Genevieve said.

"It's relevant to the discussion about all the crazy things

happening here at Château Beaulieu. Of that, I am certain. It's something I saw or something I heard over the last couple of weeks." He snapped his fingers and his eye flew wide. "I know what it was."

"What?" everyone shouted at once.

Genevieve leaned in, put her elbow on the table, laced her fingers, and rested her chin on her hands, buzzing with anticipation.

Kim reveled in having everyone's attention. "The afternoon of David and Becca's wedding, Jing asked me to bring some jasmine over."

"Ah, yes. We put jasmine in Ella's hair. You did a good job, Kim." Julia patted his hand where it rested on the table.

"I walked over. I came through the headlands and alleyways from Clos Peyra to Château Beaulieu. I dropped the jasmine off in the kitchen—gave it to Sophie. I turned right around and headed back home. When I walked by your greenhouse, someone opened the door and came out. They couldn't see me because I was in the vines, but I could see the door perfectly."

"I'm sure people were in and out of there all day." Genevieve slouched, disappointed. "You know, Kim, we *were* having a wedding that day and we were using a lot of flowers."

He held up his hand. "Wait, just wait. Can anyone guess who was coming out of the nursery?"

"Delphine," Julia said.

Philip played along. "Lizette."

"Edouard," Julia offered.

"Edouard?" Duncan questioned Julia's guess.

"Well, he *is* the vigneron. Why wouldn't he be interested in what's growing in the greenhouse?"

Duncan backed off. "Okay. Good point."

Kim shook his head. "Any one of you may be right. Sadly, it is very much like the horse thief."

"What do you mean?" Julia asked.

"I mean, whoever it was wore a long coat and had wrapped a scarf around her head and neck up to her eyes. I couldn't see her face, but, in this case, I could tell it was a woman," Kim said.

"Okay." Genevieve broke in with the question on everybody's mind. "How is her exit from the greenhouse significant? As I said, people were coming in and out of the greenhouse all day."

"I'm glad you asked." A smug smile curved his lips. "I know a thing or two about botany, don't I, Jing?"

She rolled her velvet-brown eyes. "Sure, darling. You are a plant whiz kid." She leaned into Philip, who was seated next to her and in a stage whisper said, "I asked him to bring me some peonies from the cutting garden last spring and he brought me daisies."

Undaunted by his wife's sarcasm, Kim plowed on. "So the door to the greenhouse opens. I stop, as anyone would. The girl or woman sticks her head out and looks around as if she doesn't want to be seen. I duck a little lower behind the vines, then she creeps out and in her arms—wait for it—she has three stalks of purple foxglove."

"Really? How do you know it was foxglove?" Genevieve was skeptical.

"Because my mother grew foxglove in her garden in China

and when I was very young. She took me around the garden and told me about each plant. Which plants were annuals, which were perennials, which smelled good, and, of course, which were poisonous. She had a beautiful dark purple foxglove plant that looked like it would taste like grape. She told me I should never touch it or eat it. But I loved grape. Grape candy, grape juice, grape jelly. So naturally I tried it one day when she was at one of her many clubs. I only put one blossom in my mouth, but it made me very sick." Kim paled at the memory. "Not only that, but when she got home and learned the story from my bao mu, my nanny, I was in real trouble. Being really sick and really in trouble at the same time is the worst. Anyway, my doubting friend," he pointed at Genevieve, "that's how I know it was foxglove."

"That's a pretty important piece of information, Kim." Philip cut a piece of pork and swirled it in currant sauce. He held it on his fork while he said, "It's a shame you don't have any idea who it was." He put the fork in his mouth and couldn't help but hum with pleasure.

Olivia took a drink of her wine and set her glass down. "What color was the scarf?" she asked.

"It was blue and purple. A paisley design, I believe. I was several yards away so I can't be sure."

"Do you have any other bits of information you didn't realize you had?"

"Let me dig into the vault and see what else I can come up with. Ah, yes. After seeing the person come out, I continued down the path and passed Edouard. I'm sure by then our mystery lady was gone so I doubt if he saw her." He held his empty wine glass for Philip to see. "You know, Philip, I think a bit more of your lovely claret would loosen up any information that still be lodged up here." He tapped his forehead.

Philip popped to his feet. "So sorry, Kim. I didn't see your glass was empty." He grabbed another bottle of the Château Beaulieu claret, sliced the foil in one swift motion, and slipped the cork from the bottle neck with a whish of air. "Let this breathe a minute, Kim." He raised an eyebrow and flashed a smile. "If you can."

While he was standing, Philip uncorked a bottle of La Vie Douce, the much-anticipated dessert wine, and smiled at Lian, who rewarded him with a smile of her own. As if on cue, Sophie entered the petit salon and cleared the entrée plates, which were again bare.

Very shortly, Sophie was back with Lizette, each carrying trays of individual chocolate soufflés dusted with a fine sprinkle of sucre glace, and a small offering of raspberries mounded to the side of the ramekin. As the servers laid a dessert in front of each diner, an appreciative burst of applause broke out. Lizette and Sophie nodded and grinned as they left the room, knowing their beautiful desserts were appreciated.

Philip lounged back in his chair and raised his glass. For a moment, he simply admired the rich caramel color, mesmerized by a candle dancing on the other side of the liquid.

"Philip?" Genevieve said. "Were you going to make a toast?"

Brought back into the moment, Philip chuckled at himself and raised his glass a bit higher. "Yes, darling girl, I was. All of us around this table are privileged people. And this evening we are incredibly privileged to share an extraordinary bottle of wine. La Vie Douce was the brainchild of Lian's husband Hank, and, true to its name—the sweet life—it is to be appreciated and enjoyed. We hope to help Lian resurrect this lovely dessert wine. To La Vie Douce."

"La Vie Douce," everyone echoed, and tasted their first sip. No one spoke, but the sounds of enjoyment resounded. Sighs and "mms" and second sips occupied everyone.

"This is really delicious." Julia was the first to break the silence. "This is the wine your husband created?"

"Yes." Pain flashed in Lian's eyes. "He worked so hard to create something wonderful and then had to give it all up."

"What happened to the wine, the formula, the whole operation?" Julia wanted to know more.

"Do you mind, Lian, if we talk about this?" Philip looked at Lian with warmth.

"No, Philip. None of this is a secret." Her voice had an edge but her expression was pleasant. "I know you are anxious to see if you can bring La Vie Douce to market."

"You're right," Philip said. "We are anxious to bring Hank's extraordinary wine to people who will love it and we want to do that with you, Lian. But those are conversations for the coming days. Drink up, everyone. Enjoy."

Kim clapped his hands, startling everyone. "And thanks to that very fine wine, I just remembered what else I saw at the greenhouse," he said.

"Wow. The more he drinks, the more he remembers." Julia was impressed. "Speaking strictly as a physician, alcohol usually has the opposite effect on people. It certainly does on me." She blushed as her laugh came out as a snort. "Tell us, Kim. What else did you remember?"

Leaning back in his chair, he tilted his head and gazed up at the ceiling as if to remember better. He looked back at everyone around the table and rubbed his hands for drama. "As I said before, the woman came out of the greenhouse carrying stalks of foxglove. Rather than walking toward the Château, she walked toward the stables. I didn't think anything about it at the time, but now knowing all the things that have happened, everything seems to be an alarm bell."

"So that's what you remembered?" Duncan said. "She walked in the direction of the stables?"

"That, and the fact that thirty seconds before I was about to leave, another person came out of the greenhouse. That person was in a big black duffle coat, black pants, and heavy boots. That person was wearing a hat pulled way down and dark glasses. I can't tell you if that person was a man or a woman, but I have no doubt, like the other person, they were up to no good." Kim made the sign of a mic drop.

THIRTY-TWO

"**W**HEN WAS THIS posted?"

"About ten minutes ago."

Lillie and Richard stared at the computer screen, their heads nearly touching as he looked over her shoulder.

Lillie tapped Philip's number on her contacts. She waited for the phone to connect, then listened as it rang. Three rings later, his voice came on asking the caller to leave a voicemail. "Call me. It's urgent," was Lillie's message.

She punched Genevieve's contact and the same thing happened. When the tone sounded, Lillie said, "I've just left a message for Philip. Whoever gets this first, call me immediately." She texted each of them with the same message, then pressed Finn's number. He answered on the second ring.

"Hello, beautiful girl." Warmth filled the line.

"And hello right back at you, but before you say anything else, I need to tell you this is a business call and it's an emergency."

"Talk to me."

"I'm sending you a link." She copied the link and pasted it into the body of an email and addressed it to him. She hit send. "It's on its way. And I'm putting you on speaker. Richard Durand is here so don't say anything that would embarrass me."

"Tempting. Very tempting. Bonjour, Richard. Now, what am I looking at?" he asked, after scanning an online article about dastardly deeds at the LMBA. "Who is Elise Beaufoy?"

Richard and Lillie looked at each other. "Do you want to tell him or should I?" Lillie felt as if she were living a nightmare.

"By all means. Ladies first." Richard backed away from the computer, slouched to the other side of Lillie's desk, and slumped into a chair.

"What a gentleman you are, Richard." She shot him a withering glance. "Elise Beaufoy is a friend of the Warwicks and a recently appointed board member of the Laney Museum of Fine Arts Foundation. Not only that, but she is also the president of the board of La Cité du Vin Foundation. Both high-profile positions."

Lillie's mouth was so dry, her lips stuck together as she spoke. She poured a glass of water from a silver carafe sitting on her desk and took several gulps.

She wiped her damp lips with the back of her hand. "Now, where was I?" she said. "Finn, remember when I told you about the previous museum Directeur selling counterfeit paintings to organizations, then selling the originals to private collectors and keeping the money?"

"I do. That's a clever scheme. I might want to use it sometime."

"Very funny, you. This article accuses Elise of being the architect of that scheme, which is preposterous." She took another long drink of water. "The moment we found out what

Bernard was doing, we replaced the paintings. Elise was the person on La Cité du Vin Foundation board who worked most closely with us to resolve the issue. She had nothing to do with perpetrating the fraud.

"When this happened last fall La Cité du Vin Foundation felt there was no benefit to the incident becoming public knowledge and we agreed to keep it between our two organizations. Apparently someone in one of our operations made a different decision."

Richard sat forward, put his elbows on the table, and leaned toward Lillie's phone. "Finnegan, you know all about the barrage of terrible rumors in the last couple of months, but this is by far the worst. Until now, all the stories have been focused on discrediting the House of Crosswick and all its good work. This new slur is even more treacherous. Elise Beaufoy and her husband are huge donors to the foundation. She's not going to be amused by this accusation. It doesn't matter that it's outrageous and false. The damage has already been done."

"Sadly, you're right, Richard. Let me gather the team and see where we are. I know they made progress yesterday tracking the platforms that are fomenting these stories. Is there anything else I should know that could speed up our investigation?"

Lillie and Richard stared at each other across Lillie's desk for a long moment, searching their minds for any detail they had left out.

"Hello. Did I lose you?" Finn finally asked.

"No. No, we're here." There was another brief silence before Lillie said, "Finn, yesterday just before you called, I was on the phone with Peter Fletcher, an arts reporter for *The Times*. He seems to think he has a reliable source who can confirm that the foundation, the museum and the family are all under investigation for art fraud. I'm supposed to meet with him later this week."

"I'll assume he's not going to give up his source so we could talk to them."

"Of course not."

"I think, given the evolving circumstances, you need to cancel that meeting or take a solicitor with you. I don't want you in a position to be threatened."

Lillie's heart fluttered at the note of warmth in Finn's voice, and without a moment's hesitation she said, "I'll cancel."

"Good. I'm glad I don't have to wrestle with you over that."

"Finn, there's one more thing. I'm sure you remember when we talked about Olivia a couple of days ago. She's very clever with computers. Do you think she might be the one instigating all the rumors?"

"Believe me, Lillie, she's at the top of our list."

THIRTY-THREE

WALKING INTO THE Gherkin building at 30 St. Mary Axe in the heart of the London financial district was like walking into a glass bullet. Though the building was two decades old and considered by many to be outdated technology, Finn thought of it as hip and cutting edge. He loved striding past centuries-old English architecture to the plaza where the Gherkin stood. He loved walking under the steel diamond framework into the atrium dotted with soaring potted trees.

Every time he stepped off the elevator onto the floor of MIS, Mountbatten International Security, the view of London took his breath away. He loved the deceptively serene reception, a calm façade hiding the intense energy in the offices just behind the mahogany paneling and large contemporary paintings.

In the mid-sixties, Finn's grandfather, who had a coveted appointment to the Lord Chamberlain's office, decided, much to his family's dismay, to leave the Royal Household and become an entrepreneur. He had too much vision and ambition to dedicate his life to protocol, state visits, investitures, and garden parties. When he gazed into the future, *his future*, it was filled with technology. And with that new technology, security needs would explode. Believing he could mold his fate, he walked out of Buckingham Palace and never looked back.

MIS would soon celebrate its sixtieth anniversary. In those six decades, many of the largest, most powerful companies in the world had come to rely on MIS to protect their interests, their assets, and their people.

Finnegan James Mountbatten was the new generation, the architect of the next sixty years. His mission was to ensure the firm was state of the art. MIS was on the leading edge of artificial intelligence and all it could do for their clients. They had an entire division dedicated to responsible use of all that was new and, to so many people, terrifying. There was not a better-equipped, better-staffed security company in the world, and Finn had already brought the full force of Mountbatten International Security to bear on the instigator of the trials his beloved Warwick family was suffering. His team had quickly tracked the source of many of the recently planted rumors and, though the trail was cleverly bounced from country to country with several layers of encryption, it was clear the creator was an amateur. A clever amateur to be sure, but certainly no match for Finnegan Mountbatten and his world-class security team. It was time for him to head back to Château Beaulieu and the Warwick family.

THIRTY-FOUR

"ELLA, COME BACK here! You know Mom and Dad don't want you to go in the stables alone. You're only seven! You might get hurt!" Alex yelled at his little sister, who had run ahead of him to the top of the hill. She glanced back at him then went over the crest and out of sight, no longer under his watchful eye.

He had promised his mother he wouldn't let that happen. He picked up his pace and jogged up the small rise. Just as he got to the ridge, he saw Ella pause with her hand on the doorknob.

She looked at her brother who was nearly fifty yards back up the hill.

Alex shook his head vigorously and pulled his phone from his back pocket. He rapidly punched "WAIT FOR ME!" in all caps, then sent the text. Apparently hearing the ping, Ella unzipped the pocket of her riding jacket, pulled out her phone and looked at her brother's message. Squinting into the sun, she glanced toward Alex and gave him a dismissive wave. She stuffed her phone in the front pocket of her breeches, pulled the door open, and stepped into the stables.

"Ella!" Anger exploded in his shout. "Boy, is she going to be in trouble," he huffed as he loped down the gentle slope. Halfway down the hill, a shout from Émile stopped Alex in his tracks. The vineyard worker was running toward him, cheerfully waving his hand.

"Émile, what's up? What's going on?"

"Ca va?" Émile yelled into the wind as he sprinted the last few yards up the path. When he got to Alex, he bent over, his hands on his knees, his breath rapid and shallow. "How have you been?"

"Great. We had a wild Christmas with the explosion!" Alex was pleased to have something sensational to tell the older boy. "It was really something."

"I heard. I am very glad Mademoiselle Langdon was all right. Have they found out what happened?"

Alex shrugged his shoulders. "I don't know. Maybe."

"Where is Ella? I'm supposed to introduce her to her new riding instructor. She's going to have a lesson on Commander, isn't she?"

"Yeah." Alex wasn't happy about sharing his horse, but until Jolie Fille was found, he was trying to be a generous brother.

In the background the faint, throaty growl of a motor floated on the wintery breeze that whipped across the crest of the hill.

Émile froze and leaned into the wind, ears pricked. "Did you hear that motor?"

"Ah, sort of," Alex said.

"That's a beautiful sound. It's a Ducati Superleggera V4."

Alex tried to look interested but he had no idea what a Ducati Superleggera V4 was.

"You know, a motorcycle."

"Right!" Alex still had no idea what Émile was talking about.

Émile closed his eyes, smiling at a wonderful memory. "I had that kind of bike before I came to Château Beaulieu. What a beauty she was." When he opened his eyes, they were full of hope. "I'll have another bike pretty soon. These roads would be a dream to ride on—tree-shaded, curvy."

Émile shaded his eyes with his hand and looked over the rows of vines toward the road, searching for any sign of the Ducati. When he saw none, he dropped his hand and brought his attention back to Alex. "Where *is* Ella?"

"She's already in the stables. She wasn't supposed to go in without me, but she did."

Alex was already trotting toward the barn and Émile easily met his stride. "Who's Ella's new riding instructor?" he asked, feeling very grownup running next to the much older boy.

"Her name is Felicity Coullard. She leads wine tours on horseback for some of the châteaux in the area and people say she is a very good instructor. I have met her several times and I like her." He winked at Alex as if they were friends. "She's very pretty."

"Do you want her to be your girlfriend?" Alex said.

Émile laughed and his eyes twinkled at Alex. "Ah, oui. Olivia seems to have lost interest in me, so I would like that very much."

Alex was flattered the older boy would confide in him, but he didn't understand why Émile would want a girlfriend. He had nothing in common with any of the girls he knew, except Angelique Beauville. But he didn't really think of her as a girl.

He thought of her as the best football goalie he'd ever had on his team.

When they got to the door, it stood open several inches and Alex could feel the warmth from inside on his cold cheeks. As he and Émile stepped into the barn, Alex yelled, "Ella! You weren't supposed to come in here without me. I'm going to tell Mom and you're going to be in real trouble. I bet you won't be able to ride for a week."

His little sister didn't reply. "Ella!" Alex yelled again. "Where are you?"

Only the sound of a horse's tail swishing and a pony's gentle snort could be heard. "Ella Laney Warwick, you'd better stop playing hide and seek. This is not funny." Though he tried to sound stern, Alex's voice wavered as his unease edged into fear. He and Émile trotted from stall to stall peering into each enclosure, each time expecting to see Ella's impish face grinning up at them.

Émile put his hand on Alex's shoulder and they stopped in the middle of the aisle. "Ella! Felicity!" Émile called out, then cocked his head to listen. Silence.

Alex was just opening his mouth to repeat Émile's words when they heard the faintest groan. Alex closed his mouth and the moan sounded again. The boys looked at each other, confused by what they heard.

Émile narrowed his eyes at Alex and pressed his forefinger to his lips. He pointed in the direction of the noise and together they crept toward the tack room at the end of the aisle. The moan turned to a whimper and then, just before they rounded the corner into the equipment bay, the whimper morphed into a raspy, "Help!"

In an instant the two were in the saddle room dropping to their knees by Felicity, who was crumpled on the floor, her pretty face drained of color and the blonde hair on the crown of her head matted with blood.

"Merde!" Émile said under his breath. He yanked his phone out of his jeans pocket and jabbed at Henri's number. It rang twice and Henri answered. Before he could say hello, Émile overwhelmed the line. "Henri, you need to come to the stable. You need to come now!"

The French was so rapid fire that Alex had no hope of following what Émile was saying to Henri, but he didn't have to understand the words. He knew there was serious trouble. He knew he was squatting next to a girl who was hurt and he knew his sister wasn't in the stables. His vision swam with the tears that filled his eyes and he bit his upper lip to keep from crying. He wanted to be brave, but he wanted his mom and dad, and he wished they would come through the barn door. He squeezed his eyes tight, sniffed away a sob, and wished again for his parents to burst through the door with Ella between them. As if a genie were granting his wish, he heard the stable door open at the far end of the barn.

"Alex! Ella! Where are you?"

When he heard his father's thundering voice, the dam broke and Alex sobbed, "Dad, we're here in the tack room." He could hear footsteps running toward them on the brick floor. When his parents burst into the room, Alex sprang to his feet and threw himself into his father, who lifted him and hugged him to his chest. Duncan looked around the tack room then down at Julia who squatted on the floor next to a pretty young girl with a gash on her forehead.

"Alex, where's your sister?" he said as he set his son on the floor. "Where's Ella?"

"I don't know, Daddy. Maybe she ran back to the Château to get help," he said, hoping that was exactly what she had done.

Julia looked up and swept her eyes over Émile. "Are you all right?"

"Oui, my lady."

"What happened here?"

She angled her head toward the girl beside her. "I assume this is Felicity?"

Émile nodded.

As Julia shifted from a squat to kneeling next to Felicity, something cut into her knee. "Ow!" she winced. "What the…!" She looked down to see the claw of a driving hammer, used for shoeing horses, sticking out from under Felicity's elbow. Julia lifted the girl's arm, used her knee to move the hammer to the side and noticed blood on the head of the hammer. She gently laid the girl's arm back on the brick floor, grasped Felicity's wrist, and was relieved to find her pulse rapid but strong. "Felicity, can you hear me?"

"Oui, madame," she said, and opened her eyes. Her voice was weak, but she sounded alert.

"Follow the light with your eyes, please." Julia used the flashlight on her phone as a penlight and was pleased to find Felicity could follow the light and her pupils were reactive.

"Alex, hand me the first aid kit in that cabinet." She jerked her head toward the cupboard on the far wall next to where the bridles hung on pegs. He ran to the cabinet, snatched the emergency kit, and dashed back to his mother, who gave him a quick kiss on the forehead. "Thank you, darling."

Alex sat touching her arm, his head resting on her shoulder. She glanced at him, wanting him to scoot over, but when she saw his red, watery eyes, she understood he needed to be close.

Shifting his focus from his son, who appeared to be fine, Duncan cleared his throat to get Émile's attention.

"Émile." Duncan motioned for the young man to step out into the aisle. Not wanting to miss a thing, Alex was right behind them. "What happened here?"

"Mon dieu, my lord," Émile began. "I am not exactly certain what happened before, but when Alex and I came into the écuries, the stables, we thought Ella was playing hide and seek with us and—"

Alex interrupted: "We yelled and yelled, but nobody answered then—"

It was back to Émile. "We heard a groan and found Felicity. We don't know what happened to her or where Ella is."

Duncan thought he had misheard. "What do you mean you don't know where Ella is? Alex, I thought you said she went back to the house to get help?"

"No, Dad. I said *maybe* Ella went back to the house to get help." His lower lip quivered. *I am not going to cry. I am not going to cry,* he said to himself, even as he felt the threatening sting of tears.

Duncan took a calming breath. "Okay. She has her phone.

We'll call her and find out where she is." He punched in her number and waited. The phone went directly to voicemail and Duncan felt a jolt of panic when he heard Ella's sweet voice asking him to leave a message.

Duncan's phone pinged and he looked at a text that had just come in. Much to his relief, Henri was on his way with Picard. He responded for them to meet at the Château, hit send, and put his phone in his shirt pocket. He put a hand on his son's shoulder. "Okay, Alex. As quickly as possible, tell me what happened from the time she ran ahead until you and Émile found Felicity in the tack room."

Together the boys filled in the story, trying to remember every detail. When they finished, Alex squinted at his dad. "How did you know to come to the barn?"

"Wasn't that a stroke of luck?" Duncan said. "Your mom and I came down to meet Felicity and watch Ella's lesson. We were almost here when we got a call from Henri saying there was some trouble. And it looks like he was right."

Not wanting to alarm his son, he said, "Alex, Émile, would you two go back to the house and find Ella? When she didn't see Felicity, she probably went back to the Château, just like you said, Alex."

"Sure, Dad." Alex brightened. "That makes sense. She probably went out this back door. Look, it's unlocked." He gave the door a shove and it creaked open. "If you go this way, there's a shortcut through the vineyard."

"We shall then report back, my lord," Émile said. Realizing Duncan wanted Alex back at the Château, shielded from whatever happened next, he gave his boss a sharp nod, assuring Duncan he would take care of his son.

Duncan grabbed Alex in a headlock and gave him a noogie. "Go, you two. I need to get back in to help your mother. Call the moment you find Ella," Duncan ordered as he strode back into the tack room. "We'll be there as soon as we take care of Felicity."

The riding instructor had moved from the floor to the upholstered bench running the full length of the left side of the room. Her head rested against the oak-paneled wall and her eyes were closed. Each time Julia dabbed at the small gash on her forehead with an antiseptic-soaked cotton ball, Felicity winced.

"Have you had a chance to find out what happened?" Duncan whispered.

Julia shook her head but kept her eyes on what she was doing. "I think she might have been knocked out briefly. I want to make sure she isn't concussed before we ask her any questions."

"Should I call an ambulance?"

"No. I think she's all right. I just want to be certain."

The pretty girl opened her hazel eyes and Julia gave her a smile that was a bit too bright. "No stitches required and there doesn't seem to be a concussion." She patted Felicity on the hand, then dug around in the first aid kit until she found just the right size bandage.

While she finished doctoring Felicity's wound, Duncan paced up and down the tack room.

"Duncan, darling. Could you please bring the golf cart to us? Let's get Felicity to the house, get her some ibuprofen and a brandy. How does that sound, Felicity?"

The girl had yet to say more than a few words. She had mostly whimpered and groaned. But at the suggestion of going to the Château for a little pampering, she perked up. "Oui," she said. "I would like that."

Duncan ran the length of the stables to where the cart stood at the ready, just inside the front door. Within seconds he was back.

"À votre service, mesdemoiselles," Duncan said.

As Julia eased Felicity into the cart, she said, "When we get you settled in, do you think you'll feel up to telling us what happened?"

"Ah, mais oui. I must tell you everything."

"Did someone hit you with the driving hammer?" Julia asked in her most comforting voice.

"Oui, madame. It was a beautiful woman."

"A beautiful woman?" All Julia could think of was perhaps Charlotte had made a ghostly appearance.

"Oui. A blonde woman with eyes like lilas."

"Lilas? I don't know this word."

"You know. An arbuste, a shrub that is violette and smells so beautiful."

Julia thought for a moment. "Ah! A lilac bush."

"Oui, oui!" Felicity clapped her hands and regretted the motion immediately.

Julia laid her hand on Felicity's shoulder. "Try to remain as quiet as possible for the next few hours."

"I think that is a very good idea. I shall do that." Fatigue had darkened circles around her eyes.

Julia took Felicity's hand in hers. It was icy and Julia let her fingers drift to the young woman's wrist. She glanced at her watch and counted the beats for fifteen seconds then announced, "Your pulse is excellent. You're an amazing lassie, as a friend of ours would say. One last thing before you go up to the Château. The beautiful woman with lilac eyes?"

"Oui." This time Felicity was careful not to move her head.

"What was the woman doing in the stables? Do you have any idea?"

"I thought I did." This time she nodded gingerly. "When I came in to saddle Commander, she was in his stall. She had a needle and was about to inject him with something. I thought she must be the vétérinaire who had come to give vaccinations. I said 'Bonjour,' and she asked me what I was doing here. She had an English or American accent."

"And you said she had blonde hair?" A wave of nausea swept over Julia.

"Oui. She had a blonde queue de cheval, you know, a ponytail."

Julia and Duncan locked on each other's eyes. "Olivia," they said together.

Blood rushed so loudly in her ears that Julia could no longer hear Felicity who was still telling her story. "I told her I was there to give Ella a riding lesson and she looked so surprised and happy I thought she must be a friend of Ella's. When she came toward me, I thought she was going to give me la bise, which would have been very strange since I did not know her, but she did not. Instead, she laughed and said, 'This is perfect, just perfect.' Then she struck me on the head and everything went black. When I woke up, I was on the floor in the tack room."

"Did you ever see Ella?"

"Non. I don't know if she came or not. This is all very strange and a bit frightening, non?"

Sitting in the driver's seat, Duncan was ready to hit the accelerator. "Get on the back of the cart, Julia. We're taking the shortcut."

THIRTY-FIVE

DUNCAN PRESSED THE accelerator to the floor and was getting all the speed the cart had to give. They bumped along aisles, bouncing between the vines until they shot out of the field onto the stone headland at the top of the rows, Felicity bracing herself as best she could. Before the golf cart came to a stop at the kitchen door, Julia was off the back and running into the house. That left Duncan to help the injured riding instructor through the Château and into the grand salon where she could be looked after until her family came to collect her.

"Ella! Ella! Ella!" Julia streaked from room to room shouting for her daughter, then started up the stairs

When she heard Julia yelling, Delphine strode into the foyer. "Lady Julia, Alex and Émile told us what happened. We have looked all over the house and Ella isn't here."

Julia whipped around and the panic in her eyes frightened the head of the house. "I'm going to check her room." She choked on the words. She turned back around, grabbed the wrought iron rail, and took the stairs two at a time. She ran down the hall and into Ella's room. As she stood in the doorway searching for anything that might give her a clue where the little girl might be, she choked down sobs. Her eyes raced over Ella's bed, overflowing with stuffies. Julia stepped into the pretty room and began walking from one piece of furniture to the next. On Ella's desk, books were organized in three short stacks, each pile its own genre. Julia ran her hand over the snow globe that had pride of place next to a small sculpture of a ballerina Genevieve had given her for her third birthday when she had begun dance lessons. Her phone charger was draped over her computer screen and next to her computer her iPad was plugged in. She turned toward her daughter's reading chair and was bending over to pick up a t-shirt that had not made it to the clothes hamper when she froze. She whipped back around to Ella's desk and her eyes focused like lasers on the phone charger.

"We know she has her phone," she said under her breath. When Duncan called Ella, it had gone to voicemail. But there was another option they hadn't yet tried. "She has her phone!" She bellowed it this time. She pulled her own phone out of the back pocket of her jeans, tapped Ella's name and her sweet face flooded the screen. She tapped the "KIDS" icon on her home screen, found the child tracking platform, and hit it. Almost instantly a map loaded and Ella's memoji pinpointed her location.

Julia stared at the screen but didn't understand what she was looking at. It appeared as if Ella were right here in the front yard of Château Beaulieu. Half expecting to see her little girl jumping rope on the lawn, she dashed to the window overlooking the front of the house. Ella was not there. She bolted out of Ella's bedroom, raced back down the hall, and flew down the stairs, nearly tripping twice.

"Duncan!" she screamed. "Where are you? I know how we can find Ella. Where are you?"

Just as she hit the last step, he strode into the foyer with Alex, Émile, and Delphine on his heels.

"We've been combing the house and she's not here. How are we going to find her?" The fear in Duncan's eyes made Julia wince.

"Look, look." She held up her phone. "Ella's phone is on the tracking app."

She turned to her son. "Alex, when you last saw Ella did she have her phone?"

"Yes," he said, eager to provide any information he could. "Just before she went into the stables, I texted her to wait for me. I was still at the top of the hill. She looked at her phone, waved at me, and went in. I was so mad that I screamed at her." His face clouded at the memory and Julia saw his eyes were misty.

"Well, thank god she has her phone." Julia whooshed out an enormous breath and felt an inkling of hope. "Look at this."

As she showed Duncan the map on her phone, Henri and Picard burst through the front door without knocking, Picard blazing with questions.

"Tell me everything. Where is the riding instructor? Is she all right? Was she attacked or was it an accident?"

Duncan held up his hands to silence the chef. "The plot has thickened and the most crucial thing is, Ella is missing." Though he was trying to stay calm, he nearly screamed the words. "Luckily, she has her phone, and as long as it's with her and switched on we might be able to find her." He thrust Julia's phone at Picard. "Can you tell where she is?"

The chef studied the screen, zooming in, zooming out. He was thinking so hard, Julia thought she could smell his brain sizzling. At last, recognition flashed in his eyes. "Is it possible Ella would go to visit Château Pitique?"

"What? No." Duncan couldn't imagine Picard had read the location correctly. "You think the locator says our daughter is at Château Pitique? What in the hell would she be doing there?"

"My lord, I do not know why Ella would be at your neighbor's Château, but that appears to be where she is, or at least where her mobile is."

"Let's go." Julia threw the armoire door open and yanked out a coat. When she pulled it on, its shoulders jutted well beyond her own and the sleeves hung inches below her fingertips

"This is Philip's," she said, peeling it off and throwing it on the floor. She reached for a parka she knew was hers.

Delphine had already rehung Philip's coat and was holding a blue Barbour wax jacket for Duncan. He shoved his arms into the sleeves and was ready to go.

"Moment. Moment," Chef Picard said. "Do you not think we should discuss our plan before we start?"

"There's nothing to discuss." Julia was already charging toward the door, where Henri was waiting with his hand on the knob. When she saw him standing there, her eyes widened. "You're going with us, Henri?"

She saw a flash of hurt cross his face. "Mais oui, my lady. I am always here for the family."

With a lump in her throat, Julia stood on tiptoes, kissed his cheek, then pulled the door open to find Finnegan and Becca standing on the stoop, his hand raised to grab the door knocker.

"Finn! Oh my god! Becca!" Julia burst into tears and threw her arm around Becca's neck. "What are you two doing here together?" she asked when she got herself under control.

"We happened to be on the same plane from Gatwick and sat next to each other on the flight." Becca pulled a tissue from her pocket and wiped Julia's cheeks. "We've been comparing notes for the last three hours. What's been happening here?"

"Yeah, tell us. What have we walked into?" Finn braced himself.

By now Duncan had walked the length of the foyer and was at the entrance. He pulled Finn and Becca across the threshold and nudged Julia back so he could close the door. With words flying, he and Julia gave the two newcomers a recap of what had happened within the last hour.

"Where are your parents?" Finn asked Duncan.

"Of all the times to take Wallace and Mrs. MacIntosh back to Wilmingrove Hall, this is when they chose. They left yesterday and plan to stay for a week or so."

"Have you talked to them? Do they know what's going on?"

"No, Finn. There hasn't been time to tell them. Does it matter?" Duncan snapped.

Finnegan put his hand on his friend's arm. "Just calm down, Duncan. Show me what you have on the tracking app."

Duncan breathed in, then out. "Sorry, Finn."

Finnegan shook his head, dismissing Duncan's apology. He took Julia's phone, squinted at the screen, and zoomed in. Absorbed in what he saw on the screen, he said nothing for several seconds. "Ella's mobile is close to here, just up the street, but that's not all. I came to tell you my team tracked the location where the latest rumors have been generated and it looks to me as if it's exactly the same location as where your tracking app has pinpointed Ella's mobile."

Becca followed up immediately. "And I'm here because of the pages I emailed your parents, Duncan. The entries I found in Olivia's journal indicate she and Lian have been working together for several months to destroy the House of Crosswick's reputation."

Both Julia and Duncan stood with their mouths hanging open, unable to speak, not knowing what to say. Duncan shook his head. "I don't know what you're talking about, Becca. Mom and Dad didn't say anything about Olivia and Lian working together. I don't understand. There's no way they would have that information and not share it with us, the people staying at the Chateau with Olivia. They wouldn't put their grandkids in danger like that." He looked at Julia. "I don't understand," he said again.

"I don't need to understand." Julia was heading out the door again. "Whether or not anyone else is going with us, Henri and I are leaving now. I'm going to get my little girl."

"Mom, Dad, I'm coming with you." Alex dashed for his coat, but Duncan grabbed him by the arm.

"Buddy, you need to stay here just in case Ella isn't at Château Pitique and comes back here. Okay?"

Alex thought for a moment, then nodded. "I guess that makes sense. And I'll call you if she comes home."

Duncan smiled into Alex's very grown up, very solemn face.

He couldn't help but bend down and kiss his cheek. "Thanks, Alex," he said.

Picard dashed to his police car, the gang of five stepped across the threshold and the sprint was on. With Henri at the lead, they barreled down the path toward the garage and bolted through the door into the cavernous building.

"We'll take the G-Class Mercedes." Henri pointed to a bronze SUV Julia had always thought looked like a big matchbox toy. He shot into the office, grabbed the keys, and was behind the wheel before everyone was belted in. The garage door rumbled up, the engine revved, and the boxy hunk of metal squealed out into the morning. They followed Picard's souped-up Citroën and the two cars streaked down the road to the neighboring chateau to rescue Ella.

THIRTY-SIX

"Listen to me carefully," Picard said, leaning through the Mercedes window so everyone could hear him. "All of you stay in the car. This is police business and another unit is on its way."

"No. I don't want to wait out here." Julia was defiant. She had no intention of surrendering control of Ella's rescue, if that was what this was.

Having just called for backup, Chef Picard tucked his mobile into his breast pocket and buttoned the flap. "My lady, I am the Directeur de Police Municipal and this is a police matter," he said. "We have a little girl who is missing and presumed kidnapped."

When Julia heard the word "kidnapped", dizziness flooded her brain and black wavered around the edge of her vision.

Honoring Picard's directive, Henri said, "I shall make certain everyone remains in the car, chef?"

"Merci, Henri. I shall approach the door and ring the bell as if I am simply paying a visit."

Still ready to follow, Julia reached over the seat back and clutched Duncan's shoulder. Without looking back, he covered her hand and squeezed it. Though she was skeptical of the plan, she didn't know what else to do but follow Picard's lead. They were trespassing on someone else's property. Their only clue that Ella might be here was a phone app, but the phone and Ella weren't necessarily together. She had to put her trust in someone and guessed Picard was as good as anyone: an experienced cop and a friend who was almost as anxious to find Ella as they were. So they would let the professional do his job.

The house was two centuries older than Château Beaulieu and the weathered stones loomed into the sky. Chef Picard squared his shoulders and marched up the stairs to the imposing entrance. He raised the tarnished knocker and rapped it against the oak panel. The door moved on its hinges and eased open just enough to feel the warmth from inside. Picard looked over his shoulder to confirm everyone was still in the car. He turned back around and pushed gently on the door. It creaked as it opened and Picard stopped then started again, pushing until it was open enough to walk through. He poked his head inside, looking for any sign someone was home. He stepped in, unholstered his gun, cradled it in two hands, and crept down the hall in a half-crouch, his eyes darting back and forth. He heard a rustle behind him and when he glanced back, there were five people lined up behind him like penguins, waddling to catch up to him.

With a huff of disgust, Picard motioned for them to gather around him. As everyone leaned in, Picard seethed, "Vous êtes tous fous! You are all mad!" He took a breath, then whispered, "You should not be here, but if you are, I want everyone to stay behind me."

"Frederick, is the gun absolutely necessary?" Julia said, her eyes fixed on his pistol. The idea that Picard would have a drawn gun in the same room as Ella was terrifying.

"Oui, my lady. I want to be prepared for anything we may come upon. I promise I am an excellent marksman." His voice was so low Julia could barely hear his response.

Julia felt herself shaking and her breath quivered with each inhale. Duncan pulled her back against him, wrapped his arms around her, and whispered into her ear, "We're going to find her in this house, and she's going to be fine."

Julia swallowed a sob and pressed hard against Duncan. She closed her eyes, trying to keep her fear in check, then it was time to go forward.

Picard made a move down the wide foyer and the others followed so closely they almost stepped on each others' heels. Halfway down the hall, Picard stopped. As if they were in a Three Stooges movie, they rear ended each other—Julia running into Picard, Duncan into Julia, Becca into Duncan, Finn into Becca, until Henri stepped to the side to avoid running into anyone.

"Écoutez. Listen."

Everyone strained to hear something, anything. Finally, a lively melody drifted toward them.

When she heard it, Julia gasped. She couldn't believe her ears. "Duncan," she whispered loudly enough for everyone to hear. "Duncan, that's 'Gamine'."

Duncan looked blank.

"It's Ella's favorite. You know the Zaz song with all the clapping."

His flash of recognition was all she needed. "Frederick, Ella's here." She nudged the officer forward, but he didn't go far. "Let's go!" She was ready to storm the Château, tear every room apart, follow the lilting tune, and scoop Ella into her arms.

"I am going to proceed alone. We have no idea who is in there or what their mental state is. I can go in calmly and secure Ella's safety. You five stay right here."

"But I—" Julia started to object, but Picard held up his hand.

"I am putting my weapon away," he said as he re-holstered his gun. Julia noticed he didn't put the safety on or snap the strap over the handle, so he remained at the ready.

He turned, took a deep breath and stood a bit taller. As he walked away from the group, it was all Julia could do not to run after him. She wanted to be the one bursting into the room. She wanted to be the one to tear limb from limb the people who had taken her darling child. If Duncan hadn't been holding on to her arm, she would have done exactly that.

When Picard reached the end of the foyer, he stopped at the two French doors that led into a large, elegant salon overlooking a terrace and vines beyond. The five at the other end of the hall watched as Picard peered through the glass doors. Slowly he reached for the lever, pressed it gently down and inched the right door open. Zaz blasted through the opening. Picard continued to creep the door open until it stood wide. He stepped into the room and there at the far end of the salon in front of a waning fire, Olivia Conway lay on her back on a wide burgundy sofa, one arm flung over her face and the other limply hanging to the floor.

On a Persian carpet, Lian was on her stomach, her thick, black hair spiked around her face, her slender frame limp and still.

"Mort. Ils sont tous les deux morts," he mumbled to himself, certain they were both dead. As Chef de la Police in tranquil Saint-Émilion, he never saw dead people, much less two young beautiful corpses in one room. He felt hot, sour bile rise in his throat and clasped his hand over his mouth. His breath came quick and shallow as he knelt by Olivia and placed two fingers on her neck just under her chin. He heard a sharp scream and recoiled, then realized the sound had come from his own mouth as Olivia moaned and turned onto her side.

As he turned to Lian, who was stirring, he caught sight of two Champagne glasses and three empty bottles of Veuve Clicquot filling the coffee table and he noticed, for the first time, that the room smelled distinctively like skunk. Everywhere he looked were signs of partying, but nowhere did he see any sign of Ella, except on a side table, where her phone lay blasting "Gamine" over and over on her Spotify app.

THIRTY-SEVEN

Every member of the household was trying to find busy work to take their minds off their darling Ella's disappearance. Lizette tied her kerchief under her chin, took her old tweed coat from the peg, and shoved her arms into the sleeves. She grabbed her cutting basket and opened the mudroom door, squinting against the icy wind that blew in. She loved the walk across the terrace and down the stone path that skirted the vineyard office to the greenhouse. She knew that at this time of year, the moment she walked into the steel-and-glass building, humidity would fog her glasses and her shapeless coat would sag even more. Though a pall hung over the house, she refused to lose hope that before the sun set Ella would be home and ready for her favorite meal. That is what she would concentrate on, making Ella's favorite coq au vin, stewed chicken. And for that she needed thyme, bay leaves, and parsley, which meant a trip to the greenhouse.

She wiped her runny nose with the back of her gloved hand and dabbed her eyes as she trudged along. The thought of that darling girl being kidnapped was more than she could bear.

Last year when Ella came with her parents to live at Château Beaulieu, there wasn't one person on the estate who didn't fall in love with her.

What if—

She wouldn't let herself think about what if. She funneled her mind to dessert. What would make Ella clap her hands with delight? Something chocolate. Lizette mentally ran through a litany of chocolate treats: chocolate soufflés, gâteau royal, chocolate mousse… then she remembered. Hands down, Ella's favorite dessert was chocolate-filled profiteroles with chocolate ice cream.

Lizette put her shoulder to the door, turned the knob, and gave it a shove. Someone needed to take this door off its hinges and plane the bottom. It had been sticking for ages and it was getting worse. She stepped through the opening, turned, and had to give the door a mighty shove to get it closed behind her. She loved the smell of this old glass building: the earth, the moisture, the fragrance of the blossoms. She inhaled deeply as she walked down the aisle to the herbs. She pulled a tissue from her coat pocket and blew her nose.

She heard herself sniff, then realized she had not sniffed. She heard a whimper, then another sniff. She turned around and looked under the table full of rosemary, oregano, dill, parsley, and thyme and saw nothing. A stifled sob drew her attention to under the opposite table and there, with her arms wrapped around her shins and her chin on her knees, Ella looked out at Lizette with red eyes filled with tears and worry.

Lizette was immediately on her knees. "Ella," she cried, stretching her arm toward the little girl. "Come, ma petite."

"I don't think I can, Lizette. My mommy and daddy are going to be so mad at me."

"Darling, they are looking everywhere for you and they will be so happy to know you are here, at home."

"But I did so many naughty things." Her whimpers were turning into sobs. "I went into the stables b-by myself," she choked out. "And th-th-then Alex was m-m-mad at me and I lost my phone so I'm in real trouble now." Words tumbled over each other between sobs. "B-b-ut I didn't get on the motorcycle with Olivia because she didn't have a helmet for me, but then she got mad at me and yelled at me because I wouldn't go with her without a helmet, so *everybody's* mad at me. Now Olivia will tell Émile not to like me and I really want Émile to like me because he's really cute." By now she was weeping so hard it was almost impossible for Lizette to understand her.

"Ella," she said. When the crying child didn't respond, Lizette said, "Ella," more forcefully this time.

Ella looked out from under thick lashes shiny with tears.

Lizette stretched her hand out as far as she could without going under the table. "You need to come out right now. I don't have mon portable. I left it in the kitchen and we need to call your parents immediately."

"Where are they?" Ella asked as she crawled out from under the table.

"They are at Château Pitique because your tracking app said you were there."

"Olivia must have picked up my phone." Ella nodded her head. "Good," she said. "I didn't lose it."

Lizette gasped a laugh as she helped Ella to her feet. "Everything that is going on and you are worried about your mobile. Now that's funny. Come on, petit chou. We must let your parents know you are home and well."

THIRTY-EIGHT

W HEN JULIA, DUNCAN, Becca, Finn, and Henri burst through the kitchen door, Ella was sitting at the marble-topped island in the middle of the room while the kitchen staff bustled around preparing her favorite dinner for later in the day. She warmed her hands by cradling a steaming mug of hot chocolate and kept a watchful eye on a plate stacked with cookies she was sharing with Alex and Émile.

"Ella!" Her mother cried as she raced across the kitchen and smothered her little girl in an embrace.

Struggling to keep his tears at bay, Duncan stood in the doorway and watched his two girls. To his surprise, Alex slid off his stool and barreled into his father, throwing both arms around his dad and holding tight.

"We did it, Dad. We found her."

Duncan heard the muffled words sobbed into his coat and rubbed the back of Alex's head. "We sure did," he said as his eyes met Lizette's. "Thank you," he mouthed as a lone tear escaped and trailed slowly down his cheek.

When Alex finally eased his hold, Duncan and Julia gave Ella a bit of breathing room. It was Duncan's turn. He kissed the top of her head, wrapped his arms around her, and whispered in her ear, "So is that the last time you go into the stables by yourself?"

"Daddy, don't scold me! Not now. At least wait until after I finish my hot chocolate."

He spun her around on her stool and bent over so they were eye to eye. "In addition to scolding you, I also want to tell you how proud I am. Lizette said Olivia wanted you to go with her on her motorcycle, but you wouldn't because she didn't have a helmet for you." As the words came out of his mouth, he saw the stricken look on Julia's face and added, "You know you should never go on a motorcycle, period, but if you do—which you shouldn't—you should always wear a helmet. Just like when you ride horses. Good job!" They high fived, and as Duncan popped a cookie in his mouth, he felt his phone vibrate. He pulled it out and his father's face filled the screen. "Dad! Wow! Have you missed a lot."

Duncan gave Ella one more hug before he pushed his way through the swinging kitchen door into the foyer and toward the study, ready to fill his parents in on everything that had happened.

Halfway through the story, Philip and Genevieve were ready to fly back to France immediately. A half hour later, when Duncan had shared everything he knew, he was able to convince them to wait.

"Dad, Chef Picard has everything well in hand. He did a good job keeping all of us under control when we went to Château Pitique." He chuckled. "As you can imagine, that was not an easy task. Lots of alphas with lots of opinions."

Philip laughed at the other end of the conversation. "G, what do you think? Tomorrow or the next day?"

"If you really don't think we need to be there immediately, Duncan, we'll come back the day after tomorrow. Mrs. MacIntosh and I are taking care of a few things that need attention. And of course Wallace is blustering about how everything has gone to hell in a handbasket in his absence. He's even been down to the greenhouse. I've never known him to go to the greenhouse."

"I wouldn't expect anything else." Duncan could imagine Wallace with his iPad, marching through Wilmingrove Hall. He could envision the perfectionist making notes about every tiny thing he found out of place, or every fingerprint he saw on a mirror or on a polished table. Duncan was glad he was at Château Beaulieu and not the Hall.

"Chef Picard will be here as soon as he has interrogated Olivia and Lian, and I'm assuming they'll be officially under arrest. Until then, there's nothing else we can do. We'll call with any news." He stood and walked to the window. "As I said, it appears those two were responsible for everything. I don't know how they did it, but I'm certain all will be revealed. It didn't take Finn a minute to find out who's been stirring up all the rumors, so that's a huge problem solved, or if not solved, at least we know where to begin."

"Have you talked to Lillie and Richard yet? Oh, of course not. You haven't had time." Genevieve answered her own question.

"I thought Lillie should be here for the big reveal, don't you think? She's going to want to hear everything." Duncan watched a cluster of birds peck at the bark on the lemon trees dotted around the terrace.

"That's a good idea," Genevieve said. "Then we can make a plan to get the museums and foundation back on track." She hesitated. "And how is Becca?"

"She's certainly relieved Ella's okay. Again, we haven't had a chance to talk about the journal and Olivia's involvement in everything, but I got the impression Olivia's been putting everything in motion to do as much damage to our family as possible for several months. When the extent of Olivia's crimes is uncovered, you know Becca is going to be devastated."

"Absolutely. Olivia's a clever girl. With the exception of Wallace, she had all of us fooled, including Dr. Morgan. I'd say this was her last chance. I think she'll be under lock and key for a long time."

"Hey, did you two ever get the pages Becca emailed from Olivia's journal?"

"I didn't. In fact, I forgot all about them. Did you get them, Philip?"

"I'd have to go back in my billions of emails and check. I guess it's moot at this point."

Duncan could hear a voice in the background, then his mother said, "Darling, I need to go. Wallace has discovered some silver pieces were put back in the wrong place after they were polished. I'm afraid heads are going to roll if I don't intervene. Please kiss our grandchildren and we'll see you the day after tomorrow."

"I'll do it, Mom." He could hear her brisk footsteps on the marble floor of the grand foyer and pictured Wilmingrove Hall in all its glory. Standards were standards and Wallace wasn't going to allow the benchmark for the estate to be anything but excellence.

"Okay, Dad. Let me know what time Henri should pick you up."

"That would be great." There was a pause. "I guess I need to fill Wallace and Mrs. MacIntosh in on what's happened. I'm sure Wallace will be glad to hear Olivia is in police custody, but when I tell him what Ella went through, I'm afraid he's going to go berserk, even more than her father or grandfather. You know how he feels about her."

"I do. It's very sweet. He'd do just about anything for her."

THIRTY-NINE

"**P**ICARD!" THE CHEF de la Police barked into his phone.

"Frederick, this is Duncan Warwick."

Embarrassed by his curt tone, he said, "I am so sorry, my lord. I am driving back to the station and didn't see who was calling."

"Never mind." Duncan brushed off the chef's concern. "I have news you're going to want to hear. Ella is here."

"Quoi?" Picard didn't understand. "Ella is where?"

"She's here, at home. Delphine found her hiding in the greenhouse. We'll tell you more when you come to the Château, but we wanted you to know that she is safe and sound and never left the property."

Relief washed over Picard like an unexpected spring shower. Of all the events he believed Olivia and Lian had caused, Ella's disappearance was the one that terrified him. "That is spectacular news." He heard his voice quiver. "Tell her Jolie Fille will be home this afternoon. We found her in Chateau Pitique's stables."

"Thank you, Frederick." Duncan paused for several seconds. When he spoke again, his voice, too, was filled with emotion.

"Ella will be so happy. I know you'll keep us posted about what you find out from Olivia and Lian."

"Of course I shall, but I am afraid it will be several hours before they are in a position to talk. They had quite a fête and are pretty stoned, or drunk, or both. I believe it will be their last party for some time."

As he had anticipated, by the time Olivia and Lian were sober enough to be interrogated, the sun had set and Picard was out of patience. His team of four officers had spent the day combing through Château Pitique for evidence, securing computers and searching mobile call records and text threads. After a long day of waiting, he was more than ready to hear from the two suspects.

In his twenty years on the Saint-Émilion police force, this was only the third time he had interrogated two people at the same time. The other two were hardly worth mentioning. One was a fourteen-year-old boy and his sister who were stealing bikes and selling them, and the other was two women who were selling counterfeit Chanel handbags in their posh shop. They both said they had no idea the bags were fake and each pointed a finger at her partner. In the end, they both confessed. This is how it would be today, he thought. He would go back and forth playing one against the other until he got the full story.

He buttoned the top button of his shirt and slid his tie knot up until it was snug at his neck. He stood, rolled his shoulders to relieve the tension in his back, and slipped his arms into the sleeves of his jacket. He brushed each shoulder with his hand, inhaled and exhaled, and was ready to go. He snorted a laugh as he thought about the British and American police procedurals he loved to watch where the interrogator had a sidekick and there was a separate team to question each suspect. What a luxury. In Saint-Émilion, a town of just under 2,000 people where crime was rarely an issue, *he* was the interrogation team and the interrogation rooms were normally used for community activities.

On his way to the conference room where Olivia waited for him, he stopped by the break room and poured himself a cup of coffee from the cafetiere. He knew it would be bitter and cold by now but that would be just fine.

With a file folder under his arm and his hand resting on the door handle, he paused for several seconds to calm his breathing before entering the room. Olivia sat with her back to the door, her elbows on the table and her head cradled in her hands. She didn't turn when she heard him walk in.

Without speaking, he set his cup down, slapped the file folder on the table, and pulled out his chair, the metal feet scraping on the floor like fingernails on a chalkboard. Still, Olivia didn't move.

"Mademoiselle Conway," he began. "You have been read your rights and I would like to inform you that this interview is being recorded." He was relieved his voice was steady and showed no signs of how nervous he was. He pressed the button on the recorder and sat. "You are here because we have reason to believe

that you have been the instigator of quite a list of serious crimes."
He flicked the folder open and looked at the first of several pages.
"You quite possibly will be charged with two counts of attempted
murder, threat by written word, attempted animal abuse, vol de
chevaux…" He looked up from the page, searching for the English
word. "Ah, oui. Horse theft. Also attempted child abduction,
intentional violence, and several charges of cybercrimes."

As he read from the list, Olivia slowly raised her head until she
was looking at Picard through lank strands of hair. Her mascara
had smudged raccoon circles around her violet-blue eyes. He gave
her a toothy grin then took a sip of his tepid coffee. "I assume
you didn't realize how seriously we take fake news websites in
France, or perhaps you would have been more careful to disguise
who was doing them." He tutted. "Sloppy. Very sloppy work. Not
like you at all, non?"

"You're out of your mind," Olivia snarled. "The only thing
I've done is party a bit too hard with Lian Shou. You need to
bring her here. I assure you, she'll tell you we were just having
a girls' night. I have no idea what you're talking about with that
list of absurd accusations. I've been at Château Beaulieu living
through all the terrifying events. I'm a victim just like everyone
else in the family." She dropped her head back into her hands.

"Your wish is my command, Mademoiselle Conway. Lian
Shou is in the interrogation room next door."

Olivia's head shot up but this time her eyes were wide and
concerned.

"Yes, Olivia. You should be nervous," he said, gaining
confidence as he saw her anxiety rise. "This is a game of, um, do
you call it chicken? Whoever gives me information first has the

best chance of things going well for them. The last to share… not so much. But I must say," he waved the sheet of paper in the air, "if necessary, there are enough charges to keep you both in prison for a very long time. And, while you two slept away the day here in our charming accommodations, we have gathered quite a lot of convincing evidence."

Olivia lurched across the table and grabbed at the paper. As she plopped back in her chair, tears filled her eyes and she sobbed, "Frederick, Lian Shou is a terrible woman. She hates the Warwick family for what they did to Hank and for trying to take La Vie Douce from her. Everything that has happened at Château Beaulieu was her idea. She blackmailed me into helping her." Her eyes were wide, innocent, and pleading. "I'm so relieved that the truth is coming out. She told me if I didn't help her destroy the House of Crosswick, she would tell everyone that I planned everything. She would make certain I would never get out of Blain Lodge." She leaned across the table, took Frederick's fisted hands in hers, pulled them to her, and wept.

He felt her tears dampen his fingers as she held them tight and marveled at how convincing she was. Prying his hands from her clutches, he pushed out of his chair. "The interview was paused at 18:59," he said, and pressed the stop button on the recorder. "Mademoiselle Conway, Officer Millard will bring you a glass of water. I shall return in a while." He closed the folder, picked up his coffee, and walked to the door.

"Where are you going?" Olivia snapped. Instantly, her tears were gone, her damp cheeks the only evidence she had been weeping and pathetic.

He turned and said, "I am going to see what Madame Shou has to say. Do you like this game, Olivia? I think it is quite good."

He flashed a dashing smile and pulled the door closed as she shouted, "You bastard!"

He was beginning to enjoy himself. He nodded to the officer who had been sitting outside the door, a twenty-year-old who had recently completed her training. "Millard, take Mademoiselle Conway a cup of water. Do not talk to her," he warned. "Then come back out and sit right here." He pointed to the chair next to the door.

"Oui, chef," she said, and headed to the breakroom to carry out her boss' orders.

When Picard entered the community room, Lian was standing at the window looking through the smudged glass out onto the street.

"Madame Shou," he said.

She turned slowly until she faced him, her arms crossed and her head tilted.

"Please, come sit here." He pointed to the chair facing the door.

She didn't react for several seconds but finally walked to the designated chair, put her hands on the table, and eased her slender frame into the seat. She looked up at him with eyes that gave away nothing.

He sat, opened his folder, and took out his government pen. He made the same statement he had recited in the other room and pressed the record button on the machine. "Madame Shou, I am certain you realize that you are in serious trouble and—"

Lian held up her hand. "Chef Picard," she said, in a voice so quiet he had to lean forward to hear. "I shall tell you whatever it is that you wish to know. I have shamed myself and my family." Her eyes dropped to her folded hands.

Picard looked at the machine to make certain it was recording. He could hardly believe his luck. He felt a surge of adrenaline and was careful to regulate his voice as he said, "I am pleased to hear that you wish to cooperate in the unraveling of the charges that have been made against you and Mademoiselle Conway. Before we begin, may I get you a coffee, or perhaps water?"

When she looked up from her hands, her eyes were blank. "I am fine for the moment. I would just like to answer your questions, please."

"Mais oui." He opened his folder to a clean page, ready to take notes. "Let us begin at the beginning." He cleared his throat. "Mademoiselle Conway said you hate the Warwick family and want to destroy them. Is that true?"

"I thought I did," she said flatly.

"What does that mean?"

"That means that for the last year while my husband has been in prison and I have been alone at Château Pitique trying to keep our vineyard from insolvency, I have hated the Warwick family. Though Hank was entirely responsible for his own situation, I blamed them for our misfortune. It was easier than acknowledging that the man I married—the man I loved—was a coward, a crook."

She began to sniffle and a tear slid down her cheek. She pulled a tissue from her trouser pocket and blew her nose. "I am sorry, Chef Picard. I shall do my best to control my emotions."

Picard shook his head. "It is quite all right, madame. Please go on."

"Olivia offered me a way to save Château Pitique. She needed help carrying out her plan to destroy the Warwick family and offered me a great deal of money to help her. Olivia Conway is a very clever woman. She knew she was coming to Château Beaulieu for her mother's wedding and decided it was a perfect opportunity to wreak havoc on the Warwicks. She knew—"

"Wait, Madame." Picard stopped her. "I understand why you might feel hatred toward Lord and Lady Crosswick, but why would Olivia want to cause the House of Crosswick so much trouble?"

Lian bit her lower lip. She studied her hands as she clasped and unclasped them, then finally looked across the table at Picard. "I think that is something that only she can tell you," she said.

"The recording was paused at 19:17," he said, and pressed the stop button. "Madame Shou, I shall return."

She nodded and watched with weary eyes as he left the room.

Making his way down the hall to the WC, he could feel his shoulders slump. He glanced at his watch. This was exhausting work. He was ready to go home, sit down, and enjoy a glass of Bordeaux, but it was going to be a while. He washed his hands and splashed water on his face. Feeling slightly refreshed, he walked back down the hall and pushed through the interrogation room door, determined to find out why this privileged young woman would rain foul play on a family she should love. He couldn't imagine what the answer was going to be.

She sat on the table cross-legged, her elbows on her knees,

her chin on her fisted hands. She had tidied her blonde ponytail and wiped the mascara from around her eyes and now she looked young and innocent.

As he came through the door Olivia gave him a smile he was sure was calculated to charm him. *So that's how she's going to play it,* he thought.

"Mademoiselle, if you would be so kind as to sit in the chair, we can resume the interview."

She unfolded her legs and dangled them over the side of the table, swinging them flirtatiously, first one then the other. She tilted her head and said, "I missed you."

Picard sat in his chair and she slid off the table onto hers. She leaned back, hummed a sigh, and pouted her lips.

He shook his head and pressed record. "The interview with Mademoiselle Olivia Conway is resumed at 19:24. Mademoiselle Conway, first I must tell you that Madame Shou has been most cooperative. She has admitted to helping you in your efforts to ruin the House of Crosswick and all they stand for." He watched her closely as he spoke, but her coquettish pout and wide eyes remained frozen on her pretty face.

He sat back and let silence hang between them. Finally she sat forward, leaning on the table. The flirty girl was gone and in her place Picard saw a cold, cunning adversary. As she lasered her villainous stare on him, a shiver ran up his spine and still, he waited.

When the corners of her mouth lifted in an icy leer, he braced for what was to come. "Chef Picard. You have no idea what the Warwick family has done to me."

FORTY

As Chef Frederick Picard's car stopped in front of Château Beaulieu, the foyer clock chimed twice inside the grand house. Before he could knock, Delphine opened the door just enough to keep the pelting rain out. She pulled Picard through the narrow opening and corralled him on a small carpet that had been put in front of the door to protect the floor. She took his umbrella, shoved it in the stand, then held his coat by the collar while he pulled his arms from the sleeves. After shaking as much water from his trench coat as possible, she draped it over the bench beside the door.

"Merci, Delphine," he said.

She nodded in reply and ushered him into the grand salon where seven people sat waiting.

"Drink?" Delphine asked.

"Non, merci," Picard declined. "Peut-être plus tard."

"Later, it is." She glanced at the sideboard. When she was satisfied the refreshments met with her approval, she turned and was gone.

A comfortable rolled armchair next to the fireplace had been left vacant for the chef.

"Please, Frederick, sit here." Anxious to get the meeting underway, Philip skipped all pleasantries. "While G and I have been in York, you've been hard at work the last few days, haven't you? So, chef, what do you have to share with us?"

Picard smiled at Philip's directness. "It seems as if we meet like this too often, eh?"

Everyone offered a polite chuckle, then the room was silent, waiting for Picard to proceed.

He put his briefcase on his lap and as he pressed the brass locks, the top popped up. He pulled out a notebook and a red government pen, closed the case and set it back on the floor beside him.

He crossed his legs, settled into the soft cushions, and took a moment to assess each person's mood before he began. Normally a man of easy charm, Philip clenched and unclenched his jaw; Genevieve looked relaxed sitting with her right leg tucked under her, but her left foot bounced nervously; Duncan sat forward, his elbows bent and hands on his thighs, looking as if he were ready to pounce; Julia's onyx pen was poised over her leather notebook, ready to record every word about to be said; Lillie's eyes darted around the room and she twisted the rings on her right hand around and around; Becca sat so still she could have been mistaken for a mannequin, except for her periodic blinking and her shallow breath; only Finn looked comfortable and ready for what was to come.

"I believe I shall start at the end." He rested his elbows on the arms of his chair and tented his hands. "After interrogating Olivia Conway and Lian Shou, I can say with confidence they are the people responsible for the chaos you have been experiencing for the last few months. Madame Shou particularly has been extremely cooperative. She does not have the criminal experience nor the criminal personality of Mademoiselle Conway, and she was most anxious to help us in any way that could lessen the severity of her punishment. But she is most concerned about the shame she has brought on her family.

"Mademoiselle Conway, as you all know, is very different. She is not concerned with shaming her family at all." He offered Becca a sympathetic smile. "She is clever, deceptive, and anxious to deflect blame, and we saw all of that as she was interrogated. In the case of Monsieur Wallace's attempted murder, Olivia was insistent she only wanted to make him ill, not kill him. But I am getting ahead of myself." Picard looked down at his notebook and flipped a page. Using his pen, he trailed down the paper until he found his place. "Ah, voila."

He looked up and went on. "Lian has confessed to orchestrating the dining room explosion, but at Olivia's request. According to Madam Shou, Olivia wanted to escalate the threat to the family. She decided a small explosion would serve as a notice that everyone was in danger. Again, no one was to be hurt. But, as it turned out, Mademoiselle Langdon was injured." His gaze landed on Lillie and he gave her a sympathetic smile.

"But how in the world did Lian know how to create a small explosion?" Genevieve couldn't imagine the bland, shy woman instigating such a thing.

Picard's eyes sparkled. "I am glad you asked. I wondered the same thing. It seems unlikely she would have such a skill. But it is not. Did you know her family owns one of the biggest fireworks companies in China? She knows a lot about small explosives."

"Wow," Genevieve said. "Looks are deceiving. In a million years, I would not have guessed Lian Shou was involved in all of this. Delphine was the one I was concerned about. I really thought she might be trying to hurt our family. She's been behaving very strangely lately. I'm so relieved I was wrong."

Philip shook his head slowly. "You never said a word to me. Why didn't you share you were suspicious of Delphine?"

"I'm embarrassed to tell you why." Genevieve looked at her hands, folded in her lap.

"Now I really want to know," Philip said, elbowing Genevieve in the side.

"All right." Heat flushed her cheeks. "I had a dream Delphine stole Charlotte's friendship from me. Delphine seemed very mean in that dream and ever since, I've felt uneasy about her."

"You thought Delphine was trying to bring down the House of Crosswick because you had a bad dream about her?" A laugh gurgled from Philip's throat until it exploded into the room.

"I know." Genevieve had no defense. "I sound like a fool."

Philip leaned into her and planted a kiss on her cheek. "Yes, my darling. A fool you are, but you're my fool and I love every foolish inch of you." Still chuckling, he returned his focus to Picard. "Frederick, what else do you have for us?"

He looked down and scanned his pad. "Alors," he said, and tapped his forehead. "J'ai presque oublié. I almost forgot. Speaking about Delphine: Émile told me he had seen Delphine give Olivia a card. When I asked Delphine about it, she said

Olivia wanted to write felicitations to her mother and Sir David and had asked Delphine for a notecard. In the end, the message wasn't exactly what Delphine thought it would be, was it?"

"Olivia's pretty amazing, but she doesn't have the ability to do everything. The explosion is a good example," Philip said. "So, Chef Picard, that leads me to ask two questions. First, how do Olivia and Lian know each other? Second, why in the hell would Lian get involved with Olivia?"

Picard smiled and said, "I can answer both of those questions." He pushed out of his chair and walked to the sideboard where he poured himself a glass of water from a Baccarat pitcher. As he drank, he walked back to his chair and sat, then pressed on. "As we know, when Monsieur Wallace went to Blain Lodge, he threatened and humiliated Olivia." His eyes sparkled as his story built up steam. "And that's when she decided to mount a campaign against not just Monsieur Wallace, but against the Warwick family. She decided she would destroy their reputation and hurt them any way she could."

"This is not an unusual pattern for Olivia, but how did Lian get involved?" Philip asked again.

"I promise, my lord, I am getting to there."

"I am getting there," Philip corrected, and got a blank look from Picard. "Never mind." He waved the subject away. "Go on."

Picard held up a slender leatherbound book and looked at Becca. "I must say, without Lady Weatherington finding her daughter's journal, our case against Olivia and Lian would not be so strong." His grateful gaze lingered on Becca for several seconds before he said, "Olivia needed an accomplice to do the things she could not. Last year her mother told her all about the Shous. When she telephoned Lian Shou last fall, it was just to introduce herself—a friendly chat, if you will. But it didn't take long for Olivia to understand she had found a," he looked at Philip, "shoemate?" he said tentatively.

Philip flashed a smile. "Soulmate. I believe the word you're looking for is soulmate."

Picard nodded his thanks. "At that time, Lian hated the Warwick family as much as Olivia does."

Genevieve deflated into the sofa cushion. "My god. Who knew our family was so despicable?"

Picard went on to share Lian's confession that for a long time, she had blamed the Warwicks for Hank's troubles, until she finally admitted to herself that he had brought his woes on himself.

"But there was une autre incitation, another incentive? The other incentive was Olivia's promise to pay off all Château Pitique's debts."

"That would have been an offer hard to resist. Especially since she hated us anyway. No moral quandary there." Duncan looked across the room at Julia, who was writing notes as fast as her pen would go.

"That makes sense about Lian, but why is Olivia determined to destroy the House of Crosswick when we have welcomed her into the family after everything she did at Wilmingrove Hall?" Duncan was curious to know.

Picard had the answer. "Her motive is classic. Her motive is jealousy."

"Jealousy!" Genevieve spat. "Jealous, my ass! She's young. She's beautiful. She's rich and she is privileged beyond reason. After what she did last year, how many people could have gone to a posh facility instead of prison? How could she be jealous of anyone?"

Philip reached across the sofa cushion and squeezed Genevieve's hand. "Hard to imagine, isn't it?" he said. "Go on, Frederick."

"She believes the Warwick family stole her mother from her."

Now Duncan was incensed. "What!" He looked at Becca and pointed. "What the hell is she talking about? Her mother is right here."

"All right, everybody." Philip raised his hand. "Let's let Chef Picard explain, shall we?"

"Merci, my lord. Please keep in mind that these are Olivia's words, not mine. Mademoiselle Conway believed that, from the moment her mother met your family, Lady Weatherington no longer belonged to her." He looked around the room. Some people scowled, some people shook their heads. "Oui, oui. Je comprends." He nodded. "I understand this is difficult to hear. She is a troubled young woman." He glanced at his notebook. "Ah, oui," he said, his memory jogged. "She said her mother rarely visited her at Blain Lodge because she was always with the Warwicks. Always celebrating a holiday or a birthday but never celebrating with her."

Genevieve looked across the room at Becca. She could see her friend clenching and unclenching her jaw.

He went on. "She blames your family for all of it. And Lian

was the piece of the puzzle she needed to execute her plan to destroy your family."

"Why not? It makes perfect sense." Sarcasm dripped off Duncan's words.

Finn narrowed his eyes. "What was the deal with Jolie Fille? Lian stole Ella's horse, right? Why?"

"Ah, oui." Picard sat straighter in his chair. "This is where Olivia and Lian had a bit of a disagreement. Olivia wanted Lian to steal Jolie Fille and destroy her but Lian refused. The only thing she would do is take Jolie Fille to her own stables. Olivia was très en colère, very angry about that, and threatened to withhold her money if Lian didn't do the things she was told. But Lian is not as passive as she appears. That is when she threatened to expose Olivia's attempt on Wallace's life."

Duncan barked a laugh. "Oh my god. Those two deserve each other."

"I couldn't agree more," Genevieve said. "But why did Olivia try to kidnap Ella?"

Picard raised his finger. "Ah, oui. A potential crime of opportunity. Olivia went to the stables to give Commander an injection that would have killed him. A dramatic statement, indeed. But happily she was interrupted by the riding instructor. As we know, Olivia knocked Felicity out just as Ella arrived. That is when she decided to take Ella with her. It was an impulsion du moment—I believe you say 'spur of the moment'—decision." He nodded at Duncan, then Julia. "Kudos to you that Ella is too smart to ride without a helmet."

"It's gratifying when you see your children have learned some of the lessons they've been taught, especially when it keeps them from getting kidnapped." Julia had stopped writing long enough to interject.

"Now, tell us about the rumor campaign." Lillie stood and walked to the fire. She was anxious to hear how the smear campaign had come about. "Whose idea was that, and how did they do it?"

Picard raised his eyebrows. "Mademoiselle Conway was very proud of that part of her plan. She believed that was the piece that would ruin the House of Crosswick by destroying your reputation and all the good your family has done for many centuries." He inclined his head toward Finn. "I believe Monsieur Mountbatten can walk you through the details of what she did."

Finn took a long drink from his glass of water and wished it were one of Château Beaulieu's wines. "I'll try to be as un-nerdy as possible. I know nobody wants to listen to a lot of tech talk." No one objected. "Let me start by saying none of this was difficult. The internet is like the wild west. Sadly, people believe almost anything they read on websites and it's easy to post things that can do terrible damage. According to Chef Picard and his team, Olivia admits to starting the ball rolling by setting up a fake news site. Initially, she reposted stories from trusted sources, then after a while she started publishing fake articles about the House of Crosswick. As you know, Lillie, most of the initial stories were about the museum and the foundation and keyed off the reality that last year the museum sold two counterfeit paintings to La Cité du Vin. She posted the hell out of that story and was off and running. She was able to gain the confidence of a reporter from *The Times,* Peter Fletcher, and that's how the story of Elise Beaufoy was planted. I would imagine you will ask *The Times* for much more than a retraction; I would think a front-page story in the arts section about all the wonderful things going on at the Laney museums and the foundation and, I trust, Peter will be looking for a new job."

"Finn." Genevieve leaned forward. "It can't possibly be that simple. What are you not telling us?"

"Trust me, Genevieve. For my team, it really was that simple. She used some VPNs, virtual private networks, and a few other rudimentary techniques, but there was nothing we couldn't quickly figure out. I would recommend you put all of your IT under contract with Mountbatten International Security so we can prevent this sort of thing from happening again."

"Done!" Philip and Genevieve said in unison and a heavy weight lifted from Lillie's shoulders. For the next few weeks, she would spend her time setting the record straight, soothing donors, and getting all the good press she could.

"So what happens next?" Julia asked.

"This morning our local prosecutor offered Madame Shou a choice. In France, there is a three-year prison sentence and a minimum €45,000 fine for the theft of Jolie Fille, which is one charge against her. The explosion could be charged as attempted murder, which would put her in jail for a very long time. She can either remain here, pay the fine, and serve a long sentence, or be deported. She has chosen to return to China. Her parents are furious, of course. She has shamed the family, but they have agreed she can come home."

"What a choice." Genevieve couldn't help wondering if prison might be a better alternative than returning to angry parents in China, but she wasn't going to worry about it.

"And what about Olivia?" Julia said.

"I can hardly wait to hear," Genevieve added.

"As Lady Weatherington knows, Olivia had no choice. She is already on her way back to Blain Lodge. Needless to say, she will no longer be on the open residential floor, but on the high-security third floor. Between attempting to murder Wallace, her online crimes, and assaulting Felicity Coullard, it is going to be a very long time before she is out in the world again."

"So that's the end of it?" Lillie said.

"Ç'est tout." Picard slapped his notebook closed and laid it on his lap.

"No, that is not quite all." Becca spoke for the first time. She stood up and looked at each person in the room. She cleared her throat then said, "As Olivia's mother, this is difficult for me to say, but after everything Olivia has done or has tried to do to this family, I'm relieved we won't have to worry about her for many years to come. Over this last year, I had a glimpse into what Olivia could be if she were healthy. My heart breaks knowing she is not and it's likely she never will be. Only passing years will reveal that secret. I will always love who Olivia could have been, but I can no longer love who she is." She paused and bit her lip to keep her emotions under control. "Sadly, Olivia was right. *You* are the people I love, the people I consider my family. I regret every terrible thing Olivia has done to this family and I'll do everything in my power to make certain she never touches your lives again." Her face clouded and her eyes filled with tears. "Thank you for continuing to love me through it all."

Without saying a word, Genevieve went to her friend, who over the last twenty months had become like her sister. She wrapped Becca in a fierce hug and they sobbed together, convinced at last Olivia would never be the loving daughter Becca had for so long thought she could be.

FORTY-ONE

"**A**ND THEN WHAT did she do, Wallace?" Elsie Lomax, the queen of Wilmingrove Hall's kitchen, was spellbound as Wallace regaled her with the stories of everything that happened at Château Beaulieu over the Christmas holidays. She had stopped mid-stir as she mixed the thick dough for marmalade biscuits. The aroma of bitter orange peel and Seville oranges floated from the bowl each time the spoon made a turn.

"Well, she didn't say much, but every word was like a challenge." He took the bowl from Elsie and continued mixing the ingredients. "Let me do this. You do something else."

"Thank you, Wallace. I can't believe you're going to take cookies to that horrible girl."

"It's fine, Elsie. Actually, I asked her mother if it would be all right if I visited Olivia and Lady Weatherington was most grateful. Besides, this might be my last opportunity to set things straight." He grunted as he pulled the wooden spoon through the thick mixture.

"I'll be right back, Wallace. I have to run down to the cold cellar to get some piccalilli. I have some nice sausages I thought I'd cook for lunch."

"Oh, lovely, Elsie." Wallace's mouth watered at the thought. "What a perfect winter meal. I'll just keep stirring these and they'll be ready to go on the trays when you return."

Wallace put the bowl on the counter, reached into the inside breast pocket of his black jacket, and pulled out a long vial filled with fine powder. He smiled as he pulled the cork from the neck and leaned away from the bowl as he poured the powder into the biscuit dough. He rinsed the vial, dried it with a paper towel, and put it back in his pocket. He turned back to the bowl and carefully, very carefully, folded in the powder until he was satisfied it was thoroughly mixed.

"Is it ready to go on the baking sheets?" Her arms full, Elsie had come back with more than a jar of piccalilli.

"What else did you bring from the cellar, Elsie?" Wallace took jars from Elsie and put them on the counter.

"Just a few things I thought you might enjoy."

"Oh, Elsie. You know the way to my heart. I do love a spoonful of Branston pickle on my cheese sarnie. And more marmalade?"

"I used the last jar from the pantry for that wretched girl's biscuits."

"What am I missing in here?" Mrs. MacIntosh said as she pushed through the swinging door. "Elsie, is Wallace trying to flirt his way into a custard tart? Oh, biscuit dough. Yum." Bertie took a spoon lying next to the bowl and dug out a taste. As she brought it to her mouth, Wallace boomed, "No!" took two strides and grabbed the spoon from Bertie's hand.

Stunned, Mrs. MacIntosh plopped onto a stool and stared at Wallace, her mouth wide.

"Wallace, what was all that about?" Elsie took the spoon from Wallace and tossed it into the sink.

"I'm so sorry, Bertie." Wallace took her hand. "You know you shouldn't eat anything with raw eggs in it and at your age, well…" He had no idea how to finish the sentence but hoped he had sounded convincing.

Not taking her eyes off Wallace, Bertie shook her head. "Something's going on with you, Reginald Wallace."

"I think I know," Elsie said as she put small dollops of dough on three prepared baking sheets. "He's taking these marmalade biscuits to Olivia Conway tomorrow and I think he's nervous."

Wallace gave Elsie a withering look. "I wasn't going to tell Bertie until I came back." He turned to Mrs. MacIntosh. "I told Lady Weatherington I would go see Olivia and she was most grateful."

Elsie shoved the trays in the oven then put the timer on.

"Thank you, Elsie, for doing that. I'll take care of the biscuits from here. You've done me a very great favor and I appreciate it. Now, as head butler, I am directing you both to go into the lounge, put your feet up and have a sherry. I shall clean up here, and later we'll enjoy a lovely dinner."

"But—" Elsie started.

"Please don't object. It would give me great pleasure if the two of you would go into the sitting room and relax for a moment. I shall be in to join you directly." He untied Elsie's apron and shooed the two confused women out the door.

He checked the timer. Just five more minutes and he could

take the biscuits out of the oven. His armpits felt clammy and his breathing was too rapid. *Calm down,* he told himself.

When the timer dinged, his heart nearly popped out of his chest. He laughed at himself, found an oven mitt, pulled out the three trays and slid the biscuits onto the racks Elsie had laid out for him. Every few minutes, he checked to see if they were cool enough to package. Twenty-five minutes later, he decided they were fine.

Using a piece of waxed paper, he began placing the marmalade biscuits one at a time into the pretty presentation box Elsie had insisted he use, instead of the plain paper box he had chosen. When there were twenty-four confections nestled in the carton, he folded the tissue paper over them and closed the hinged top. Elsie had thought of everything, even a red ribbon. He draped it over the top, twisted it on the bottom, and brought it back to tie into a pretty bow.

"Who could resist that?" he said out loud, admiring his work. He took the other twelve cookies to the sink where he turned on the water and, grateful they had a waste disposal, flipped the switch and poked the soggy bits down the drain. He washed and dried every dish and utensil Elsie had used, then found sanitizing spray under the sink and sprayed every surface in the kitchen. When all that was done, he put the dish rags in the laundry. He went into the cooler, selected a bottle of Veuve Clicquot, and put it in a wine bucket. He chose three crystal flutes, checked them for spots, and went out to join Mrs. MacIntosh and Elsie.

"Reg," Bertie said, surprised to see the Champagne. "What's the occasion?"

He set the bucket and the glasses on the coffee table in front of the two women, selected a log, and tossed it on the fire. As sparks shot up and the embers snapped back to life, Wallace whipped the foil off the cork and eased it from the neck of the bottle, enjoying the satisfying *pfft* sound it made.

Bertie and Elsie watched him pour the perfect amount. He handed each woman a glass. Then, still standing, he said, "To Olivia. She is where she should be, securely away from our family." He drained his glass and was refilling it before his partners had even brought theirs to their lips.

Bertie took a sip then said, "Olivia has been trying to destroy the Warwick family since they inherited the Crosswick title and fortune. Is it a bit harsh to wish that she languish in misery at Blain Lodge for the rest of her life?"

"Oh, I don't think so!" Elsie said. "Wallace, what do you think?"

"I think that is a fine wish, indeed," and he drained his glass again.

EPILOGUE

WALLACE HAD TAKEN pains to look immaculate for his meeting with Olivia. He had pressed his black suit and brushed it until not a speck of lint could be found on the fine worsted fabric. His shoes were buffed to a high luster and his shirt was so starched it chafed his neck. He had laid his topcoat and suit jacket flat in the back seat of the Moroccan-blue Bentley he was driving, making certain to smooth any wrinkles before closing the door. His hands felt clammy on the steering wheel and he would have wiped them on his pants, but he didn't want to disrupt his sharp crease. It was to be expected that he was nervous, he told himself. This would be the last time he faced Olivia Conway... ever.

Stopping at the iron gates that guarded Blain Lodge, he thought of the last time he was here and a ghost of a smile flickered across his face. His pulse pounded in his neck as he rolled down his window, pressed the red button, and announced himself.

"Reginald Wallace to see Olivia Conway on behalf of her mother, Lady Weatherington." He used his poshest accent and most officious voice and knew he sounded like an important man on an important mission.

As his window eased up, he thought about Shylock's words in *The Merchant of Venice*, "If you wrong us, shall we not revenge?" He slammed his hand on the steering wheel. "Bloody right we shall," he hissed.

He waited until the gates opened completely before advancing up the long driveway. The sun dappled the car until he emerged from the tree-lined lane. He pulled into a parking spot marked "Visitors". When he took his hands off the steering wheel, his fingers ached and he realized he had been gripping the wheel harder than necessary. He checked his face in the visor mirror, wiped a dot of spittle from the corner of his mouth, and opened the door. As he heaved himself from the car and stood, a wave of dizziness made him sway and he grabbed the door frame.

Stress, he thought. The lightheadedness passed in an instant. He opened the rear door, shook out his jacket, and put it on. With the sun beating on his black suit, he was pleasantly warm so decided to leave his topcoat in the car. He reached in and picked up the box of marmalade biscuits and was ready to go.

"Good afternoon," the receptionist said. "You are Mr. Wallace, aren't you?"

Wallace glanced down at the nameplate on the desk. "How kind of you to remember me, Mrs. Powell." Wallace offered the tidy, middle-aged woman his most charming smile and included an elegant head-bow.

"I believe you are here to visit Olivia Conway, is that right?"

"It is, indeed. I come bearing a gift from her mother." He offered the box for inspection.

"What lovely presentation," she said, and shook her head. "An attendant will run it through the metal detector when you go upstairs. I hope you don't mind. Protocol, you understand. I'm sure you know Ms. Conway is no longer in the open residence, but rather is currently residing on the more secure third floor."

"Of course, Mrs. Powell. I understand completely."

A printer hummed behind her and Mrs. Powell swiveled around to retrieve a card that said "Reginald Wallace, VISITOR". She slipped it into a plastic holder attached to a black lanyard and handed it to Wallace.

"Go down the hall to the lifts and press three." Mrs. Powell pointed in the direction of the corridor. "The screen will ask you for a code. It is on the back of your nametag. An attendant will greet you at the lift." Her smile seemed genuine as she said, "It's lovely to see you again, Mr. Wallace. I do hope you enjoy your visit."

I'll enjoy my visit when it's over, he thought. "Thank you, Mrs. Powell." He turned and continued his journey to Olivia.

When the doors slid open, Wallace was greeted by the blinding smile of an attendant who was about his height and about his weight. The similarity ended there. It was obvious that the young man, whose brass nametag said "George," spent time in the gym and time whitening his teeth.

"Mr. Wallace?" he said, his smile still broad. "Ms. Conway is expecting you. Please, come with me."

They walked toward double doors that George opened with a swipe of his card and entered a room that looked more like a foyer in an elegant hotel than the entrance to a secure floor in a psychiatric hospital.

"Emma." George stopped in front of the woman behind the reception desk. Her hair was pulled so tightly into a severe bun that Wallace was certain it must give her a headache.

"Mr. Wallace is here to see Olivia Conway."

She looked at Wallace over her wirerimmed glasses, stared at her computer screen as she tapped on her keyboard, frowned, looked at him again, and tapped some more. Wallace could feel sweat prickle at his hairline. He pasted a tight smile on his lips while he inhaled and exhaled through his nose, trying to steady his breath.

When she was satisfied with what she saw, she said, "Take Mr. Wallace to the lounge. Ms. Conway is waiting."

They walked through a metal detector and down a corridor to the second door on the right.

George tapped his card on the pad beside the long, narrow window next to the door. Wallace heard a buzzing sound, George pushed, and the door eased open.

"Just use the call button beside the door when you're ready to leave, sir," George said, then turned and left.

With his heart thudding in his ears, Wallace peeked around the door, and there was Olivia. He didn't know what he had been expecting, but it wasn't this. Sitting on a sofa upholstered in pastel paisley, she looked like the subject of an Impressionist painting. The sun slanted into the room from tall windows, bathing her in winter's soft yellow light. White cashmere sweater and pants draped her lean body in casual elegance. Pulled up into a loose knot, her blonde hair looked like a halo around the top of her head, and her perfect bow mouth was tinted the same rose as her high cheekbones. Angelic was the word that sprang to mind, but when he looked into her blue, violet-rimmed eyes, Wallace saw that the cold, calculating woman behind this beautiful façade was still alive and well.

She didn't rise when Wallace entered but remained seated with her hands folded to her side and her legs crossed. "Forgive me for not getting up, Wallace, but you and I are not exactly friends, are we?"

And the game is on, he thought. "Certainly not, Ms. Conway." The ice in his voice chilled the air between them.

"I can't imagine why you've come. I'm sure it isn't to see if I'm well. Shall we dispense with the pleasantries and make this as short as possible?" She leaned forward. "I have dastardly deeds to plan, as I'm sure you can appreciate."

Wallace saw a flash of humor in her eyes. He might enjoy staying a while and bantering with this clever adversary, but he was here with a purpose and it wasn't to match wits with Olivia Conway.

He crossed to where she was sitting and offered the gift. She raised an eyebrow and took the present, then adjusted the red bow so it was a little perkier. "Is this from you?"

"It is not," he lied. "Ms. Conway, I am here for two reasons. The first is to bring you these marmalade biscuits from your mother. I understand they are your favorites."

In spite of herself, Olivia looked like a child as she pulled the tail of the ribbon, eyes glistening, lips slightly parted. It came easily undone. Wallace watched as she opened the box and a smile of anticipation tugged at her lips. She looked up at Wallace then back at the box and plucked a cookie from the package. His eyes were riveted to the pastry as she brought it to her mouth. He watched her teeth bite into the biscuit and her full lips close over the bite.

She shut her eyes and moaned as she chewed, while Wallace stood mesmerized, not sure what would happen next. Finally, she opened her eyes and said, "Wallace, these are without a doubt the best marmalade biscuits I've ever had. My compliments to the chef, whoever that may be." She studied what was left of the cookie and licked a crumb from the corner of her mouth. "They have a perfect bitterness that I don't think I've ever had before. Bitterness is my favorite part of a marmalade cookie. I'd offer you one, but I'm certainly not going to share with *you,* of all people." She threw her head back and laughed, then popped the last bite of cookie in her mouth. As she was chewing, she asked, "What was the other reason you came?"

"Ah, yes, Ms. Conway. I simply wanted to remind you of what I told you on my last visit. Do you remember?"

Olivia narrowed her eyes and tilted her head to the side. "I don't really remember what you said, but I certainly remember when you dumped the coffee in my lap. You know that's why I decided to give you a little taste of foxglove in your Champagne the night of my mother's wedding, right?"

"Yes, that was very clever."

"But refresh my memory. What did you say?" With her first biscuit finished, she reached for a second.

"I told you I would make it my mission to see you spend the rest of your life here, at Blain Lodge. Today I am going to add perhaps it will be a shorter stay than you would imagine." He couldn't read the look on Olivia's face but he decided he had just spoken the perfect exit line. "With that, Ms. Conway, I shall bid you adieu." He walked to the door and pressed the call button. The door buzzed and he pushed it open, but before he walked through it, he turned back to Olivia and said, "Don't eat all of those biscuits, Olivia. You will make yourself sick."

He pressed the elevator button and when the doors opened, the tea lady pushed her trolley filled with cups, saucers, tea sandwiches, and petit fours off the elevator. *Perfect timing*, he thought. *She's going to eat all those marmalade treats before teatime is over. At the very least she's going to be an extremely sick girl, but with any luck…*

As he pressed "G" he couldn't help but smile.

Did you enjoy

VENGEANCE

at the

VINEYARD?

Please leave fellow readers a review!

AND SO IT BEGINS

I'M QUITE SURE my first memory is floating in moist darkness, waiting for something extraordinary to happen. And then it did. I remember my surprise at the waves that rhythmically ebbed and flowed. The longer it lasted the more it annoyed me and just when I decided I'd had enough, the biggest wave of all shoved me against an elastic band. Of course, I didn't know at that time what an elastic band was, but in retrospect, that's what it felt like. And then, another big shove through a small hole, and I was blinded by bright lights bouncing off white walls, white uniforms, white sheets, white faces. I think I was upside down, though, again, I have to say, I didn't know what upside down was. I whimpered, but when someone smacked my bottom, I gave them what they were asking for—a big, fat wail. I remember thinking, "What a set of pipes!"

That was 3 August 1921. I've been telling that story since I was four and every time I do, someone pats me on the head, well, not so much anymore, since I'm, well, dead, but they used to, and they would say, "What a funny story, you clever boy." I would roll my eyes knowing, even at four, that they didn't think I could possibly remember my time in the womb and my journey out into the world. But I did.

And I remember my mother. She always smelled of roses. When I was six, she told me that Rose Otto was her favorite perfume because my grandmother Lady Caroline, had given her a vial of the treasured scent on the day she married my father. Our family believes in tradition and Rose Otto was a tradition that began with my great-grandmother, the magnificent Charlotte Chaubert, the toast of Paris and London. According to my mother, who loved to tell a lively story, Charlotte was my grandfather's passion. Lord Philip adored her, denied her nothing, but in the end, the love of his life was taken from him far too soon.

Sometimes I wonder if I had heeded their story as a warning, could I have veered from the events that took my life down a path I did not choose, or want? It's a bit late to ponder these things, but sometimes my mind still goes there.

The London Times, August 6, 1921

THE COUNTESS OF CROSSWICK HAS BEEN DELIVERED OF A SON

The Countess of Crosswick was safely delivered of a son at 05:26, 3 August, at Columbia-Presbyterian Medical Center, New York City, New York. The baby weighed 7lbs 2oz.

The Earl of Crosswick was delighted to greet his first child.

Lord and Lady Crosswick will reside with their son, Jonathon William Wallace Laney, at their home, Margrave House, Kensington, upon their return to London.

And so I was announced to the world. An auspicious beginning, to be sure. A proper English babe wailing his way into the world, not in the serene, shaded lanes of Kensington, London, but into the noisy, brash streets of New York City, surely a harbinger of how I would live my life.

I'm not certain that my parents wanted more children, or actually any children at all. It seemed to me they were delighted with each other and would have been perfectly happy to live their interesting lives surrounded by artists and musicians rather than a brood of young savages. Regardless, I was the only savage they produced, and it suited me that they stopped at one, as long as I was it.

It was said that I was a bonnie baby, but that was my mother and my granny speaking. I doubt if my father said the same. I believe he preferred the attractive swirl of paint on canvas more than the red face of a newborn. He tended to avoid me in my early years until I could ride well enough to join him on The Hunt at Wilmingrove Hall, our family seat in Yorkshire. Or when I could give him a good run for his money on the chessboard. Then he began to take an interest in me and my development.

I had a nanny I loved nearly as much as I adored my mother, but my nanny was my friend and my mother was, well, someone I worshiped. She was a charming, brilliant, and stunning woman who never tired of bringing life and laughter into our home. No matter what I did, she delighted in it. If I colored a picture for her that was nothing more than a few scribbled lines on the paper, she would declare it to be the work of a burgeoning young talent. If I made a mudpie and insisted it was a plum pudding, she would pretend to eat it all and insist it was worthy of a Michelin star. She read to me. She tutored me in the vast and spectacular art collection that was my parents' pride and joy and because she loved it, I loved it.

And she told me stories. The night she told me the tragic tale of my great-grandmother, Charlotte, the wife of the 9th Earl of Crosswick, it was raining and cold. I was six. My mother and I huddled together on a small sofa in my father's study, which would one day be mine. I remember how cozy we were with a lap robe tucked around us and a fire crackling on the hearth. My hands cradled a cup of hot cocoa, and my mother kept stealing sips, smiling at me each time she did, a little cocoa mustache painting her upper lip. The smell of cocoa still reminds me of my mother. The smell of cocoa and Rose Otto.

"Your great-grandmother was a beauty," she began. "Everyone adored her, but no one as much as your great-grandfather." As she spoke, my mother's forehead nearly touched mine. Her voice was so quiet, I watched her lips to make certain I didn't miss any words. "It was your great grandparents' fortieth wedding anniversary, and this house was filled with guests who were here to celebrate with them." My mother's hand was cool on my cheek. "Everyone gathered at the bottom of the staircase, waiting for Charlotte to make her grand entrance. When she appeared, she was stunning in a shimmering silver dress with a train that curved around her feet. Even at sixty-four, she was breathtaking." My mother looked deeper into my eyes. "You have her eyes, darling boy." And she kissed the tip of my nose, then went on. "The 9th Earl raised his Champagne glass and said, 'To my magnificent bride of forty years. No one else has ever walked the earth, whom I could love as I love you.' At the end of the toast, the band struck up Charlotte's favorite song 'Oh You Beautiful Doll' and Charlotte blew a kiss to the Earl." My mother's eyes were glistening with tears. I didn't understand why she was crying. "When she started down the stairs, the toe of her shoe hooked on her gown's silver train. She tried to grab the banister but missed and tumbled head over heels down the stairs. By the time she reached the bottom, she was…." My mother's voice trailed off, but I understood.

"One day, darling boy, I'm sure you'll meet her," she said. I know my mother intended to comfort me, but when she saw my eyes, wide with fear at the idea that I was going to run into an old, dead lady, perhaps in the middle of the night when I got up to go to the loo, I'm certain she realized she had miscalculated. She quickly tried to recover, pulling me close, kissing my forehead, and laughing. "Don't worry darling. I just meant we'll talk about Granny Charlotte again, and the more we talk about her, the more you'll feel you know her."

I didn't believe her, and for the next year, I lived in fear of great granny jumping out of my wardrobe, every evening when I opened the door to get my dressing gown. Other six-year-olds were frightened of monsters or goblins. I was terrified of my beautiful, kind, dead great-grandmother. And then I learned, purely by accident, that Granny Charlotte was a ghost.

OTHER BOOKS BY
TANA L.H. BOERGER

Money, Murder, Mayhem
Art, Wine, and Crime

ACKNOWLEDGEMENTS

FOR MANY WRITERS, writing is a solitary occupation. For me it's just the opposite. When I write I bounce ideas off anyone within earshot, that's usually my indulgent husband, Tom. I yell out things that need to be researched, mumble the names of characters I might kill, muse aloud about locations my characters might go. The tapping of my computer keys does not exist in a quiet environment. There's music playing—jazz, classical, always wordless—I have more than enough words rattling in my brain trying to get out. In the months it takes to write a book, imagine all the folks I suck into my vortex as I pour my stories onto the page and how many people need to be thanked.

To my first line of defense, Rosie Walker, my even-keeled, consistently encouraging English editor. You are the best. Please don't ever fire me. And to my designer, Caerus Kourt, how do you keep designing covers that are interesting on their own, but keep the creative feel of their predecessors? It's magic. To Jayne Ryder, you came in and saved us from ourselves with your mastery of PR, social media, and all things that move a book from the shelf into the reader's hands. Thank goodness you did. To

Stella Boerger, who pushes me forward with her constant desire to learn about everything. I am in awe of you. To Cody Boerger, who asks daily how my writing is going and who will never allow me to slack off or accept mediocrity. To Alana Davidson, my sister and alter ego. I'm sure one day when I ask you to read one of my manuscripts for the millionth time before it goes to Rosie, you're going to say no! To Tom Boerger, my very best boy. When you whistled at me across the quad fifty-eight years ago, who knew we'd have such adventures?

A huge shoutout to Karen Glasser for her sharp eye and unerring insistence on continuity in a plot line. You've saved me more than once. To all my dear friends who support me, bolster me, stroke my ego, and cheer me on, you know who you are. Thank you for always being there.

And the most enormous thank you to my spectacular readers who have fallen in love with Philip and Genevieve Warwick. You come to Book Signing and Bubbly and allow me to sign your books, you ask me to speak at your book clubs, and your meetings and your events, you write reviews, you write me notes and share your stories with me, all of which I cherish. Knowing that readers around the world are enjoying the adventures of Lord and Lady Crosswick is more than I ever hoped for.

Enjoy *Vengeance At The Vineyard*, it was written for you.

ABOUT TANA

WITH THREE BOOKS under her belt, Tana is looking forward to writing the final book in the Lord and Lady Crosswick Mysteries. With the next series already bubbling in her brain, she is anxious to get words on the page. With her-first-and-only husband, Tom, she spent years in Hawaii, Germany, and England before forging a life as an entrepreneur in Washington, D.C. and North Carolina. As a result of her international experiences, her life is bulging with stories to tell. If you ask her, she will tell you that becoming a novelist is the best adventure yet. As she says, "When you're writing, all things are possible. You can create worlds, you can destroy worlds. You can create characters, you can destroy characters. You're the boss and nobody, except your editor, can argue with you."

WWW.TANALHBOERGER.COM

𝐟 TANALHBOERGER

www.ingramcontent.com/pod-product-compliance
Lightning Source LLC
Chambersburg PA
CBHW030134310726
48970CB00005B/1429